Also by Susan McGeown:

A Well Behaved Woman's Life

Rosamund's Bower

A Garden Walled Around Trilogy:
Call Me Bear
Call Me Elle
Call Me Survivor

Rules for Survival
Recipe for Disaster

The Butler Did It

Published Faith Inspired Books
3 Kathleen Place, Bridgewater, New Jersey 08807
www.FaithInspiredBooks.com

A Garden Walled Around Trilogy

Book II

Call Me Elle

By Susan McGeown

Faith Inspired Books

To My Parents

Marylynn and Herb

My Faith is because of them and the examples they set…

Hebrews 11:1

Table of Contents

May the paths from every direction

recognize each other.[1]

From a Cherokee Sacred Formula

Elle Graves

The fierce Indian brave walks towards me strong and sure. He's naked except for his breechclout and bright feathers tied in his hair. He doesn't smile or laugh or make any motion 'cept to walk toward me in an easy, long legged stride. When he gets close enough to me he stops, raises his hand and touches my cheek. "Are you ready to go, my mate?" he asks in his best white person words that I've taught him.

Before I can answer, the door behind us opens and out comes our friend, Deer, looking a bit sheepish. "Got any more room on those packhorses? Seems as if Possum has found still *more* things to send back to the village with you ..." He rolls his eyes like he can't believe what his mate has done.

"There would be *plenty* of room still on those horses if you had not insisted on sending those sacks of new fangled seed you want the village to try planting," comes an impatient voice directly behind him. Possum,

Deer's mate, comes into view holding a basket, covered carefully with a piece of muslin cloth.

Deer and Possum are the mirror images of Bright Feather and me, he with his white face and she with her Indian one. Of all of us today, only Deer looks truly white instead of his Indian self, choosing to look like the proper white trader known as William Holland Thomas with his homespun shirt, tan trousers and cloth suspenders. For you see, even though Possum wears the clothes of a white person, no one would be able to mistake her for one with her dark snapping eyes, beautiful long black hair and red Indian skin. She is Possum, of the Turkey clan of The Real People of The Maple Forest. But you can call her Mary. She'll answer to either name as long as you speak to her proper like, with respect.

Which is the problem, you see. For many a white person would call her a savage no matter what she wore or how she behaved because they can't see past the red skin. I was like that for a time. Until I was taken from my white home. Until I was made a slave even with my proper white skin and all. Until I had to realize that it wasn't the skin color that made you a slave or a savage or anything else. It was what was *inside* that made you the person you *chose* to be. I have white skin, I wear savage clothes, I love an Indian brave, and I call The Maple Forest of The Real People my home. I'm not white anymore. I'll never be red. If you need to say a color, you best call me pink.

I grin at Possum. "I've still got some room, but you'll have to help me fit it on Willow's pack." As Possum and I start to walk to the horses, I realize that even Possum looks more white than I do from behind at least with her proper cloth skirt and blouse.

We are almost ready to leave with our pack horses piled high and final shouts of best wishes from Deer and Possum's three children: James, *Red Bird*, Eliza, *Sleeping Rabbit*, and Richard, *Small Turtle*. This being my first trip to white territory since Bright Feather and I have joined together, I was powerful worried about just about everything. Would I be safe? Would Bright Feather be safe with me? What if we met others besides Deer and his family at the trading post? What should I say? How could I explain my circumstances? Do I have the right words to tell my story? All of my worries are needless in the end. Even with soldiers showing up unexpectedly at the trading post, by keeping quiet and in the shadows they thought I was nothing more than a "thievin' Injun squaw" I think is how they put it.

In the end, this trip to Deer and Possum's has filled in a powerful large hole in my puzzle of life. Things I'd wondered about, like why I was taken in the first place from my home in Ward's Mill, Virginia, to Great Elk's village in The Maple Forest.

And then there are the things I never thought to consider. I glance at Bright Feather as he talks quiet like to Deer. I had no idea that so many of my choices had been so right. I had no idea how my presence has brought healing to so many.

Bright Feather stops talking to Deer and turns to look at me across the hard packed dirt of the yard. For a moment there is no Deer or Possum, no horses stomping and flicking away annoying flies with their tails, no Eliza, *Sleeping Rabbit,* pulling on my arm and asking me the last few one hundred questions she needs to ask before I leave. There is just me and Bright Feather. Standing separate and yet joined so strong I feel as if he is touching me, can smell his manly scent, can hear his thought whisper in my ear, *Are you alright, my mate?* I sigh and give him a brief nod and a small smile. *Yes, I am fine, my husband.* He turns back to finish speaking with Deer.

I have promised Deer and Possum's daughter, Sleeping Rabbit, for that is how Eliza now insists on being called, that perhaps in the coming summer she will travel back to Great Elk's village with us and stay for a bit. Their son, James, already had the chance this past summer I am surprised to learn and Sleeping Rabbit feels that she is ready now, too.

"Think *long* and *hard* before you make the final decision about her coming," Possum says to me in pointed words while rolling her eyes as Sleeping Rabbit shouts her last few questions to me as Bright Feather joins me and we mount up on our horses in the chilly morning mists.

I feel adult and grown up but look at Possum and smile thinking back to me and my endless questions. "I remember," I say to her as I turn to answer Sleeping Rabbit's latest question, "When I come to visit Great

Elk's village and stay with you, can I have a tunic to wear made just like yours?"

"Perhaps," I say to Sleeping Rabbit with a smile, "we can make you a tunic that is decorated with rabbit fur. What do you think of that?" She claps her hands in excitement.

"I will remember your words," I tell Possum for she has asked me to send greetings to a number of family and friends in the village. "Thank you for everything."

"*Thank you, too*," she says and she looks up with meaning at Bright Feather as he guides his horse, Companion, near me and says, "Are you ready to go now?" Possum must grin a wide grin every time she calls Bright Feather "Bright Feather" instead of the name she has known him by for so many years – One Who Is Always Alone.

Because of me, the name no longer fits him, you see.

That makes me smile a bright smile as I cast a glance back at the trading post at Forest City, North Carolina, and wave to the family of red and white skin that has made three beautiful pink children. It is a peek at my future that I hope sometime soon will come true.

The journey back seems much faster than the journey there. I have nothing to worry about and many stories to remember and sort through. I think about all the pieces to the puzzle of my life and am amazed at how large the puzzle truly is! I ponder over why I came to be taken from my white home in Ward's Mill, Virginia, and all the heartache and sorrow that went along with it. I now know the gift Bright Feather gives me in choosing to love again for I have learned of the heartache and sorrow that brought him to be called One Who Is Always Alone for so long. I now know that the choices I made were wise ones.

I think in particular about the times that Bright Feather came so close to bringing me back to Virginia. I wonder what I would have done with the chance had he offered it and how much I would have missed about finding out about me as a powerful woman. I think about the flier telling others about my capture and pleading for my safe return. I think about Cornelius Cooper of Cooper's General Store and wonder just what he would have done with me had I shown up on his doorstep at any one of those times? Just what would he have done with an orphaned white girl who had lived for a time with the *wild Injun savages.* I remember his face and his store and his kind, plump wife who I only knew to call *Mrs. Cooper.* I can't recall any children although they were both older so perhaps their children were married and gone. Would they have adopted me like One Who Knows has done in The Maple Forest and would I have become their daughter and learned all about their store and married some white settler and gone on with my white life just as I have here in this Indian life? I look at Bright Feather's straight back in front of me Companion and I think, *Would I have even missed you? Would you have even missed me?* A wave of sorrow deep and sharp cuts through me at the thought of being without him. It's different from the sorrow of losing Pa, Henry and Eli. This sorrow feels like all of my insides are being carved out and thrown on the ground to be trampled and left to rot. It's a pain so strong I decide maybe not to think on this subject anymore and make an effort to turn my thoughts away.

But then I hear Bright Feather's words in my ears from last night when we talked about different places, different languages and different words and how we still found each other and what it meant. In between his kisses, Bright Feather had whispered to me, *It means we are each other's destiny. No person, no situation, no thing will stop this that we have,* and I feel certain that at some point even if had I become the adopted daughter of Mr. and Mrs. Cooper of Ward's Mill, Virginia, a tall handsome Indian brave with bright feathers in his hair would have crossed my path somehow. *Destiny.*

The village of The Maple Forest is glad to see us and is happy to receive the many, many things that we have brought. I tease Bright Feather that now I understand why everyone always seems so glad to see him when he returns each time. I thought it was just because they missed him. He pretends he does not hear me.

As soon as I have finished kissing and cuddling Little Bird and answering my friend Otter's many questions, I make my way into the village to deliver Possum's words and gifts. Possum, I have come to learn, has a sister and an aunt in the village who are happy to receive all the things I bring with me. It was here that James spent his summer last year while I struggled with the unexpected directions my life had taken through no fault of my own. I answer their polite questions and tell them of Sleeping Rabbit's hope to visit next summer. I laugh in understanding when they seem to hesitate (Sleeping Rabbit has quite a gift at making a body tired with all the questions that she asks) and things become more comfortable after that.

My final stop before I return to our hut is to One Who Knows. My adopted mother. A woman who at first I was a slave to and now I am a daughter to. One Who Knows is as her name replies: she is a healer and she can sometimes tell directions for the future. She is also old and mighty crabby. Age has made her impatient with stupid questions, annoying people, and, well, most things in general.

Turtle, the young Indian woman that lives with her, is preparing the evening meal and tells me that One Who Knows is somewhere out in the forest gathering her precious herbs. I smile at Turtle and ask if she is ever allowed to help prepare the herbs. For sure I never was. She gives me a horrified look and says, "Oh No! The worst slap I ever received was when I accidentally ruined some of the herbs she had drying in the sun. I am *never ever* to touch *or even look at* the herbs she uses for healing."

"I suppose she told me that too, many times, but I couldn't understand her words then."

A sharp voice behind me says, "That is true. When you were with me you were more of a trial than Turtle ever was, as slow as she is. Head as thick as rock, you have. How was I ever supposed to get anything done with a fool white girl that always seemed to draw trouble to her quicker than ants to a tasty crumb?" Turtle scurries to get back to work and I remember the fear I see in her eyes.

I turn as she is speaking and her expression is as hard and dark as how I recall it to be when I was in Turtle's place, only called Mouse. But I know many things now as I stand there in the late afternoon shadows and I know that there are many differences from when I was Mouse and now: I am unafraid, I am Bear, and *I am her daughter by her choice.*

"I come to wish you well, *Mother*, and inquire how things are with you. I bring greetings to you of Possum of the Turkey Clan of the Real People of the Maple Forest."

She snorts through her nose and rolls her eyes. "Help me with these things, *Daughter*," and she says the title with not the same kind meaning as I meant mine, "they are heavy and anyone polite will have done it without being asked." I remove her precious gathering basket from her back and am amazed at how heavy it really is.

"Tell me," I say politely and with great respect, "when I was Mouse here in this hut with you, did you speak to me like this even when I did not understand you?"

She looks at me for a beat and then I see the twinkle in the eye. "I speak to *everyone* this way and that was one of my greatest frustrations with you. How can I cause you to jump with fear at threats you cannot understand?" She sighs as she settles on her furs at the opening of her hut. "I was well rid of you."

"You claimed me for your daughter the night I was named Bear. I did not know that until Bright Feather told me. I thought you claimed me as your daughter the night we celebrated my joining with Bright Feather."

She begins to sort through her basket and hands me some herb I don't know. "Goat's Beard," she says. "Good for poultices for bee stings and to be brewed as a tea to stop bleeding after childbirth." She whispers quietly to me, "I like to soak my swollen feet in it at times, too." I watch her speed and skill as she works. "Best picked right before the end of the growing season. You must immediately break off the roots and hang it in a bunch in a dry, dark place or it loses much of its power. Here." She thrusts a pile of the plant in my hand and I watch as she works to prepare it for hanging. I am pleased to be allowed to help and carefully begin to follow her directions. "Bright Feather has a big mouth," is all she will finally say about my comments.

"If you claimed me for your daughter, why did I not go back to live with you in your hut?"

She looks at me and I sense impatience. "Do you ask questions of me because you like the sound of my voice? I have some songs I can sing you that might be more interesting than just repeating things you already know."

I look down at the herbs and study them closely while I think. At last I say, "If I were to come back to your hut, without understanding the language well enough, I would have just thought that I was going back to being your slave again."

She nods ever so slightly. "And Otter needed companionship. And Raccoon needed someone to stir him up a bit. And One Who Is Always Alone needed someone to make him remember he was a *man* not some solitary creature of the forest. And I needed someone I can threaten more with my words." She smiles a sweet innocent smile at me that can almost be more frightening then her dark looks and I can't help it; I burst out laughing.

"I have brought you a gift," I say finally and I hand her a package wrapped in an old seed sack and tied with twine. "Two, actually."

She puts down her herbs and for a flash seems almost like a child as she unties the twine (and carefully wraps it up for future use) and opens the seed bag and draws out what I have brought her. "It is a collecting bag," I say all of a sudden worried that it is a foolish thing to give a woman who has been gathering herbs for longer than three of my lifetimes – at least. "The whites use them when they are planting and it is used for carrying large quantities of seed." I stand up and demonstrate, "It sits comfortable like at your shoulder like this – see the padding here? – and then drapes across your body to rest at your hip. They are not usually decorated like this but Possum showed me some stitches and gave me some thread and so I added some decorations on it so it didn't look so plain." In the face of her silence at the gift I add, "If you prefer your basket, then you can always use it for something else ..." She examines it with quiet concentration; the fabric, the stitching, and the decorations. But remains silent.

"And this," I draw out the other thing that I have brought her from the seed sack, "Deer tells me is called a *mortar and pestle* by white doctors and such. It's heavy because he says it's carved out of a kind of rock! I think it will be easier to grind your herbs with it. White folks use it for the same thing." This too she examines with great interest, turning it over in her hands.

"I have no use for two gathering containers," she says at last, "and lately the gathering has gotten to be harder with these tired old legs." I feel the disappointment in me well up almost like tears and then she says. "But to have company sometimes along for the walk to talk and listen and that I can share things with, now that might just give me a new passion for things. You would have to be content with that old basket though for I am not inclined to share this new gathering bag with *anyone*. And I am not inclined to say things more than once, well maybe twice, so you are going to have to carve a hole in that thick skull of yours to quick catch all the things I would be teaching you. You are far too old to learn to be a healer, but there is a skill in just knowing the herbs that you can probably master in time."

I grin at her a great wide grin. "I will be back again tomorrow. Is this time of the day good?"

"Of course not! I am just about done for the day. Come as soon as you can and it will still be too late." She picks up her herbs and starts working on them, but not before she carefully folds the seed bag and places it by the rolled up twine.

"Good night, Mother," I say to her as I walk away.

"Good night to you, too, Daughter." She says it with no sharp words or tones. I think she liked my gifts.

I tell Bright Feather that I have given One Who Knows her gifts and of her reactions and words to me. In my excitement over the gifts it's not occurred to me that he has made no comments during the preparation of the gathering bag nor my plans to give One who Knows the gifts. "I am happy that she is pleased," he says at last.

I sit down next to him and look at his face. "I did not ask you about the gifts, should I have?" I ask for all of a sudden I think I'd like to hear his thoughts.

He shrugs. "One Who Knows is difficult to understand," he begins carefully and I can't help but laugh quietly at his way of description. "There has been no one in many years that has helped her in any way with her gathering and healing. At one time, many sought her out to learn her thoughts and seek her advice about important things in their lives. These past years she has kept most of her thoughts to herself except when it suits her to hurl them at you almost like a sharp rock. At one time, she anticipated people's needs and wants and almost knew before you did when you needed a special herb or other special care. These past years if you needed her you knew where she is. She rarely ventures out among the village except to sit at council circles. And often even then she is silent and unwilling to voice her thoughts.

"I did not know how she would react to your gifts, especially since they had to do with her healing arts. I think it is best that you did not speak to me about my thoughts before you gave them to her for I would have had to tell you these things that I just did. Then maybe you would not have chosen to give her your gifts and things would be unchanged.

I spend the rest of the fall tramping through the forest with One Who Knows trying my best to crack open my thick skull and shove as much knowledge as I can inside. More than once I feel that I'm hopeless and should just give up. Very soon, she tells me, there'll be nothing to look for until the spring comes. Today I'm walking in the forest with One Who Knows, she with her new gathering bag and me with her old gathering basket. I feel much the way I did when I struggled to learn the Indian language and the words always seemed to come and go too fast for me to keep them in my head. One Who Knows seems to me to be made entirely of knowledge about the forest and its plants and the more time I spend with her the more I begin to realize that I'll never, ever know all she knows about these things. I tell her that finally in frustration when she scolds me for not remembering correctly the uses and care of an herb I *do* remember she tried to teach me about the first or second day we began gathering together.

"I was not so quick with learning these things, either," she finally tells me as we walk slowly back to the village. "I was young and beautiful and smart but was more interested in other things than the silly dried herbs

I had grown up with hanging from the roof of my hut and smelling in the baskets around my head while I slept."

"What was more interesting to you?" I have to ask and wait for a sharp word for asking such a question.

"Boys," she says, "quite a few of them," and she giggles the most wonderful giggle I've ever heard. It sounds like happy water in a quick flowing brook.

I grin at her. It's hard to imagine at first the stooped, gray haired old lady walking slowly and carefully beside me as a beautiful Indian maid chasing boys, but the giggle manages to paint a good picture in my mind. "I never, ever thought of boys much," I say to her in all honesty, "until Bright Feather."

"You had survival on your mind," she says quickly. "The mind is very wise and works on important things one step at a time. You do not make plans to build a hut to live in while you are still a baby in a cradle board. Once you do decide to build a hut, you make sure each step is sound: choice of location, choice of materials, care of construction. Who wants to live in a house that is unsafe? Who wants to rest each night in a house that threatens to collapse in on you with the first stiff breeze? Life is filled with hard choices that correctly made lead to an existence of harmony and peace. But it can take a long time to get there.

"You will not learn all I know about the herbs and the plants around you. Do not frustrate yourself over the things your brain will not have the time to do in this lifetime. Concentrate on the things you know you can do. Learn one piece at a time, just like you learned our language." She mimics me shouting, *DANGER! FIRE! STOP! BEAR! HORSE! NO! COME! FIRE!* the day that Bear John came to attack our village. I remember the fear in my heart as I struggled to decide what I should do and how I could make my slow tongue explain it to those I cared about. I remember the look of puzzlement on Otter's face at my shouts and screams and then the terror when she realized what was coming fast behind me. I remember the feeling of power that poured through my arms as I picked up the burning stick and killed a white man to save my red friend and her baby

. . .

One Who Knows grunts and shakes her head in disgust at the obvious shortcomings of my brain bringing me back to my present difficulties. "Maybe, walking through the forest with me pointing out things is too much for your thick skull. We will do it differently in the spring. We will start with the herbs you already know and I will tell you all the things I know about just them. Then, I will send you out on your own for these old legs are just not what they used to be anymore and I cannot do this every day, and you can bring me back things you find and I will tell you what I know. How does that sound?"

I worry that she is disappointed with me. "I want you to be pleased with what I learn from you. I want you to understand that I am doing my best and trying my hardest," I say to her with great emotion.

She dismisses my words with a wave of her gnarled, old hand. "You are foolish to worry about such things. Mothers always understand that about their daughters." She looks at me and I have learned to watch for the brief twinkle of fun that flashes very quickly now and then. "No matter how stupid they appear sometimes."

Sometimes she says things to me that I have no answer for. We fall into an easy silence as we walk through the beautiful forest not unlike my times hunting and riding with Bright Feather. My mind wanders and I think of Otter and Raccoon and Little Bird. "Otter is expecting another baby," I say to One Who Knows after a time. "She says the baby will come in the late summer."

"You worry about not one but two things," she says to me casual like and I feel the goose skin run up my arms across my neck and into my hair even for she is right.

Her bent old legs carry her with purpose through the forest as she says to me over her shoulder, "They call me One Who Knows because I know more than most people but I don't know everything. Sometimes it is a terrible thing to see only parts of the future, not enough to know anything for sure, only enough to be afraid." She is quiet in her thoughts and I know she must think of her daughters Raven and Black Fox that she could not save from an early death. And perhaps even Weasel and how she could not keep his evil from those she loved and cared about. She shrugs. "But I see good things, too, like the brightness I spoke about seeing where you are concerned.

"You worry first about whether you will have a child with Bright Feather for it has been some months since you first mated." She turns and smiles a rare, sweet smile at me. "You do not need to be One Who Knows to know of that concern for it is something almost every young woman thinks of – I am sure white *or* red – if a baby does not come with the first time you are together with a man.

"But a bigger fear you have still is that you worry that you *will* have a child with Bright Feather. That," she says with certainty, "is another fear that one does not need to have special skills to know about. All women worry of such things for all women know of those who have gone on to the spirit world during the hard battle of childbirth."

I am silent just as she is lost in memories. We walk for long moments, she with thoughts of her daughter Black Fox, Bright Feather's first mate, and the grandson that never lived to see a sunset. Me with thoughts of Ma and how Eli knew only ever me as his Ma even though I was just a girl of eight. I wonder, what do I dread more? Do I fret that I never will have a child with Bright Feather or that I will? I can't decide which path is more filled with worry.

We walk for a bit more and I know we are close to the village. "Men worry about such things, too, but their worries show in different ways. Maybe the baby I know you will have with Bright Feather waits until it knows the worry of *wanting* a child will become greater than the worry of *having* a child – for both of you." I had not thought of Bright Feather worrying about me and the dangers of childbirth. It was the death of Black Fox and his son that caused him to go from being the great hunter known as Hawk to the man I first met known as One Who Is Always Alone. I sigh and shake my head at the tiny hole I peek through to view my world. I realize I must work more on seeing how others think and feel than just my selfish self.

She touches my arm. "When the worry gets great about the *having*, look around you at every single living being you see and know that the *wanting* usually wins out eventually." She snorts loudly at her own joke. "And have fun with the practicing in the mean time."

We enter the village with her hand still on my arm and I'm certain my face is red with the thoughts of the 'practicing fun' to make a baby with Bright Feather. As we get towards the center where the council circles are held, her hand tightens on mine in caution and warning. "Watch and listen carefully for the brightness, my daughter, for darkness is here in this village again." I raise my head in concern to see a strange Indian brave talking with our village chief, Great Elk and War Woman, his mate. He wears the clothes of a white man but it does not change who he is. But the darkness One Who Knows speaks of, I realize, is more probably in the form of the white soldier standing stiff and surprised and looking right at me.

One Who Knows stumbles and I stop to catch and steady her. "Are you alright? Shall I take you back to your hut?" I ask quick with concern. My mind scrambles to still the millions of thoughts buzzing around in my head like an angry hornet's nest. My heart thumps and thumps. *Don't forget me too!*, it seems to say with a panicked shout.

She places her hand on top of my hand and looks deep into my eyes calm and unconcerned. "I am fine. *So are you.* Remember who you are and what you have learned and where you choose to go. You have handled many situations much more difficult than talking to a white man here in your own village." I realize she has stumbled on purpose to give us a moment for *me* to gather my thoughts.

I grin at her serious eyes. "I am Bear, daughter of One Who Knows, of the Elk clan of the Real People of the Maple Forest and the mate of Bright Feather, son of War Woman of the Wolf clan and Great Elk, chief of the Real People of the Maple Forest. I am a Powerful Woman."

She nods her head satisfied. "*Now*, you can take me home. We will meet these men tonight I am certain."

I realize something about myself as we walk casual past the strangers in our village. I feel my heart slow and my thoughts still and my eyes take stock of who is present and who is not and my senses register the feelings around the council circle group. I realize I do particularly well in unexpected situations; my brain and heart get the sudden shock – like getting struck by a bolt of lightning I suspect – and then everything settles into a hum of high alert. *Experience is the best teacher, Elle,* I hear Pa say loud and clear in my head. Lord knows I've had some experience with unexpected situations! Kidnapped by Indians not once, but twice. Responsible for the death of one white man and pleased about the death of at least three red ones. All before I turned sixteen years. I sigh and shake my head at the passel full of experience that I've been educated by as One Who Knows and I make our way to her hut. *Proper schooling would have been a might easier I suspect,* I think with a quiet chuckle to myself. *Oh well...*

By the time I have the council fire area to my back, I already know that these strangers have just arrived for they are not seated nor have their horses been tended to. I see that Great Elk and War Woman are alert yet do not appear overly threatened. I see a number of others who sit regularly in council circles making their way towards the council area. I am certain that the brave has white blood in him. And I know that the soldier is powerful curious about me for he follows me with his eyes like no other.

I leave One Who Knows at her hut and am glad to see that Turtle has begun the evening meal. She gives me a shy smile and then gets back to her work. At our hut, I have not even finished the preparations of our meal before Bright Feather, Raccoon and Red Fox show up; Red Fox has obviously gone and got them. I stand as they approach and see the concern in their eyes. "They have seen me," I tell them, "and they are powerful curious who I am." Then I tell them what I have seen and know.

As it is with almost every night in the village, after the evening meal is completed many travel to the council circle to talk and hear the way of things. Tonight has a different feel to it as Bright Feather and me make our way through the dark and light spots of the village to join the evening's discussions. Just before we enter the bright spot of the council circle fire, Bright Feather pulls me into the shadows for a long embrace. I feel his tension and know his desire to protect me; it is a good feeling. But there is something more I realize as I reach up and touch his face and kiss his mouth and smell the wonderful smell of him. I realize with a start that I am right calm about things. I reach up and touch my husband's face and smooth my fingers through the three colorful feathers tied in his hair – red for cardinal, yellow for goldfinch and blue for blue jay. In the darkness and shadow the flickering firelight flashes brightly on his long dark hair. "These people were once my people," I say to him quiet like in the safety of the shadows. "I know *both worlds*. More than anything, I remember what One Who Knows and Great Elk have said that I bring brightness to this village. I think this village is much better off with me here than without. I think that much of what has happened to me so far is to make sure I am right in this spot right now. So let us go see just what I can hear and understand about these people who think they still *are* my people." I draw him down for a long and lovely kiss.

When the kiss is finished, Bright Feather takes long moments to search my face, in no hurry to go into the light. Then he grunts, the closest I have ever heard him come to outright laughter. He's apparently satisfied with what he sees. "Do you think this soldier is afraid? I think maybe he should be." He kisses me again holding my face between his two big red hands and then takes my white hand and leads me to the brightness of the council circle.

The white soldier seated in the council circle cannot conceal his surprise as Bright Feather and I arrive hand in hand. It is Bright Feather's way of making a statement to these strangers, I know, as we rarely show affection to each other within the village and never in the council circle. The Indian brave that has traveled with the soldier shows no expression whatsoever but watches us both just the same. Seated with the newcomers are War Woman, Great Elk, One Who Knows, and Raccoon. I realize that this group is specially called for others that regularly join the council circle are not here. All wear their serious faces, even Raccoon who enjoys nothing more than to cause me problems and confusion with his teasing.

"My name is Major Alexander Everett and this is my interpreter, George Maw," the soldier with fair hair and blue eyes says to me. He looks strange among the ring of dark faces and dark hair and I realize that with my brown hair and tan skin I go more with the dark than light. Even his partner has dark brown hair and brown eyes. "I am a member of the Second United States Calvary, Division of the Army, Company A. Our unit is presently based in Virginia, and we work with Ninth Virginia Cavalry, Company D out of Fort Winston, Virginia, of which George Maw regularly works." He looks at me seated across from him sitting between Bright Feather and Raccoon.

"I am here because of a communication I have received regarding one," here he searches through his pack and takes out a letter which he begins to read aloud to the group. He speaks in English and I translate to all those in the circle ignoring George Maw.

"- *poor young woman of obvious gentle breeding for her manner and way was most kind and solicitous to all she came in contact with when treated with care and compassion. She was brought to this Indian settlement as a rescued captive and spent approximately six weeks with us this April last, 1829, however, it was our understanding that prior to her arrival she had spent a considerable amount of time north of here in the Indian village that is frequently referred to as "Indiantown" for want of a better name. Upon her arrival here, she was fully acclimated to the Indian way of life and was fluent in the language and customs to the point where she was unwilling to reveal her white name or history. She departed with three Indian braves, one being the eldest son of Chief Dark Cloud, and one French trader by the name of Martin DuBois with the destination I understand to be the hopes of returning her to her white relations. None in the party have been seen or heard of since. The Cherokee Nation has made every effort to cooperate and become a civilized partner with the United States of America. The United States Government has been supportive and eager to encourage a solid alliance with the Cherokee nation. It seems to be an easy matter to join these two like mannered forces and to inquire into the safety and well being of this young woman whom my wife and I have embraced and taken to heart as if she were our own daughter. We would be most appreciative to any assistance you could afford us in securing information regarding this young woman's whereabouts and health. Your Humble and Sincere Servant who in His Holy Name I entrust my soul and safety, Reverend James Francis Wilder, New Echota, Georgia, July 15th, 1829"*

His blue eyes meet my green ones and I feel the silence stretch across the fire growing longer and longer. At last he says, "Are you the young woman Reverend Wilder refers to in this letter?"

"Yes, I am," I say but I answer not in English but in the language of the Real People. George Maw translates to Major Everett and when he finishes I explain, "I will speak to you in the language of The Real People as that is the language of this council circle."

"I understand," Major Everett says politely, "and I will trust that you will continue to translate my words as carefully as George Maw does yours." I nod my head.

He reaches into his pack and takes out another paper, one that I recognize before he hands it across to me for I have seen the likeness drawn on it. "Have you seen this?" he asks, and I translate his words and then read aloud the words about me and my capture to the council circle:

"On the evening of TUESDAY, the 22nd of March in the year of Our Lord 1828, the peaceful homestead of Andrew Graves, Esq. of Ward's Mill, Virginia was violently and savagely attacked by a marauding band of blood thirsty Indians. No surviving witnesses were found to provide an accurate account, however, it is with the Utmost Hope and Desire that the person of Mistress Elle Graves might still be Alive and with the Most Extreme Care and Speed be found and returned post haste. All leniency will be afforded to those cooperating with authorities in the positive outcome to this tragic occurrence. April 10, 1828, Cornelius Cooper of Ward's Mill, Virginia." Beneath the writing is my picture, roughly drawn with the description: *"Orphaned white girl whose mother has died and father and brothers have been murdered by marauding Indians, who answers to the name of Elle.."*

I look up when I have finished reading and translating and look and Major Everett. "Yes, I have seen this," I answer, "I saw it just this past month in the trading post of our friend and brother, Deer, also known as William Holland Thomas, in Forest City, North Carolina." I hand the paper back to him.

"Are you Elle Graves?" he asks, taking the paper and holding it casual like in his hand.

"No, I am not," I answer strong and sure and I meet his eyes. I try not to even blink. "I am Bear, of the Elk Clan, daughter of One Who Knows, mate of Bright Feather, son of War Woman of the Wolf Clan and son of Great Elk, chief of The Real People of the Maple Forest."

"I see," he says, after listening to the translations and carefully studying each blank Indian face in the council circle. "I had suspected that you would say that. You understand that there are those that still search for this Elle Graves and wish for her safe and speedy return?"

After I translate, at first I am silent. But then finally I say, "Yes, I can see that there are those that search for her. But none of them are her family it seems."

He looks down at the flier and I see him read through the final bits and see *Cornelius Cooper.* He puzzles for a moment and then he finally says, "Often the proprietors of general stores or trading posts are listed as the point of contact as they are more easy to find and more well known. She might have other family members besides the ones that are spoken of." His answer from all is silence.

Major Everett looks at all of those around the council circle but then settles on me and finally he asks, "How is it that you sit here in Indiantown when last you were seen on the trail with four men charged with the assignment of returning you to your white relatives? Are those men here and we do not know it?"

"You have been misled if you think that I am not where I wish to be." I tell him. "You were also misled if you believe that *the four men charged with the assignment of returning me to my white relatives* had anything such as that planned. I am not a prisoner here, I have never been tied nor have I ever been attacked or brutalized here. The only time that I have ever been hurt by anyone was under the *care* of Dark Cloud's son of whom I refuse to speak for his name is dirt in my mouth. I carry scars from him and his treatment on my arms," and I hold up my hands that show wrists forever marked by rope burns, "and on my body," here I open my tunic to show the scar that is still pink and new over my breast. "I carry more wounds such as this made from a knife and from teeth – eleven in all, do you wish to see more?"

Major Everett swallows and appears even paler than before. He does not need the translations I think from the sound of my voice as I speak, the scars I show on my body and the anger I flash in my eyes. "No, I do not need to see more," he finally manages to say.

I continue. "As for the whereabouts of these men, I do not know and I have never known. I am back here where I want to be in the village of The Real People of the Maple Forest. I know only that I was taken by force by this son of Dark Cloud and held against my will at that village. The only people who showed real concern for my safety were the Reverend Wilder and his wife, Miss Rebecca. They were unwilling to believe anything less than what they were told by those in charge and I was never in a position to convince them otherwise. I am grateful for their concern over my health and safety. Please assure then that I am fine, wish them well, and," I smile a little smile, "I am still saying my prayers."

Major Everett is smart enough to realize that to discuss my white life will not benefit him much in this council circle and the talk finally turns to other things. Food is brought and enjoyed and I feel the tension up my back start to ease just a slight bit. I learn that Major Everett has been part of the 2nd Division of the United States Calvary for more than fifteen years. George Maw has been many times to Dark Cloud's village, but always in the capacity of the cavalry's need for a translator. Both soldiers agree that the opportunities within the cavalry cannot be equaled anywhere else within the military. "There is an independence that cannot be equaled in riding your own horse, scouting new and different places and viewing the world from a higher place than most," Major Everett says with a shy smile.

Bright Feather and I decide the next morning to have me ride out early on Willow and avoid any more contact with either Major Everett or George Maw. Bright Feather will stay in the village and watch the way of things. Willow is glad to see me and dances in excitement as I ready her to ride out. "That's a beautiful horse you have," a white voice says to me and I turn around startled to see Major Everett leaning against a large oak.

I take a deep breath to still my jumping heart and stroke Willow's soft silky side. "She's white and learned to be an Indian, just like me," I say. "Miss Rebecca Wilder said that I couldn't go back to being white but would never be red and that perhaps I was more closely pink. Willow's the same way."

"I know you are Elle Graves," he says in the quiet of the forest as I mount up onto Willow as fast but as casual as I can. "The picture is not a good likeness, but the age fits and Dark Cloud was able to share with me when he knows you came to be a part of this village and where he suspects your family is from."

"Seems powerful interesting to me how much he seems to know about me considering I never had the *pleasure* of knowing him until a few months ago and even then I told him *nothing* of myself," I say, and I remember how very, very much I hate him and his dead son.

Major Everett surprises me with a laugh. "Do you know, that is exactly what I said to him." He looks at me, "Considering the Wilders insisted that you never revealed anything about your white past to them, I found it hard to believe that you would have chosen to tell Dark Cloud anything of a personal nature and I said so to him. He told me that in his capacity for leadership he had many connections and had heard information about you from a number of sources." His face tells me that he finds those words hard to believe. "You have nothing to fear of me. I am not here because of Dark Cloud but because of the Wilders. Rebecca is my aunt, you see."

I don't know what to say to him but I search his eyes and think, *Why would he lie to me?* I can't think of a reason.

"They are tenderhearted, the two of them." He smiles shyly at me and sighs. "I'm glad that God watches over them for they need all the help they can get."

I remember my time at Dark Cloud's village and the danger I feared for them more than for myself. "Almost nothing is as it seems in that place," I finally say. "Yet, whenever they spoke, I knew that their words meant just what they said and had no hidden meanings. There was never a time that I didn't believe that they were truly worried for my safety and my well being." He smiles a smile of gratitude for the way I think of his aunt and uncle.

I will him to go away. Far away. Away from me and my life here, leaving me safe and sound and where I want to be. He looks at me with concern and kindness. And a fair bit of stubbornness, too, I realize with regret. Finally I say, "The flier says that Elle Graves' father and brothers were killed and that her mother was already dead. She's called an orphan. Seems to me that there isn't much for her to go back to."

He sighs and walks away from the oak to mingle among the other horses and view the beauty of the autumn forest with its floor of golds and reds and yellows. "Indiantown is an aberration. Do you know what that means, Bear?" he asks me and I shake my head 'no'. "It means that it is a place unlike any other place that people know of." *A Garden Walled Around … chosen and made peculiar ground*, I think of the words of the Isaac Watts song. "It is an Indian village that has barely any signs of the white world in it. That alone is stunning in this day and time. It is like going back in time to before the whites' arrival before the sicknesses, before the lies, before the Old Ways were called the 'old ways.' But this is not an Indian town, is it?" He laughs and sweeps his arm out towards the sounds of the stirring village. "This is a *United States of America town* full of *citizens* of that country. Here is the problem which you might find surprising, but unfortunately you probably won't: *No one wants this place or knows what to do with it.* The United States of America doesn't really want it. The State of North Carolina certainly doesn't want it. And here is the saddest thing: The Nation of The Real People don't want it anymore either. They would *all* just like this Indiantown to *go away.* Disappear. Cease to exist. Never have happened. Every single one of those powerful institutions would like you all to just vanish and they would love to find a reason to make it happen."

He walks over to stand next to me and I look down at him from Willow's back and he gazes up at me. The last remaining fall leaves drift down around us like colorful snowflakes. "*You* could be an excellent reason to make trouble for this place called Indiantown. *You* could be a reason for the United States of America to reconsider the citizenship status of this village of *red savages. You* could be a reason for the State of North Carolina to reconsider its *magnanimous* offer of money in replacement of the land reservations they promised but could not give. *You* could be the reason that The Nation of The Real People does not step forward in defense of this place for they have done everything in their power to secure your freedom and have even had blood shed over it. *You are exactly what all these powerful institutions are all looking for.* The unanswerable questions that surround you and the voices that call you still from the white world could be music to the ears of those who wish this place serious harm."

Major Everett's words are awful words to hear. I want to throw my hands up over my ears and keep them from getting into my head and heart. I feel like I have so often felt in my life that there are no choices for me, just action I must do. "So what do you tell me to do? For it seems to me whether I am this Elle Graves or not, just the fact that I am a white woman in this Indian village seems to be a problem. I have heard that from Dark Cloud already and even from Great Elk and War Woman."

"Seems to me that you have only one choice," he begins to say but I interrupt him.

"Choosing between two things is a choice," I say with bitter words, "choosing between one thing is not a choice at all."

I really think he is sorrowful for me as he says the next words, "You must go back to Virginia and tell them what has happened to the young woman named Elle Graves." I feel the fear and the tears begin to build and turn Willow into the forest so that Major Everett will not see either feeling. As I ride into the woods I hear him say to me, "We will wait another day before we leave. We would be a good escort for you should you wish it." I want the black fur earplugs that Raccoon gave Bright Feather to shut out Major Everett's words but I know it is already too late for they are colliding around in my brain sucking my life right away.

I ride the whole day alone on Willow feeling powerful sorry for myself. My heart is full of sorrowful questions that tear me apart. What is it about me I think? Why does disaster seem to be the course of my life whether I live in the white world or the red? Does everyone have a life like mine and face choices that are no choices? I listen in my head for wise words from Pa and try to remember important things I have learned from Bright Feather and One Who Knows but my thoughts are silent. Then quietly, I hear Miss Rebecca's words, *Then shall ye call upon Me, and ye shall go and pray unto Me, and I will hearken unto you. And ye shall seek Me, and find Me, when ye shall search for Me with all your heart.* So I try praying to this God that is supposed to be so loving and I am told cares so much about me and I ask

Him, *Why? Why must I do this thing? Why must I leave those I love to go back to a life that has nothing for me? Why?!*

And then the answer comes to me like the start of a soft breeze that grows and builds with force until it becomes a blasting force that whips your hair across your face and tears the branches off of trees. *For Love,* the answer says. *Only for Love.*

I ride into the village that evening just before the evening meal, and as I expected with guests in the village, many including Bright Feather, Otter, and Raccoon are seated around the council circle eating and talking. Bright Feather stands as Willow and I walk into the flickering firelight. I have returned as planned and I can see just passing concern for me as he walks towards me. He touches my cheek and murmurs for only me to hear, "I missed you, my mate, but I hope your day was a good one. Things have been quiet and easy here in the village today."

I smile at him - a sad smile - and he stops short for he can tell that tears are close and that is powerful unusual for me. "Are you well?" he asks in concern and I nod my head 'yes' but choose not to speak for I am uncertain if my voice will work.

"Will you join us to eat?" I hear Otter call from the circle with her usual bright smile and she rises to get a bowl for me. I can see all eyes are on me. I slip my hand in Bright Feather's and still concerned he grasps it tightly. Together we walk closer to the group. I see Major Everett and George Maw seated amongst the group relaxed and at ease.

At the edge of the circle, I look at Major Everett and his eyes tell me he knows I have made a choice that really is no choice at all. I struggle on the words that I manage to push out of my mouth as I look at Major Everett and clutch onto Bright Feather's hand. "My white name is Elle Graves, late of Ward's Mill, Virginia," I say to him in English and the words just about choke me. Bright Feather, of course can understand what I say although no one else in the village can. He looks at me and then to Major Everett and back at me again and I look at him and think how much I love this man. The feeling bursts from the very center of me and is greater than any sorrow or hurt or loneliness I have ever felt or imagined. As I look in Bright Feather's very troubled eyes, I say clearly to Major Alexander Everett of the Second United States Cavalry Division, Company A, "I am the girl you are looking for and the one that must be returned to her people in Virginia."

I've never seen Bright Feather angry I discover right quick. The talk around the circle swirls around me as I stare at the uneaten bowl of rabbit stew that Otter has placed in front of me. For once, it seems, my stomach is not hungry. George Maw is hard pressed to do all the translating back and forth for I'm not inclined to do any talking and he must do the part I did last night. Major Everett explains the same things he has explained to me. Bright Feather, Raccoon and even some others around the circle argue that there are other ways around these things. They're all ways I have thought of over the course of my long, terrible day alone with me and my sorry thoughts and there are still a few more I've considered that they haven't gotten to yet.

It's One Who Knows who at last speaks and causes the arguments to stop. "My daughter, Bear, is right. She must return to the whites just as our brother Deer had to return although for different reasons." She looks at me fiercely but it sends me love and strength just the same. "Bear knows who she is, Deer was uncertain. Bear knows where she belongs. Deer could not decide. Things must always be done in the proper order. *Life is filled with hard choices that correctly made lead to an existence of harmony and peace. But it can take a long time to get there.* This village must gain strength and prepare for fierce battles that are coming. That involves fixing things inside our borders *and outside.* Deer has warned us; only but the greatest fool would deny that great battles are still ahead. Bear must return and carefully put out all fires that could spread to this village and threaten its existence of peace and harmony. But she will return to us for she is no longer *Elle Graves* and though many will force her to look for her, she will not be able to find her."

"I will travel back with my mate," Bright Feather finally says in a tone that asks no permission and denies any discussion.

"No, you will not," I say to him for I've prepared myself for this argument that I knew would come. His look tells me that he's prepared to argue with anyone but me. "They will not understand that you are my husband, even if we say it is so. You can be blamed for my taking and for the killings that happened at the homestead. It would be your word and mine – a foolish young girl who's been kept with red *savages* for nigh onto two years – against an angry group of homesteaders powerful hungry for revenge. You will not go, you will stay safe here. Major Everett will travel back with me."

It's War Woman who speaks, but many nod in agreement. "She is right, my son, you cannot travel with her."

"In fact," I turn to Major Everett, "I do not want them to know where I was found. Is that possible?"

"I see no reason why we need to be specific about the location of your *rescue*," he says after thinking for a moment. He looks at George Maw who shrugs his shoulders.

It's Raccoon who speaks next. "It is obvious that Bear feels that she can trust you, Major Everett. I mean no disrespect when I question the character of Mr. George Maw. Tell me, what is your opinion on the way of things here in this village and beyond its borders?"

George Maw finishes the translating of Raccoon's question and then answers for himself. "My mother is full Cherokee," he says, "and my father is full white. I was raised with a strong taste of both worlds. I grew up away from the lands of the Real People but returned each summer to spend time with my mother's family and learn their ways. When land was taken again in the Treaty of 1819, most of my mother's family chose to travel west of the Mississippi. I am a translator because I can do it and do it fairly." He looks across the fire at me and smiles a small smile, "Major Everett has told me what his aunt has said to you. I am a different shade of pink than you, but I am pink just the same."

In our hut that night the silence continues from me. I've nothing to say and am tired to the bone. And for sure there is nothing that anyone can say that will make me feel any better. I lay down on the furs and curl up into a tight ball willing my thoughts and worries and tears to go away and leave me in peace but that doesn't work. Bright Feather seems unable to settle down, too, and finally walks out into the night leaving me to my own sorrows. I understand his helplessness, I think. I lay there tense and miserable wishing I could just escape to a place with no sorrow or pain or worry. But there is no where to go.

Time passes but I don't sleep. My mind struggles to remember pictures to carry with me that will help me once I'm away from this wonderful place. I must keep my memories sharp and not let them grow cloudy. I listen to the noises of the village and the woods and try my hardest to remember every speck of it. I listen to the nightingale sing and hear Companion and Willow stomping and snorting in their place nearby. Then I realize that the nightingale sings a powerful lonely song, one that I'm unfamiliar with and I know that it is no nightingale at all.

I step out into the dark night and follow the song for I know all of a sudden that it is Bright Feather. He's seated in a clearing that's so bright that there are shadows of the trees on the ground cast by the light of the full moon. I sit down next to him and rest my tired, sorrowful head against his shoulder. He makes no move to touch me and for the first time in many, many months I remember how he was when he was called One Who Is Always Alone.

"It was a choice that was no choice," I begin. "It was not something I could discuss with you for it was my decision to make and not one that you could have helped me with. You said one time to me, *The only way you can keep your other choices is to make this one.* This was just like that, Bright Feather. I had to make the choice to go back for otherwise I could lose these other choices that mean so much to me: you, the Indian way, this village. A wrong choice could mean that it could all be lost." I weave my arm underneath his and find his hands clenched in tight balls. "I will come back. I will go back and say, 'Here I am: Elle Graves, but I am no longer her. I am healthy, strong, happy and smart. I am Bear. I am the mate of Bright Feather. I wish to go back and live with them always. Where is my horse? Thank you, good bye.' I will be back before the first flower buds."

He is silent for a moment and then he grunts and shakes his head. "That is a ridiculous plan but you are the only one I know who might be able to succeed with it." His tight fists open and he wraps his big warm hands around my one small one. "As soon as you leave here I ride to Deer. I will tell him what has happened and ask him what we should do." He lets go of my hand and turns and grabs my face and holds it tight, almost too tight, and says fiercely, "If you have trouble, *any trouble* you send word to Deer's trading post by letter or a messenger you trust. As soon as you can, you go there to his place and I will come to get you there."

"I promise," I say. "I will do as you ask. Now it is my turn to ask a promise of you."

His hands release my face and he lays back on the grass, throwing his arm across his eyes. "What," he says in a tired voice and I realize that he is as day weary as me. "What would you have me promise?"

"No matter what you hear or what concerns you have, you will not leave Indian territory to come for me. I cannot have that fear tied around my neck forever worrying that you will risk your life for me."

Still without looking at me he sighs and says with angry words, "And tell me, Bear, how that is different from what you are doing now."

It is my turn to be angry for I realize the importance of this promise. "There is a great difference and you know it! I can never be in as much danger as you would be just by crossing a border." I lean over and pull his arm from across his face and his dark eyes look at mine hovering over his. "Give me your word," I demand.

In a flash I am flipped on my back and he is above me, looming in the dark night. "I promise … that I will not lose you. I promise … that we will be together again. I promise … that I will always love you. I promise … that I will not put myself in danger unless it is the only way to help you. Those are the only things I will promise you, *ever.*" The fierceness of his look tells me I know I must settle for that.

I touch his face and try to smooth away the fierce look and the lines of worry I see around his eyes. "You must remember, I am much more than I was the last time they saw Elle Graves. I am a powerful Indian woman with much knowledge and … only a little fear. I will watch, and listen, and learn, and be very patient. And then I will come home to you," and I pull him down to kiss him.

"You seem to be in some danger now," he says quietly after a time, but I laugh at the threat.

"If I could only be in this kind of danger for the rest of my life," I say and I sigh a wonderful sigh as he kisses the hollow between my neck and shoulder and I feel his warm breath send shivers up my back. I force the fears and worries away as I wrap my arms and legs around him and try with all my might to draw him right inside of me.

"I love you, *Elle Graves*," he says to me in my ear.

The chill of the autumn night finally forces us back to our hearth and the warmth of the furs. A full moon's brightness does not warm like the sun. Still neither of us wishes to sleep. I stir up the fire and add a few sticks to the red coals. By the time Bright Feather has dragged out two big wraps, the fire is warm and inviting.

"Tell me how you got your permanent marks," I ask him suddenly as I stare at his face in the firelight and will myself to remember every single speck that I see.

He shrugs. "It is a little bit like names for you often get them to celebrate an important part of your life. For me, I received them when I received the name of Hawk. Three lines for the three claw marks a hawk often leaves on its prey. Great Elk did them for me."

"I would like some," I say all of a sudden before I can change my mind. "One Who Knows has them. I wish to have some so that no matter what clothes or skin color I have, people when they look at me will know that I am more red inside than white."

He looks at me for a moment, pondering my face as an artist would. "And what would you have?" he finally asks. I think as an afterthought he adds, "It is painful, you know."

I shiver but it is not from the cold. I draw my bearskin around me and Bright Feather moves closer to me. "I do not know," I say. "I do know that I have many marks on my body from my times since I left Ward's Mill, Virginia. There are few people who see them, but I know they are there just the same. I would have some marks on my body that speak of other times that I would choose to remember with love and happiness."

He reaches over and studies my face and his hands touch the smoothness of my forehead and my cheeks and my chin. He is like an artist searching for the right place to do a design I realize and I shiver again. He takes his knife out and places it in the hot coals of the fire. "Do you know of the four sacred directions?" he asks me finally.

"No," I say concentrating hard to stop the shivering nervousness that seems to be slowly creeping through all parts of my body. I shut my eyes and concentrate on the gentle rhythm of his voice.

"Well," he says, "the direction in which the sun rises from is called *The Direction of Beginnings*. It speaks of family, togetherness, sharing, and spiritually-same thoughts. Within a family or group of friends there is a certain freedom that comes with that sense of belonging and unity." As I listen to his voice my shivering slowly stills and I close my eyes and remember my family here in this village and I know exactly of that sense of freedom that comes with that feeling of belonging. "This first mark on your chin," he takes the knife from the coals and I hear the sizzle of it being cooled in the birch bark container we keep nearby to drink from, "is for the *Direction of Beginnings* and I feel a sharp pain as he cuts my chin and a greater sting as he rubs the wound with ashes from the fire.

He puts his knife back into the coals. "The direction in which summer comes earlier and winter comes later is called *The Direction of the Natural,*" he says in a quiet soothing voice. He blows a cool breath on my stinging chin. "It speaks of the natural way of life and the boundaries that must be kept in place to make all things harmonize. It reminds us of respect for Mother Earth and the importance we have in protecting her. It is rooted in innocence, play, and the respect of learning." I think of the contrast of the way of life between the whites and what I have learned here in the Maple Forest. I think of love of my Pa and how I think he was more Indian than he was white with the way he wanted to live his life. I think of all that I have learned to love and respect in my time here in the Maple Forest. I hear the sizzle hiss of the hot knife cooling just before feel the second sharp cut in my chin.

"The direction in which the sun sets," Bright Feather continues, "is called *The Direction of Introspection.*" This time he blows warm breath and follows that with a light feather kiss on my trembling lips. I work to concentrate on his words and not the pain that screams so loudly on my face. "Our strength, our will, and our self-awareness comes from this direction. Belief in one's abilities and the understanding of what should be valued and what should be forgotten is a part of this direction, too." I think of the changes that came about in me when I realized what a Powerful Woman I am. When I realized that I was no longer white and could never go back to the frightened white girl I once was. I think that perhaps this Direction of Introspection is one that has grown the most in me. I feel the third cut get made and the sting of the ashes as they are rubbed into the wound.

With my eyes squeezed closed I am held in place only by Bright Feather's words and touch. I take short quick breaths to forget about the pain as Bright Feather blows, then kisses and then finally, this time, trails hot, wet kisses down my neck. He bites me careful where my neck and shoulder meet and I jump and for a moment I forget just about everything else but his mouth.

At last he says to me, "The final direction is called *The Direction of Sharing* and it comes where it is always coldest." He places his knife in the fire and I feel him kiss my mouth gentle and careful one more time but I still do not open my eyes. "This direction is a quiet one for it comes on the whisper of the winds. It speaks of generosity and sharing like the deer who is gentle and kind and Mother Earth who is generous with all nature has to offer. It is my direction for it is like when I used to be alone all of the winter and it is yours, too, for it is from you that I have learned of the *sharing of love.*" And he kisses me again just before he makes the fourth cut and then does the final piece of smoothing in the ash.

The shivering starts again and it is not from chill I realize but from the thoughts of being far away from this man I love so fiercely and fear of being on my own with strangers who do not know me and do not care and I feel the tears building up behind my eyes and slipping out from my still shut eyes. "*Remember me, and I will always be there*," he whispers soft into my ear and gathers me close on his lap and wipes my face of tears and just a little blood I think. Silently we sit there, the two of us as one dark shadow, rocking back and forth, sharing our love and sorrow and fear. *"Destiny,"* he whispers then, *"remember destiny,"* he reminds me of our pledge on Deer and Possum's porch not so long ago, "no person, no situation, no thing will stop this that we have." And he loves me again in the warmth of our hut and furs and I try hard to remember every single moment and believe that I will be back here before the first flower blooms.

"I love you, Bear," is the last thing I remember him say before I finally fall fast asleep.

'Twas in the watches of the night, I thought upon thy power,
I kept thy lovely face in sight, amidst the darkest hour.[3]

~Isaac Watts

Guest

The next morning Bright Feather and I say our final goodbyes in the privacy of our hut. We speak less with words and more with looks and touches. Words can't tell what we both feel deep inside.

"Remember you are not One Who Is Always Alone anymore," I say as I move to walk outside our hut.

"Remember you are not Elle Graves anymore," Bright Feather says back to me with a fierce growl.

We prepare to ride out me, Major Everett and George Maw. I sit on Willow and feel like the last lone autumn leaf on a tree that's been battered by storms all night. My mind is foggy and slow from the nervous shivers that I still feel now and then and the near sleepless night I've had. And let's not talk about the pain of the permanent marks that I now have on my chin.

Otter reminds me of Miss Rebecca sobbing quietly next to Raccoon who has his most menacing look on. I can't work up the notion to say a word to either of them.

One Who Knows approaches me and I see the twinkle in her eye as she looks at the very sore cuts on my face. "Hurt something terrible do they not?" she says. "I regretted mine for days after. You should have asked me." She studies me a moment and then says, "But maybe the pain will give you something else to think about, eh?"

"I've a gift for you," she says in the same way I had spoken to her just a few weeks back and she hands me her old gathering basket to place in among all my things. "I've filled it with important herbs that will be no good to you if your thick skull can't remember what to do with them. At least most of them will smell good when you are sick."

She studies my sorrowful face that can't fight the tears that now and then escape. "I am proud to call you my daughter. He," she gestures her head to Bright Feather who I see is in a serious conversation with Major Everett, "is proud to call you his mate. And all of us," she gestures around her and I see what must be the entire village standing quietly watching, "are all proud to call you *ours*. Remember," and she holds both of her old hands up and weaves them together, "You are destined for great things but I have told you once: *There is much difficulty as well as joy to come for both of you.* You do not need to be close enough to hold hands to still be together. Now is a time for the difficult, but there is still more joy to come." She smiles a rare smile. "Joy never comes without a bit of work to get it." As she walks to stand beside War Woman and Great Elk, I hear in my head what she has told me before, *You were always a powerful woman even before you knew it.*

Bright Feather comes and stands beside me as I sit on Willow. He rests his warm hand on my thigh and says, "See you before the first spring flower buds." He smiles at me and quotes Isaac Watts, *"Were I in heav'n without my God, 'Twould be no joy to me; And whilst this earth is my abode, I long for none but thee*." He mounts up on Companion and rides out of the village without looking back at me. As he has promised, he leaves for Deer's place to learn what should be done.

Major Everett, George Maw and I travel that whole first day with no conversation and set up camp in a place I take no note of. I work hard to feel nothing for otherwise I will just die from the pain of it I think. I have no thoughts or words in my head. I just work at being empty.

I sleep like the dead that night making up from exhaustion in my head, my heart and my body. The morning dawns bright, shiny and cold and we travel out after a quick meal that I don't taste. As we stop for a moment's rest in the middle of the day, Major Everett at last breaks the silence and asks me, "What are your plans?"

I stare at him for a moment, with a dumb look I'm sure, and think, *Why are you talking to me? Can't you see I'm not alive anymore?* But he continues to stare at me with his polite, interested look and I struggle to spark some life in me.

"I don't understand what you are asking me," I finally say.

He gives me a sideways smile and looks at George Maw. "First off, you might be better received if you switch over to English for a time." I don't even realize. I repeat my question in English.

"Well, as a first point," he says. "How will you behave? Will you be cordial or hostile? Will you be polite and helpful or will you be silent and withdrawn? Will you make every effort to be Bear or will you be Elle Graves?"

I realize that I've not thought a moment past the leaving of my people and have no answers for them and say so.

"Can I make some suggestions?" George Maw asks polite like. I look at him but don't speak. He continues in the length of my silence. "Looking at you here, now, you appear remarkably *savage*; the bow and arrow, the knife, the tattoos, the dress. You are going to walk into that general store and the whole world is just about going to stop and take note. You can behave like a *savage* and prove many people's first impressions correct or you can behave *civilized* and shock them right down to their toes." He shrugs. "The first way will make a strong point but will gain you little in the way of support. The second way will confuse even the greatest critics and may win over a few sitting on the fence."

I mull over his words in my tired, slow, sorrowful mind. "I thank you for your suggestions," I say in my politest English I can manage. I look at Major Everett. "What did Bright Feather speak to you about before we left?"

He takes off his hat and scratches his scalp and chuckles a little quietly to himself at the memory. "Well, we had a right polite conversation, him and I." He looks at me pointed. "In perfect English I might add," and I work to hide a little smile at the fun Bright Feather must have had. "He spoke at length about the *Real People's* belief in balance and harmony and how *the only purpose for The Real People of the Maple Forest* here on earth was to keep the way of things correct here within the bounds of Mother Earth and all those things that she holds dear." I nod my head, for I know this to be true. "Then he very politely told me that if anything were to happen to you before you are returned to him he would hold me personally responsible and hunt me down and kill me in the most painful way he could come up with." I don't have anything to say about that but I hear his voice in my head, *Remember me, and I will always be there* and for a brief moment I can almost smell his smell and feel him sitting next to me. It's a good moment.

The ride to Cornelius Cooper's store, of Ward's Mill, Virginia, takes us fourteen days. I remember that with Weasel the trip took less time, but we're not running from anything and I suspect Major Everett and George Maw think I need a slower pace. Maybe I do for by the time we have arrived I've at least been able to do some planning and make some decisions.

In my whole life, I've been to Cornelius Cooper's store five maybe six times, I think. That's the best my memory serves me. It was always just a two day trip with Pa and there was so much to see and take in all the while caring for Eli that it was usually more than my brain could take in completely. I can conjure up the image of plump Mrs. Cooper for she always gave Eli and me some sweets that tasted right delicious. I can remember her kind smile and voice. Mr. Cooper I remember being a big man with a huge white apron that I think Ma could have used for a tablecloth had it not been so filthy. He was always busy bustling with the customers and I don't recall ever having spoken one word to him.

Ward's Mill, Virginia, as best as I can recall has a blacksmith and stable, Cooper's General Store and the mill. Cornelius Cooper has owned the mill along with the store for as long as I've known. I can remember at harvest time traveling sometimes with Pa and Eli and Henry and waiting with the other farmers for their turn to have their grain ground. The rule was always "whoever came the farthest goes first" so there were times that we camped a night or two or three waiting for our turn. During harvest time the mill runs day and night, but I know it'll be silent now in the late part of autumn, early part of winter. That's all that I can remember but as we ride into town it causes my heart to pound practically right out of my chest because it is so *white civilized* and I am, after all so *red savage* inside now.

"Perhaps I should go in and prepare them," Major Everett says as we sit there on our horses and hear laughter and conversation spilling out from the store. "No need putting you into any more awkward of a situation then there already is," he says as he dismounts. "George, you wait with her."

We sit on our horses and almost immediately as Major Everett walks in, a man walks out. He stares at me like his brain can't believe what his eyes are seeing. "Well, well," he says after a time. "Lookit what we've got here." He steps down into the dirt by me and Willow and I sense that Mr. George Maw has gotten almost as tense as I am. "It's a pretty Injun squaw." He takes his hat off and squints at me and begins to walk slow around Willow. "No ... no ... it's a pretty white maid all done up like an Injun squaw. Now that's something we haven't seen around here in ... I don't think forever. Why don't you come on in and enjoy the hospitality of Cooper's? Here, I'll help you down ..."

"I appreciate the welcome and the invitation," George Maw says and the man seems to see him for the very first time. "But Major Everett has gone in to speak with the Coopers and we were told to wait outside here for the moment."

The two men eye each other, and I am reminded of two male dogs at Great Elk's village that were always fighting amongst themselves. "Is that so," the man says. "Well, I'd be a fool to carry on home and miss all of this, now wouldn't I?" He turns and steps back up into the store and disappears inside.

Major Everett comes out a few moments later and looks at me, "Are you ready?"

I think it is a powerful foolish question and choose not to answer. But I dismount just the same. *I am Bear, of the Elk Clan, daughter of One Who Knows, mate of Bright Feather of the Wolf Clan, son of War Woman and Great Elk chief of The Real People of the Maple Forest.* The look I give Major Everett says, *Let's go.*

Cooper's General Store is absolutely stone quiet when I walk in. There's not a sound as I step into the darkness of the inside. I feel eyes on me taking in everything there is to see and I hear George Maw's voice saying, *Looking at you here, now, you appear remarkably savage; the bow and arrow, the knife, the tattoos, the dress.* That suits me just fine I realize and I stand and let them all drink their fill of me while my eyes adjust to the dim light.

It's Major Everett who must speak first for it seems that all present are stunned into silence. "Mr. and Mrs. Cooper, may I reintroduce to you Miss Elle Graves, late of this town and who we have been searching for nigh onto two years."

My eyes can now see the couple I remember to be Mr. and Mrs. Cooper and the looks they have on their faces tell me that they never, ever, *ever* thought to see me standing in their store being reintroduced to them. I step forward and extend my hand, "It's good to see you again and I'm right grateful for your offer of hospitality."

"Well, well," I hear the same voice from outside, "seems like the Injuns didn't change her manners none," and there's some laughter.

Mrs. Cooper finally manages to make herself come to life instead of being carved out of wood and she says, "My dear, Elle, welcome home ..." But her voice fades away. She doesn't know what to do with me, I realize. And she never takes my hand.

Mr. Cooper steps forward and he's as big as I remember and his apron's as stained as I recall, too. I look at him and he says, "Where've ya been all this time?"

Major Everett speaks before I can even form thoughts. "She was brought into the Cherokee town of New Echota down in Georgia. My aunt and uncle are missionaries down there and so I was contacted and asked to escort her home as my company is currently stationed in Virginia and I was heading back north anyway." I am impressed with his words, for they are not lies actually, they just don't tell the whole story.

Major Everett looks at the Coopers and must finally ask, "Do you have accommodations for this young woman? Or are there nearby relatives I should escort her to?"

"Her Pa's dead," Cornelius Cooper says and he talks in front of me as if I cannot understand his language.

Major Everett looks a bit annoyed. "We are aware of *all* the sorry details of Miss Graves immediate family." He reaches into his coat pocket and withdraws the notice that speaks of my disappearance and has my likeness drawn on it. "We are here first because of this flier that has been circulated. Am I correct in bringing her here or should I take her someplace else?"

For a brief moment I have a rush of hope that is so overpowering I am afraid it will knock me over. *Please say you do not want me* I will him to speak with every speck of me. *Please say there is no place for me here.* My mind plays mean tricks of me riding happily into Great Elk's village and enjoying a welcome embrace from Bright Feather. "Oh, of course we have a place for her," I hear Mrs. Cooper say. "We have a bedroom in the back that would be just perfect for her. Come dear, let's get you settled and, er, cleaned up a bit," she says.

"I have a horse that needs to be cared for," I say, "and things I need to carry in."

"I'll not have no bug infested Injun things in my home," Cornelius Cooper says quick like and I hear a snicker from the background audience of nameless people.

"Cornelius!" Mrs. Cooper says in a shocked tone. She turns nervous eyes on Major Everett and George Maw and then finally on me. "Benny, will you help Miss Graves stable her horse round back and find a safe place to store her things *in the barn?*"

"Sure, Miz Cooper," I hear from behind me. "I've already offered once to assist *Miss Graves* and I'm more than happy to help now." There's more snickering behind me. "Come along, *Miss Graves.*"

I turn to follow Benny out as I hear voices begin to start up again as everyone talks at once. Willow's waiting quiet and calm outside and I work real hard to be just like her. Benny says, "This a ways …" He walks around the store towards a small barn and I lead Willow around back to it. There's space for four horses although only two are in use. As I care for Willow and carefully stack my things in the corner of the stall, I feel Benny's eyes on me. Finally, he says, "I just can't believe you're still alive. We'd all taken you for dead long ago."

What do you say to something like that? I wonder to myself. *Surprise!* Or *I'm sorry to disappoint you.* Or, *Let's just pretend that I am,* and ride away. I sort through the stuff I want to bring inside and the things I can settle to leave outside for a bit. I settle on my book from Bright Feather and my basket of herbs from One Who Knows. I smile to myself, *I can always smell them to get some comfort since I probably can't remember what they're good for!*

"Cornelius said he didn't want any bug infested things in his home," Benny observes as I walk out of the stall carrying my bits.

"There's no bugs, I checked," I say matter of fact and walk past him but not before I see him puzzle over how I could have done such a thing.

Major Everett and George Maw are waiting outside as I come around the corner. Major Everett looks powerful uncertain about everything and I can't help myself. I look at George Maw and say in Indian, "Seems like he worries for his life a small bit," remembering Bright Feather's threat.

"Hey! No speaking Injun in this town!" Benny shouts and looks as if I've just shot his pet dog.

"I remember listening to a private conversation was rude. Have things changed since I've been gone?" I ask him in clear English.

He looks mighty put out and mounts his horse. "Welcome home, Miss Graves," he says in a voice that means no such thing and rides off.

I know Major Everett and George Maw can't stay no matter how welcome or unwelcome I am. They know that too. "Where is the Second United States Calvary, Division of the Army, Company A that is presently based with the Ninth Virginia Cavalry, Company D located?" I ask matter of fact. "Just in case it suits me to stop by," I add but they know what I am saying. If things are difficult for me here, they're much closer than Deer's trading post in North Carolina.

George Maw spends time with me explaining the route to Fort Winston, Virginia. North of Ward's Mill by a bit, it would take me two days to reach by fast horse riding he tells me. I work hard to remember all the details and then repeat them back to him. He nods his head that I've spoken correctly.

"We will come through here anytime we pass by. We will be happy to carry messages then too," Major Everett says. "Will you be alright?"

I study him and think it's kind that he has concern for me. I think it's genuine and not just because of Bright Feather's threat. I tell him, "This is the third time in my life that I have been brought to a place that caused me fear. So far, each time I have become stronger. Each time I learn good things about myself. I trust One Who Knows' words that there will be joy again in my life and that I just need to go through some difficult times to get there."

But I don't tell him I will be alright, because even I don't know that.

I watch Major Everett and George Maw ride out of Ward's Mill, Virginia, and when I cannot see them anymore, I go back into Cooper's Store. "Here you are, dear," Mrs. Cooper says to me. "Come let me show you where you can sleep." She starts towards the back of the store to what seems to be a back room behind the main counter.

"Hang on there, girly," I hear Mr. Cooper say to me. "I told you no Injun things with bugs in them in my house." Mrs. Cooper looks nervous but says nothing.

"I'm sure they've no bugs," I start to say.

"What's this?" he says and the basket of herbs is taken from my hands. "Looks like a lot of weeds and such. This is best left in the barn. Anything gonna have bugs, this is sure it. And what's this? A book!?"

I clutch it to my heart and will my voice to stay calm and my heart to beat slow and steady. "It's a book of Christian hymns," I say.

"Surely she can keep *that* with her, Cornelius," I hear Mrs. Cooper say. He walks away without answering and I take it to mean *yes*.

After I have brought the basket of herbs back to the stable, Mrs. Cooper takes me to my room which is no more than a storage closet with a cot and pitcher and bowl for washing in between the sacks of grain and other bits of store supplies. There's a looking glass hung on the wall and after she leaves me, I study my face in the mirror. Even at Pa's there was no looking glass and I find it amazing what I see for I do look like a wild Injun savage! I study my permanent marks proper healed now and no longer painful and I touch the robin's feathers in my hair. My green eyes stare out at me from my tanned face and I touch the bear claw necklace that hangs around my neck. "I am Bear," I say to my face looking back at me and I decide that I like very much what I see.

I wash my hands and face and put my book down on my bed. I sit on the edge of the cot for a moment and I think, *Now what?* and a huge wave of loneliness just about swallows me up. I press my hand to my mouth to stifle the moans that boil in my throat and begin to rock myself back and forth for I feel the panic and the shivering coming over me something terrible. "I want to go home," I hear myself moan and I rock and rock and try to comfort myself in the quiet of the tiny cramped closet.

"You are our guest, my dear," Mrs. Cooper says to me the next morning over breakfast. I hear Mr. Cooper call her *Naomi*. They are both horrified to discover that the marks on my chin will not wash off no matter how hard you scrub them and no matter how strong the soap is. They've a habit of discussing me as if I'm not there or at least as if I don't have a brain in my head to understand what they say.

"Can you imagine doing such a thing, Cornelius?" Mrs. Cooper says in shocked tones when I tell her the lines are forever.

"Injun savages do all kinds of horrible things, Naomi," Mr. Cooper says in a voice filled with great knowledge. "I know for a fact that they eat the hearts of their enemies right on the field of battle, that they sometimes sacrifice their own children to gods that they worship, and they sometimes have three, four, even five wives at a time."

"NO!" Mrs. Cooper says, and clutches her hand to her chest as if to still her shocked heart. It never occurs to either one of them to ask me if these things are so, so I remain quiet. She does eventually look at me as if to see if any of those evil possibilities are lurking across the breakfast table in the form of one Injun-looking white girl. I try not to blink.

"We must do something about your clothes and your hair, dear," she says. "You cannot be seen around town looking as you do. You'll put a scare into everyone." *That would suit me just fine,* I realize but again I keep quiet with my thoughts.

"Anything she takes from the store she'll be required to work to pay off the expense," Mr. Cooper says. "This ain't no charity place and never will be. If she's to be a *guest,* she will be a *paying guest.*"

"I'd be happy to help around the store in anyway you can see fit," I say polite like and they both look startled that I speak civil and proper. *George Maw was right,* I think. I will win more battles being civilized than savage.

I forget how cumbersome white clothes are once I'm dressed a week later in button down chemise and over blouse, skirts and petticoats, stockings and shoes, and a bonnet for my head when I go out. I stand in front of the looking glass in my room and I can hear Raccoon laughing all the way back in the Maple Forest. For the first time I think, *Perhaps it's best that no one's here to see me* as I smile too at how silly I look. I'm careful to store away all of my clothes in a secret spot I've found out in the woods aways from the general store. Once again, in front of me, the Coopers have discussed burning all my bug infested things and the next morning I search for a safe place to put everything to stop them.

Mr. Cooper keeps a tally of all the monies I owe him as a result of staying with them. He charges me for rent of room and meals and for the materials I used to sew the clothes on my back. He charges me for the stabling of Willow and for her food as well. He regularly reminds me of the debt I owe him and that it must be repaid. I think back to my imaginings of becoming the adopted daughter of Mr. and Mrs. Cornelius Cooper of Ward's Mill, Virginia, and how wrong the thinking was. I work hard and am willing to do anything they ask of me. I try to be very polite and kind and never voice the unkind thoughts about the Coopers and what I think of them that regularly roll around in my head like big stone boulders down a steep hill.

Mr. Cooper jokes that I've been good for business, for word has spread throughout the surrounding areas that I'm here and there's always a steady stream of curious people coming into the store to have a look at me. I, once again, am polite and respectful despite the fact that they discuss me like I am a stabled horse they've come to check out rather than a living, breathing person. The women in many cases are worse than the men.

"Can you *imagine* what it would have been like to live with *savages* for almost two years?" they say with voices filled with horror.

"What do you suppose she had to do while she lived there to stay alive?" they say as they whisper loudly behind their hands as I work at counting stock.

"Even dressed in proper clothes she has a vicious streak about her, don't you think?" one of the old biddies says to her friend and I think, *And you don't even know about the knife strapped to my thigh from the white man I killed.*

"I hear that white women when they are captured often have to immediately be married off to a brave." I walk away when I hear that conversation begin for I can't manage to think of Bright Feather without tears and moans and I *will not* do such a thing in front of mean - spirited, curious eyes.

"How do you suppose she got those marks on her face? I'd never be able to go out in public if that were me." I lift my head with pride and straighten my back as I sweep the floor.

"Have you seen her wrists? She's got scars from being *tied up!*" My head thinks of Weasel for a few moments and how full of harmony my life is now that he is dead.

I keep a running conversation of things I'd like to say to these mean spirited women. These thoughts running around in my head sometimes get funny enough that I have to fight to keep the laughter down. *I've got a mighty big scar on my left breast when Weasel bit me there. Shall I show you? Or, I suspect that I am capable enough with my knife to fight all of you women and a few of your men. Would you care to try? Or, I suspect I'd be less inclined to appear in public missing my two front teeth like you are, Mrs. Bekeman. I'll take my permanent marks any day. And Mrs. Jamesway, about your powerful body odor ...?* The men, particularly the ones who visit the liquor corner of the store, seem more harmless than hurtful.

"I hear Injun squaws are better wives than white women."

"I hear Injun women are responsible for torturing and killing prisoners during war time."

"I hear Injun women fight right along side the men and some can even handle knives and bows and arrows just as well."

I have a big chuckle to myself when I think of the looks on all their faces when I imagine telling them that all of *these* comments are actually quite true. Now *that* would be worth all the commotion it would cause, I suspect.

I have little time to ride Willow but I visit with her every day and try to walk her a bit to get some exercise. I brush her and talk to her and bring her treats I sneak from the root cellar. I care for my bow and arrow which I have hidden in my secret spot in the woods every day, too. My knife strapped to my leg under my skirts is kept sharp and well cared for, too. (That was the only time I was thankful for all the foolish layers.)

By the end of the third week with the Coopers, I know the way of the store enough to wait on customers that will allow it (some won't even talk to me) and have a regular routine of chores I do. I become familiar with some of the faces that come into the store and there are even a few that stir vague memories from the occasional times I might have met them on a visit with Pa.

Old Mr. Hobson comes in once a week, every Friday. He says it's for supplies, but I suspect - since he spends most of his time in the liquor corner - that there are only certain specific supplies he's looking for. Benny

Stokes is the blacksmith and it's my opinion that it's unfortunate he lives within walking distance of the store. He's married to Emily who's one of the people who'll not allow me to wait on her nor will she talk to me. She just stands there looking right past me to a spot on the wall waiting for Mr. or Mrs. Cooper to come and serve her. She and Mrs. Cooper spend time each visit whispering quietly in the corner somewhere out of earshot of me. They glance at me often and I am the obvious topic of discussion.

Jane and Ezekiel West live on the nearest homestead and are kind of shy and unsure around me. She smiles kindly which is more than I can say for many. She's expecting what I learn to be her first baby and whenever she visits, there's much talk about babies and birthing and pregnancy and such. I hear One Who Knows saying to me, *It is something almost every young woman thinks of – I am sure white or red – if a baby does not come with the first time you are together with a man.*

I ask the Coopers one time what I get paid for all the work that I do, since I'm always reminded of how much I *owe* and I'm told that figures and figuring are not something any lady should concern herself with, *ever.* And that came from Mrs. Cooper not Mr. How will I ever be able to settle a debt if I can't worry my "ladylike head" over figures?

I learn that the Coopers have a son named Johnny but it's a sad topic that often makes Mrs. Cooper cry and Mr. Cooper look angry. I take it that there's been disagreement over "sweet Johnny" as Mrs. Cooper calls him and *"that boy"* as Mr. Cooper calls him for years and years. Mrs. Cooper tells quiet bits at times about him how he loved horses and loved to travel in the forest and she has me taste "sweet Johnny's favorite candy" but she does it mostly out of earshot of Mr. Cooper.

I find by the end of my first month with the Coopers that I feel sorry for the both of them at times because neither of them seem happy ever. *Life is what you make of it, Elle,* I hear Pa say in my head and I realize that he's right. For me, the first month's best described as wandering through a strange forest that's thick with fog. My brain's slow and I'm often tired. Like my first days in Great Elk's village my nights are filled with thoughts of those I love but now the faces are white *and* red. I dream busy dreams that make me wake in the morning more tired than ever but I can never remember them. I work hard over the course of each day to stay busy and preoccupied, even welcoming the distractions of unkind and nosy customers rather than face the chance to be alone with my thoughts. I'm happy to just have something – *anything* – to fill in the huge hole of loneliness that I feel constantly in my stomach, making it ache and roll and pitch with the sickness of my sadness.

One night, over dinner, as the first serious snow fall blows outside, I finally feel comfortable enough to ask the Coopers why they felt inclined to put the flier out about me not knowing me too well and all. They look at each other in a puzzled fashion for a moment and then Mrs. Cooper finally says. "Why my dear, we didn't put that flier out about your disappearance. Your brother, Henry, did." A loud whining starts in my ears like a hundred tiny mosquitoes all buzzing at the same pitch at the same time. It interferes with what Mrs. Cooper's still saying to me and I hear only snatches like, "I thought you knew … Asked our permission … Been searching since that terrible day … Sent word out to him but haven't heard anything yet …" and then the buzzing's so loud in my ears I can no longer hear her words. For the third time in my life a blackness descends on me and the lights begin to dim and everything at last is dark and quiet.

When light returns and I open my eyes, I'm lying on the floor with Mr. and Mrs. Cornelius Cooper looking down at me like some kind of spill they don't quite know how to go about cleaning up. Both look shocked but neither make any move to help me to sit up and eventually I seat myself back in my chair. My forehead stings and I reach up to find my fingers wet with blood. I stare stupid like at my bloody fingers all the while my thoughts whirl around in my head. *Henry's alive? Henry's been here? Henry's put out the flier?*

A large hand pushes a rag into my hand. "Why would you have thought that we would've put out the notice?" Cornelius Cooper says in a tone that lets me know he knew I was an idiot and now this proves it. "We hardly knew your Pa, let alone you." I've no answer and just look at him.

"Major Everett said that first day you arrived that you 'were aware of *all* the sorry details of your immediate family,'" Mrs. Cooper says, "So we rightly assumed that you knew all about Henry's posting the note." She thinks of something. "Do you mean that Major Everett has made no effort to contact your brother? Does that mean you have been here all this time and Henry has not been informed?!" She looks at Mr. Cooper. "Dear me ..."

Mr. Cooper's angry. "That Major Everett assured us that all involved parties had been informed and taken care of! He said that there was *no need* to make any further inquiries into 'the situation known as *Elle Graves' Kidnapping and Abduction.*' He said that you had been returned safe and sound and that he'd taken care of everything that needed taking care of!" Mr. Cooper's voice gets louder and louder as he speaks until he is shouting. "DO YOU MEAN TO TELL ME THAT YOU'VE BEEN HERE ALL THESE WEEKS TAKING ADVANTAGE OF OUR KINDNESS AND HOSPITALITY AND NO ONE'S COMING TO TAKE YOU AND SETTLE THESE DEBTS?!? DO YOU MEAN THAT YOU ARE PROBABLY HERE FOR THE ENTIRE WINTER??!"

My thoughts swirl as I try to unsort this big tangle of things that all of a sudden I've tripped over. I've a brief moment of thought wondering if all of this had been said in the language of the Real People if there would be so much confusion? I understand what Major Everett was trying to do in those first few moments of my arrival here. He meant to settle any swirling dust and cover all tracks that would have led back to The Maple Forest. Just like I asked him to. I sigh a deep sigh as I dab my head.

"The flier said that my father and *brothers* had been killed ..." I say looking back and forth at Mr. and Mrs. Cooper in confusion. "I ... thought ..." I frown with puzzlement. *What did I think?*

"Fool printer made an error," Mr. Cooper mumbled. "No sense spending money to print the thing again."

Except for the fact that I thought my brother was dead and he isn't, I think. I work to form words. "What was your understanding from Henry," and it feels *so strange* to say his name and realize he is alive somewhere out there, "that you should do if I showed up on your doorstep?" I ask finally.

Mr. Cooper walks over to a jug of liquor he keeps for "family and medicinal use" and pours himself a cupful. He takes a long swallow. He looks at me with great anger and spits out, "Your fool brother paid cash money for me to allow him to put my name on the fliers. He told me that he would satisfy any debt that you incurred if you should show up and that we should keep a running record until he came and got you. That was *over a year and a half ago*, you little idiot! *No one* thought you'd turn up after all this time." He takes another long swallow. "Henry went off and joined the Army," he looks at Mrs. Cooper, "how long ago?"

"Oh, I'd think it was early last year at least ..." Mrs. Cooper says thoughtful like.

Mr. Cooper looks at me and I realize that he has worked very hard to conceal a hatred and disgust that he no longer makes any effort to disguise. The only reason he's tolerated my savage self is for the money he was certain he would get from Henry. Money he now realizes he's not so sure he's going to get now after all this time.

He's the only businessman in the area, Elle, I hear Pa say to me in a tired voice as we ride into town that very last time. *Anyone who deals with Cornelius Cooper knows that he follows every penny in and out of that store.*

"We've tolerated your stinkin', bug infested, Injun presence here in this store because I plan to collect a tidy sum for all the trouble you've put us through. And that's *the only reason*. I have a *signed piece of paper* that says that should you arrive that he will pay me *cash money* for all expense that you incur. It's called a *Promissory Note* and I can have him *or you* locked up if you do not settle this debt as *promised. Just watch me!* Anyone who's associated with *red savages* for nigh onto two years, whose *lived with them*, and *eaten with them*, and *God knows what else with them*, is not welcome in this town let alone this house. If your fool brother wants you, *he can have you.*" The wind rises up and the snow sounds like it has turned to hail as it pelts against the outside of the house. "And by Christ, he'll have a *hell of a bill* when he finally shows up, too."

"Now Cornelius, things have worked out so far …" Mrs. Cooper starts to say.

"*Shut up, Naomi,*" Mr. Cooper says. "You don't think for one moment I'm going to listen to you *again,* do you? You don't for one minute think that *your opinion* is ever something I want to hear, do you? Just like I listened to you over your "precious little Johnny?" Mrs. Cooper gets the look she usually does when she knows that Mr. Cooper is going to speak ill of their son. It is a look that makes me think of a cowering dog in a way. "How can you defend this," he waves his hand at me like he can't think of a word that's low enough to mean me, "this *Injun lover* when you know what the Injuns did to your *precious little Johnny*? You made excuses for him his whole life even though we know he was more stupid than a mule. Couldn't learn to even count bales of hay in the back let alone money to help me run this store! So stupid he couldn't remember to do the basic things in life like *take a bath* or even learn to *not piss in his own bed* for Christ's sake!" Mrs. Cooper has begun to cry and puts her hands up over her ears to block out the words her husband's throwing at her. "You would've allowed him to stay here forever even when the stench of his presence became so bad that customers wouldn't even come to the store because of it!!"

Mr. Cooper has worked himself in to a state of fury that I've never seen in my whole life. I watch him take another long, long swallow of the whiskey as he paces around the small dinner table. He glances at me before he continues shouting at his wife. "And you would have loved him, *your precious Johnny, even after he brought his stinkin' self and A STINKIN' INJUN WHORE* home, wouldn't you have? Would you have ignored *him and his Injun slut* just like you ignored everything else, Naomi? Huh? Would You?

"Where is he now? We heard those blood-thirsty savages *murdered him,* remember Naomi? We heard they hunted him down and killed him. I heard they *scalped him* and *ate his heart for revenge.* And you can sit here and feel any sympathy for this, this … *red and white whore?!*"

He looks at me and I feel my stomach clutch and tuck and roll and I think, *Oh no, I think I'm going to be sick …*

Mr. Cooper is not done for he turns to me with fire in his eyes and disgust on his lips. "I hated the Injuns from the start because that is *the proper way of things*! I tolerated the idiot son we had because Naomi said it was the proper way of things, too, for a father to tolerate his son no matter what. But even Naomi knew that we were done with *precious Johnny* when he showed up with his squaw tied at the end of a rope like a pet dog! Grinning like an idiot, wasn't he Naomi. 'Look what I got, Ma!' he said to you like he'd brought you a bunch of *damned flowers!!* Even you couldn't swallow your *precious Johnny* being an Injun lover. Could you, Naomi? Could you?"

Mrs. Cooper is sobbing and sobbing. Her head is cradled in her arms while her hair half lays in the remains of her dinner plate. The shouting stops and aside from Mrs. Coopers crying there is no sound except the storm that is blowing and blowing outside. My thoughts are clear as a bell for once.

So, these are Bear John's parents.

I have Bear John's knife strapped to my leg.

I have Bear John's horse out in the stable.

I'm the one who killed your 'precious Johnny'.

And then a more curious thought enters my head. *Am I sleeping in Bear John's bed?* I add another sound to the wailing cries of Mrs. Cooper and the blowing of the winter storm outside as I vomit on the floor in front of me.

Things are different with the Coopers after that night. Mr. Cooper can hardly stand the sight of me and makes that plain to me every day. Mrs. Cooper's quiet and withdrawn and it becomes obvious to me right quick that she thinks little of me, too, aside from what money I'll bring in when Henry arrives to claim me and pay the bill. Outside it's a winter unlike any winter I've ever remembered for it snows and snows and snows. Aside from the brave customer that surprises us every now and then (Ezekiel West comes occasionally searching for something for Jane, but even Old Mr. Hobson misses a few Fridays) there's little business at the General Store. Mr. Cooper spends much time in the evening drinking his 'medicinal liquor' and watching me with dark looks. I try to go about and do my chores as quick as possible, trapped by the weather and by my own circumstance. Mr. Cooper talks aloud for me to hear sometimes about Injun squaws and what they're good for and what they're not. I realize I'm only good for the money Mr. Cooper hopes to collect from Henry and a small fear begins to grow in me when I think *What if Henry never comes? How long until things become different yet again and I become a paying guest who can never pay?*

This winter with the Coopers offers me little joy trapped with people who hate me and with no place I can go. I remember the winter learning to ride Willow with Raccoon and to shoot with Cloud and Red Fox and must think of it only in tiny bits for it makes me powerful lonely and sad. I remember talking and talking and talking with Otter that whole first winter and having a friend for the first time and I again must put those thoughts away for I find that tears come too easy try as I might to keep them hidden behind my eyes. I can't, under any circumstances, think of Bright Feather unless I'm in the quiet of the room I sleep in (which I find *was* Bear John's) for it brings about a misery so complete that I often lose whatever was the last meal I managed to choke down. I sometimes try to read my book of songs that Bright Feather gave me but more often than not I end up just curled up in a ball rocking myself back and forth and trying to make the loneliness find another place to stay.

One snowy cold day, Ezekiel West braves the weather once again for something for Miss Jane. He smiles shyly at me and asks, "Do you have any jarred peaches still available? Jane has a powerful hunger for it that just can't seem to be satisfied."

I search the shelves and find just one carefully preserved and labeled jar. I ask how Miss Jane's feeling. "She's been told she's doing better than most. Her main complaints are that she's powerful tired and hungry, although nothing much appeals to her to eat." He looks at the peaches on the counter and smiles at me. "Except peaches it seems. Put them on my account, will you?" He says. He puts his hat back on his head and tucks the precious peaches inside his snow covered coat. "She's been told by some ladies that they were sick to the point of vomiting sometimes in the morning and sometimes all day!" He blushes something fierce.

"Having a baby's more complicated than I imagined." Taking a deep breath to prepare himself as he ventures back outside he gives me a kind smile and says, "Much obliged."

That night as I lay on my cot I think about Ezekiel and Jane West and the complications of having a baby. I think about Otter and wonder how she's doing and try to imagine Little Bird and how much he's talking now. All of a sudden my head thinks, *When was the last time you had your monthly?* and I realize I have no recollection of having had them ever here with the Coopers. And I've been here more than two full months. Suddenly, the sickness and the tears and the tiredness and even the time I had blackness happen to me the awful night when things changed here at the Coopers makes more sense to me. I reach down in wonder at my stomach and think, *Is there a baby in there?* I've a brief moment where I'm flooding with warmth from the top of my head to the tip of my toes like one great Whoosh. *Bright Feather's and my baby,* I think in delighted wonder. *Remember me and I will be there.*

Gradually, however, the thought of all the things that I'll have to face with *that* new bit of information causes me to run to the basin and throw up again. As I stand there in the dark, the way of things for me seems more than I can handle. On my own, with no one I can depend on, trapped by the weather, and now, *with a baby on the way.* I feel the easy tears begin to flow again and all of a sudden I think with a pile full of disgust, *Is this how a powerful woman behaves?* My mind looks hard at myself and aside from the permanent marks on my chin, there's nothing to see of the powerful woman that I'd become. These past weeks and months seem to have sucked all the power out of me and I feel like I'm in a big deep dark pit that has no way out. That fills me with great sorrow. *I've got to find this Powerful Woman again soon,* I think, *before she fades away forever.*

"Help," I hear me say quiet and whisper like in the dark and I realize that it's a prayer. "I need to find some help." I remember Ma saying, *Thou preparest a table before me in the presence of mine enemies:*[5] and later on Henry saying, *Shall we start cooking dinner, Elle?* I realize I need to find someone I can cook with.

In the morning I make some decisions. I do my chores and then inform Mrs. Cooper that I'm taking Willow for a ride. I don't ask her, I tell her and she seems to not know just what to say. I leave before she can think of something. Riding Willow in white clothes is not something either of us likes. I do my best to tuck my skirts and petticoats down about my legs so that their flapping in the wind does not spook Willow too much. It's not snowed since Ezekiel West's visit yesterday and I'm able to follow his tracks and within a bit of time I find myself looking at their small cabin thinking, *What am I doing?* But my head also tells me plain and clear that of all the people I've met since my return to Ward's Mill, Virginia, these two are the only ones who seemed to show me true kindness. I hear Deer's mate Possum say to me, *It does not matter what they call me as long as they speak polite and respectful to me.* I tie Willow near a tree that's sheltered from the wind, gather up my courage and knock at the front door and wait.

Miss Jane opens the door and she looks as pale as the snow that I'm standing in. "Why Miss Graves!" she says in a mighty surprised voice and she makes a motion to smooth her hair and straightens her clothes. After a moment's hesitation she says, "Won't you come in?"

It's a small but tidy cabin and I can tell right away that she's still been in bed for the place is cool and the covers on the bed are thrown back and rumpled. "May I offer you some tea?" she asks, but she seems at a loss as to what to do first.

"I'd be much obliged," I say. "Can I help you stir up the fire?"

"Oh, yes, please, that would be a help. Ezekiel got it going before he left but I must have dozed off for a bit…" She sets out two cups and a tea pot and I stir up the fire and swing the iron kettle over the flames to heat the water.

Tucked in the pocket of my skirt I draw out another jar of peaches and place it on the table. "I found another jar on the shelf this morning while I was doing my chores and I thought you might appreciate these," I say.

She picks the jar up like it is a most precious thing and looks at me real grateful. "Thank you, *so much*," she says and she hugs the jar tight. "I've had a terrible craving for these for about a week now and it's driving me fair crazy. This isn't exactly the best time to hunger for fresh peaches," she says as the wind picks up and moans outside. She looks at me, "Won't you have a seat?"

I sit at the table and look around the place. It's neat and tidy and she's made an effort to make it look homey. There are curtains on the window and a fresh clean tablecloth on the table. I spy a drawing hanging on the wall and am moved to look at it. It's a beautiful sketch of man staring thoughtful and intent at something in the distance. His hair is tousled and there's a slight shadow of a beard. Even though it's only a pencil sketch, it's alive and breathing almost. You can sense the man's intensity and almost find yourself straining to hear what he's listening to. It's Ezekiel West.

"That was the first time I saw Ezekiel," I hear shy like behind me. "At the town meeting in Richmond concerning the availability of newly available homestead lots. I was there with my Ma and Pa for the same reason. I was bored and started sketching things." She laughs a quiet laugh. "He was the most interesting subject."

"You have a fine talent," I tell her and she looks pleased. The kettle boils and she makes the tea. We sit in silence for a bit.

"How are you doing?" she asks me but her look says she already knows.

I take a deep breath. "That's why I am here. I've no one to talk to or ask questions and I hope you'll not think I am a bother. Please tell me if that's so and I'll just go."

"No, no, I'm glad you're here. Ezekiel's told me of the general opinion of folks from what he's heard and seen. We would've made more of an effort to welcome you but I've just been so tired with this baby coming and all. Next week I start my fifth month, so I'm hoping that things will improve." She looks a bit unsure. "They told me things would get better after the third month, though."

I start to talk. "I'm not sure where to begin or just what to tell you for I don't want to cause you upset. Perhaps I'll just ask you how you knew you were pregnant and what were the symptoms and what you know about it all." She studies me across the table and I look direct back at her. "Or maybe I should tell you a little about myself first and where I've been ..."

She puts her teacup down, folds her hands in her lap and says, "Well, I was hoping to become pregnant so I'd been watching for signs. I think the first thing that happened was my breasts got terrible tender. Then of course, I missed my monthly. Then came the tiredness unlike anything I've ever felt and it seems no matter how much I sleep I'm still exhausted." She points to the peaches. "The cravings are something new. Up until then, I felt hungry but never really wanted to eat anything. Some of the ladies I've seen at the store have told me horrible stories about constant sickness and dizziness and even passing out. I'm glad I haven't felt any of that though." She blushes. "And there's one thing else, and I'll tell you since you've asked. Ezekiel says I have a funny dark line that travels from my belly button downwards…" She blushes an even darker shade of red. "He says that's new since I've been pregnant." She picks up her teacup and tries to hide behind it as she takes a sip.

"I've not had my monthly for going on three months," I tell her. "I've had passing tiredness, and I've had the sickness – often late at night, and I did collapse one time and wake up moments later. And I've cried more in these past two months than I think I've cried in my whole life."

She stares at me for a moment and then the blush returns full force. "Of course," Miss Jane says to me, "you know that you must be, er, well, *intimate* with a man, right?"

I wait a moment and then finally say, "I am Bear, of the Wolf Clan, daughter of One Who Knows, *mate* of Bright Feather, son of War Woman and Great Elk chief of The Real People of the Maple Forest."

She stares at me for the longest time with her teacup in her hand midway between her mouth and the table. Finally she sets the teacup down and stares at me for a while longer. At last, she licks her lips, clears her throat, smiles a tiny smile and extends her hand. "How do you do, Bear. It's a pleasure to meet you. My name's Jane West. Please call me Jane."

I burst into tears.

At that very moment, Ezekiel West blows in. "Jane …?" he says, his voice full of concern. "Are you all right? There's a strange horse outside …" He takes in the picture before him. "Oh. How do you do, Miss Graves?"

"Not too well, as you can see, Ezekiel," Jane says as she hands me a clean cloth to wipe my face and nose. Her look at me asks, *Can I tell him?* I nod my head to her. "It would seem that things are much more complicated than they would appear for …" she hesitates and I see she struggles with what name to call me.

"I don't care what you call me as long as you speak to me polite and with respect," I say to her in all seriousness.

"… Elle," she settles on, "seems to be in the same condition as I am," and she gestures to the peaches.

"She's got cravings for the peaches?" He says in confusion and he looks back and forth between me and my tear stained face and his wife's pale tired one. "She wants the ones back I bought yesterday? I thought you ate all those already?!"

Jane looks first at me and then at him and then at me again and we both can't help it, we burst out laughing. And we laugh and laugh and laugh until the tears roll down both our faces and we're gasping for breath. "Glad I'm so powerful entertaining," he finally says as we struggle to pull ourselves together.

"No, Ezekiel," Jane finally manages to say to her husband as she wipes her face on her apron. "It would seem that Elle is *pregnant* just like *I* am."

"Oh …" he says and then as he thinks it all through his brain and I watch him slowly fit all the pieces together, he looks at me and says, "*OH*," more loudly.

"Elle informs me that she is married to an Indian brave named," she looks at me to correct her if she's wrong, "*Bright Feather*," and I nod, "who happens to be the *chief's son* of the tribe in which she's been living these past years."

"Oh …" is all Ezekiel can say again, but he's moved to pull up a stool and sit down.

Jane gets up and refills the kettle and swings it over the flame. She adds more wood to the fire and goes to the cupboard and takes out some biscuits and a bit of jam in a dish. "You'd better tell us the whole story as to *why you're here* instead of *there.*"

So I tell them all I know, except I leave out the Bear John part of the story. I bring them right up to the point where I'm with the Coopers and how I'm am no longer such a *welcome paying guest* because there's now a concern as to whether Henry'll ever be found to pay my bill. I tell them how the mood has changed in the house and how I don't know how they will react when they find out I'm with child.

"Well no one says you have to tell them about the baby right away," is the first thing Jane says. She stands up, turns sideways and beneath her skirts and apron there's just a hint of a bump. "You can easily hide things for another few months I'd say so the child part is not a primary concern. As long as they are not suspecting, it's probably the last thing on their minds. Do you agree, Ezekiel?"

Poor Ezekiel. He has a look of stunned confusion like he's stepped bare foot into hot horse dung and not sure where to go next. He looks at his wife, "I suspect so, Jane," he says finally.

Jane looks at me with fear in her eyes, "You are in danger, however, should Cornelius come to the conclusion that your brother Henry will never come, claim you, and pay your bill. And don't for one minute think that Naomi will lift a hand against him to help you. She is quieter and less obvious, but they are the same those two. Do you agree, Ezekiel?"

Ezekiel seems to finally spark to life. "Cornelius Cooper of Ward's Mill, Virginia, is ruthless," Ezekiel says with feeling. "He keeps careful records and charges heavy interest when you're late in paying. He has no desire to hear any excuses, he just wants the money that's due him." He looks at me serious like. "He was not the original owner of the mill. Seems Jonathan Ward, who could not read or write, signed a loan agreement that stated that should he ever be late with his bill to the general store or reach a certain level of debt, he'd give the ownership of the mill over to Cornelius as payment. When he reached a point where he owed so much and was indeed late for a bit on his payments, Cornelius took the mill." Ezekiel looks at me, "Debt and uncertainty is the way of life when you make your living farming, you know."

"Jonathan Ward was my father," Jane says quiet like. "He was a good man, a loving man. Always ready with a smile or a moment to stop what he was doing should I stop by to see him. He was fair, too, never ever cheated a soul out of even a grain of wheat. When in doubt he gave more than less." She looks down fondly at Ezekiel and smoothes back his hair that is damp from the melting snow. "Maybe that was his downfall, he just didn't believe that there were people who could be so evil and cruel."

Ezekiel reaches up and puts his arm around her waist as she stands next to him at the table and says, "Jonathan Ward took his family back to Richmond, where they both had family. He still owned some property here in Ward's Mill and so when Jane and I married, I staked a Homestead Claim that bordered on the Ward Property. It's a sizeable piece that we have to offer our children, now, but without the mill."

Jane smiles a sad smile. "My mother died just before we married. I was determined not to let Cornelius and Naomi Cooper keep me from my father's inheritance. Our success," she says as she looks at Ezekiel, "is their defeat."

Ezekiel says, "He owns Old Man Hobson's place, too, you know. Reached a point where the bill was so great he forced Hobson to hand over his deed. Charges him *rent* now, plus takes most of the crops that are grown over there by Hobson to sell them for his own profit and to "settle Hobson's continuing debt." Only allows Hobson to live there because he's just like slave labor." He studies me for a moment and then decides to tell me. "He owns the property that once was yours, too. When your Pa was killed," he swallows and looks at me, "I'm sorry," he says, "your Pa had just ordered and received a full season's worth of seed, plus he owed some money for other things needed for the season. Cornelius claimed he was due payment and I understand that Henry finally gave the property over to him when it became obvious he couldn't pay and couldn't handle the place all by himself. Henry went into the army because there wasn't much else left for him to do."

I stare at my empty teacup and then at the sorrowful faces of Jane and Ezekiel West. I'd not realized that there were so many puzzles to life. Here's a new one that truth be told I would have been happy to just leave undone. At last I say, "Thank you for your hospitality," and I stand to leave.

"Wait! Where are you going?!" They both say together.

"It's getting dark. I need to get back. I need to think." I look at them with very serious eyes. "Thank you for listening to me. Thank you for talking to me."

Jane comes to me and puts both hands on my shoulders. She's a small bit shorter than me, but not by much. "Our door is always open to you, Elle," Jane says as I wrap my shawl around me and pull on my wool mittens. "Should you have trouble, need a place to stay ..."

Willow and I travel back to the store and it's dark and freezing cold when we get home. My stomach rumbles in hunger and a bit of nerves, too, I think. What a mess I'm in. Here I am, back in the white world to put *out* any fires that could burn problems towards The Maple Forest and I've probably started more than ever now. If Henry sold the homestead to Cornelius Cooper because he didn't have the funds to pay what he owed, how will he ever be able to settle any bill that I add to each day with simply sleeping, eating and breathing *now*? And if I try to sneak away without paying what I owe, suppose Henry shows up sometime after that? Would he be arrested? What do they do to people who don't pay their bills and have nothing to give in trade? And how many months do I have before everyone in the world knows that I'm pregnant *with an Indian baby*. I do figuring in my head and think maybe three months more, *at the most*. It's almost the end of February. That brings me to May. Right after the first spring flowers bud. *Bright Feather*, I think with a sob, *I miss you.* I work hard to put Bright Feather thoughts away.

I stable and rub down Willow and come in through the back door, not the main front one. The front one is for customers, the back one enters the space that the Coopers consider their home. I'm cold and tired and powerful hungry, but my terrible big problem is what causes me the greatest thought.

"WHERE THE HELL HAVE YOU BEEN?!" I hear roared at me as I step into the house and before I know it I am lying on the floor with a bloody lip and a ringing head. Cornelius Cooper towers over me just about purple with anger. "YOU HAVE BEEN GONE <u>ALL DAY</u>. WHAT RIGHT DO YOU HAVE TRAIPSING ALL OVER CONDUCTING SOCIAL CALLS? YOU HAD WORK HERE TO DO!"

I stand up and dab my dripping mouth and growing fat lip with the edge of my icy shawl. "I did my chores this morning."

"You did *morning chores*," I hear an angry female voice say and to Cornelius Cooper's left appears Naomi Cooper and she is just a few shades lighter in anger then her husband. "You have *afternoon* and *evening* chores that you're responsible for that because you chose to disappear I was stuck doing."

I take a deep breath. "I apologize," I say. "I meant to cause you no trouble." It's just about the hardest thing I've ever had to say.

Cornelius Cooper's hand shoots out and closes around my throat. I feel my feet lifted off the ground so that only my toes can barely touch and I struggle and grab at his hand to loosen it and let some air in to breath. "You don't leave here without permission. Do you understand?," He says real close to my face. I nod my head as best as I can 'yes'. "And forget about dinner, you're not around to prepare it, you're not entitled to eat it. What do you have to say about that?" He sneers as he releases my throat and I sag against the door gasping for breath.

I struggle to get breath into my lungs and I look at him and her and this time *I* make no effort to conceal what I think about either one of them. "Just make sure you don't charge me for it," I say cold and flip and I brush past them into my closet room.

The next morning I do my best to get on with my chores and avoid the two of them as much as is possible in a smallish place with no where to escape. When I finally do manage to go outside for a brief moment to feed and care for Willow like I always do, I stand for a few moments unable to understand why I'm looking at an empty stable. A wave of terror washes over me and I go running inside as fast as the snow will allow. As soon as I come in, huffing and panting from the run, I realize what I missed this morning as I went about my business trying to avoid the two of them. They appear happy as they both look up at me, pretending curiousness at my state.

"Problem?" Cornelius Cooper says cordial like to me.

"Where's my horse," I say from gritted teeth and I feel the cold blade of the knife strapped to my leg and I think about who and where I would like to stick it in first.

"*Your horse?*" Mr. Cooper says. "I find it mighty strange that someone in your *position* would claim to own *anything*. Your bills are more than three months past due as of today. I sold *your horse*," he says with a quiet chuckle at the foolishness of it all, "to get some much needed payment towards the bill that you continue to mount. The gentleman that bought her, saw no need for all the bug infested bits that went with her so I burned them. At least now, your bill will only reflect the care and feeding of you and not *your horse* as well." I struggle with the words he's said to me that feel just as painful as his punch and choking of last night. Maybe worse I realize as the misery of the loss of Willow seems to grow and grow. The pain of Willow's loss will still be there long after my bruised lip and throat have healed. *Do not cry. Do not cry.* I'll not give them the satisfaction. I clench my hands into a fist and feel the knife through my skirt and concentrate on my breathing. *Think, think…*

"Elle, I need you to help with the noon meal," I hear Mrs. Cooper say from behind me as if nothing is unusual or out of place. I turn to look at her and she gives me a bright, friendly smile like my first few days here. *I guess her friendliness depends on the size of my bill,* I realize and I feel a calmness grow slowly in me as I take stock of my situation and what I can and cannot do. I look back at Mr. Cooper and he gives me a look that says, *Go ahead, I dare you.*

I think of Bright Feather then as I stand there and rather than make me cry as it has done in the past months I feel strong and powerful and not alone all of a sudden. *Remember me and I will be there.* I think of the baby nestled in my stomach and that there are *two* of us here now. I feel my brain snapping and crackling like a just caught log on fire and feel a wave of relief like finding something you thought you'd lost for good. I feel, all of a sudden, more like Bear of The Real People of the Maple Forest than I have felt in a very long time.

I think about my pink horse and all that she has meant to me. She's been with me longer even than Bright Feather. She's filled empty spaces made by my separation from Pa, Henry, Eli, Otter, Raccoon and Bright Feather over that past two years. I think about Bright Feather calling his horse Companion and understand now clearly the way of things between a person and their horse.

My awakening brain says loud and clear to me, *You are free. Willow's sale has settled your bill.* And then, what did Jane say? *They told me things would get better after the third month.* I've been here three months so that must mean that I'm three months pregnant then. *Guess I'm feeling better,* I think.

I walk real slow over to where Cornelius Cooper is standing and he watches me approach with a guarded look. "How much did you get for my horse?" I ask quiet like.

"Enough to pay your bill and give you a few more weeks of grace, before you start owing us again," he says flip back to me. "Course that's just for food and housing. It doesn't pay what you owe for all the clothes and such. You still owe us for those things we've been kind enough to provide you with."

"Did you keep a list of all those things as well?" I ask.

"Sure did," he says smug like. He reaches underneath the counter where he keeps his ledger book and flips through the pages and says, "Here it is …" and proceeds to read every stitch of cloth and thread and button that I've been given. He finishes with, "one pair of stockings with garters – dark black, one pair of boots and one bonnet." I can see neat little columns of figures listed on the page that says 'Graves, Elle'. One column has many, many numbers, while the other column appears to have only one lone entry. *Willow's sale.*

He looks at me with hate and I return the feeling. I begin to unbutton all of the tiny buttons down the front of my overblouse, which I take off and drop to the floor. I unhook my skirt and that drops in a heap at my ankles, followed by one petticoat, two petticoats, and finally my chemise. I hear "Oh my God!" behind me as Mrs. Cooper watches me disrobe before the two of them. Cornelius Cooper can't believe what's happening before his very eyes. I see him take in my scars of Weasel's treatment of me, the bite and knife scars that are long healed by now but still show. I bend over and unfasten my boots and stockings until all that's left on me is my knife strapped high on my right thigh. I'm glad for my still flat belly; no one would suspect that there are two of us bare naked in this room! "Make sure you mark down in that book of yours that I gave it all back," I say low and quiet. "Make sure you make note that I left here with *nothing* on my body that you were *kind* enough to give me." He's stunned by my nakedness. Perhaps by my knife strapped to my leg as well, I think as an afterthought. He just sits there and stares and stares unable to move as I turn to look at Mrs. Cooper.

Mrs. Cooper has her mouth hanging open in a big, wide stunned "O". Sometimes it flaps in an effort to form words but she cannot manage it it seems. She too, takes in my scars and my knife, but she's the one that sees the hate in my eyes when I say to her, for I cannot resist, *"Precious Johnny's knife,"* as I pat my thigh. I turn and walk to my closet room where I pick up my book of Isaac Watts hymns and then walk out the back door into the freezing snow. The shock of the cold's not something I care to describe. Not ten steps into the snow and I can't feel my feet but that's good for the pain of the cold's bitter. I start to shiver and realize that I must move fast before I die from this crazy foolishness. I can hear the back door creak open just as I begin to run into the forest trying to keep my head calm as I search for my hidden place of Indian clothes and my bow and arrow and other bits. I've never, ever walked there in a direct route always fearful that I was being watched and they would find my secret place. As I run through the woods I feel the cold gradually rob the feeling from my body. My feet go numb first, followed by my fingertips and my nipples. I stumble twice and try to be more careful with my frozen feet. I don't think I'd be able to feel enough things to get up should I fall. The snot in my nose freezes as I run and it runs. I see the large fir tree that I chose - green all year round despite the season - and I must stop just once to look back and make sure that a purple faced monster's not following me. I'm alone, I see, just me and my baby freezing quickly to death. I crawl under the fir tree and dig through the layers and layers of evergreen needles that make a prickly floor for me to kneel on. Out comes my bear cape, my fur lined trousers and boots, my long leather tunic and even my beautiful dress and matching shoes One Who Knows made me and that I wore a lifetime ago when the village celebrated my joining with Bright Feather. I put it all on but am so cold that the shivering doesn't seem to know that I'm not naked anymore.

It takes the last bit of my strength to make me step out in the biting cold and wind and stomp my feet and wave my arms like Raccoon has taught me in those early days of teaching me how to ride Willow. I feel my feet begin to prickle and my fingers begin to sting and worst of all is my nipples that feel like they are on fire. But the pain is good I know. When I finally feel more warm than cold, I crawl back under the fir tree, hunker down out of the wind and wait for night. And think. Always think.

What is an Indian?

Is he not formed of the same materials with yourself?

For "of one blood God created all the nations that dwell on the face of the earth." [6]

~Elias Boudinot

Journeywoman

Every night like clockwork, Mr. Cornelius Cooper of Ward's Mill, Virginia, drinks exactly three cupfuls of 'medicinal' liquor. At the completion of the third cup, with steps unsteady, he lumbers outside to the necessary house, does his business and then buttons the house down for the night bolting both doors front and back.

I figure, given the excitement of this day in particular, perhaps Mr. Cornelius Cooper will have four cupfuls of medicinal liquor tonight which can only work in my favor. I wait quiet in Willow's empty stall in the dark of the night waiting for the necessary stop and sure enough out he stumbles just as expected. While he does his business, I sneak into the store and hide quiet like behind the counter and the last two sacks of flour he's still hopeful to sell. I'd forgotten how wonderfully quiet a body can be dressed in comfortable Indian dress. I hold my knife in my hand just in case.

I hear Mr. Cooper stumble in through the back door and place the bolt in. Three or four times since I've been there he's forgotten to do this and he and Mrs. Cooper have had an argument in the morning when it's discovered. He'll think he's forgotten in the morning once again. The dim glow of the one lit candle flickers and dances as he carries it into the bedroom and I can hear Mrs. Cooper's snores get louder for a brief moment as the door's opened and then shut. I hear the creak of the bed ropes and the rustle of the cornhusk and hay mattress. I hear three loud farts. I wait and finally I hear the start of thunderous snoring that joins in horrible tune with Mrs. Cooper's. I'm all alone until morning.

Slowly my eyes grow accustomed to the darkness so that I can see dim shadows. There's no moon or stars for the sky is heavy with snow clouds. I'm not stealing, I tell myself, for I still have some money *on account for a few weeks of grace* just as Mr. Cooper has said. I must be wise with what I take for I can only carry what I can fit in One Who Knows' gathering basket and I'll be on foot. I can hunt for meat, but there are other things that I should bring along. I go to their family store of food and take what's left of day old bread and the biscuits that I baked early that morning. I wrap in an old cloth the remains of the salt pork that we've been eating for a few days. There are three apples from the root cellar. While I think, I sit on the floor and eat an entire jar of strawberry preserves for they would be far too heavy to carry. They taste mighty good. I decide to eat a biscuit with some of the butter I find, the remains of a wedge of goat cheese, and finally one of the apples. There's a pitcher of milk and I drink that, too. Finally, my belly is happy. I take nothing from the store supplies and only a few things to keep me for the walk I plan to make to the West's. I know I'll not be fast enough to escape an angry purple man on a horse in the snow should he decide to follow and I don't want to have anything great to be guilty for should I be caught.

As I head for the door, something makes me stop and go into the store once more to behind the counter where I know Mr. Cooper keeps his precious ledger book. I think about my Willow and how it was the only thing that Mr. Cooper could take from me that would cause me grief and pain. I look at that ledger book and finally after a moment put it in my basket. I'm a powerful woman settling a score that needs to be settled. I suspect I need to restore a bit of balance and harmony, too.

It's begun to snow again. That's good and that's bad I know as I head out in the direction of the West's cabin. Good because any tracks I may have made'll be gone by morning and good because believe it or not it feels warmer than it did this afternoon with the bitter wind and cold. Bad because I'd thought that if I could find Willow's tracks in the snow perhaps I would follow them and see where they lead. That'll be impossible now.

I walk a large portion of the night. Things are slower because I'm on foot and because of the snow. I also decide to take a more round about route because I'd like to avoid getting found by Mr. Cooper for at least a day or two. Will he come looking for me? Would he bother? Perhaps not when I ran naked into the snow and he thought I would be frozen dead inside a few brief moments, but once he realizes that I've been in his home he'll be angry. And once he finds the ledger book gone he'll want to kill me. I have a brief thought of perhaps I should've left it, and then I shrug. No chance to go back now.

At the West's cabin I wait out in the cold in the same place where I tied Willow only the day before. I wait until I hear sounds from inside the cabin and I know the Wests are awake. I pluck up my courage and knock on their door for the second time in three days.

Ezekiel opens the door this time and if he looked surprised to see me the other day sitting in his kitchen he looks absolutely stunned to see me in full Indian dress standing at his doorstep at the crack of dawn. "Miss Graves!" he says in startled tones.

"Ezekiel?" I hear a sleepy voice from the corner where I know the bed is. "Who is it Ezekiel?"

He grabs me by the arm and pulls me in and I blow in with wind and snow and cold. "We have a visitor, Jane."

"Elle! Are you well?" she says with true concern in her voice struggling with the covers to get out of bed.

"I am," I say, "although I'd appreciate if I could sit down. I'm a bit tired from walking."

"You walked out here in the storm?!" Ezekiel explodes. "Are you out of your mind?"

I tell them what has happened since they saw me last and I remember as I speak the big bruise by my mouth, the split lip and the bruises around my throat. As I talk Ezekiel insists that Jane stay in bed while he works at preparing breakfast. I grow weak from hunger and tiredness at the smell of the frying potatoes and onions, eggs and bacon and hot biscuits baking in the oven pan. I sip on hot tea which dribbles a bit down my chin because of my lip.

Once my belly is full from Ezekiel's mighty fine cooking there is nothing else I can possibly consider doing but sleeping. I refuse the kind offer of Jane and Ezekiel's bed and curl up on a quilt on the floor. I don't even remember putting my head on the pillow, sleep takes me away so quick.

It's dark when I wake and I've slept the day away. The smell of more food cooking is what rouses me and I try not to look at the large pot simmering on the fire. "How are you feeling?" Jane asks and I'm handed another cup of hot, steaming tea.

"Better," I say with a smile. "Thank you for your continued kindness."

"Ezekiel and I've talked all day about what you'll do." She looks frustrated and worried. "We can't think of any good solutions. You're welcome to stay here but he and I do not think you'll be safe here for very long."

I shake my head as she's talking. "No, I can't stay here. It'd not be safe for me but it'd also be dangerous for you. You two will live here in Ward's Mill forever and you don't want to be on the wrong side of Mr. Cooper. I came here last night only because I knew that no one would be able to follow my tracks." I smile a kind of smile. "Snow can be a good thing, you know."

"Then what will you do?" Ezekiel asks with concern.

"I'll go to Major Everett and the Ninth Virginia Cavalry, Company D and ask that he escort me back to William Holland Thomas' trading post in Forest City, North Carolina. George Maw said that it would take two days by horse to get to Fort Winston, so I figure I can get there in four maybe five days on foot."

"*You plan to walk there?*" Ezekiel says.

I look at him serious for a moment. "I've no other choice. I cannot stay here. I must get there. As difficult as it'll be for *me* to get there, it'll be just as hard for anyone to follow me." I try to reassure him. "I've traveled and lived outside in the winter time. I can start a fire and make a shelter. I can track and hunt. I'll be okay." I smile at him and then must stop real quick for I feel my lip start to split again. "I'll be much better off than as a guest at Mr. and Mrs. Cooper's home."

He's nothing to say to me and at the mention of their names I remember the ledger. I stand up and my muscles remind me that they've not had so much walking experience these past many months. I go to my basket and take out Mr. Cooper's precious ledger book. "I took only one thing that I was not entitled to," I say to the Wests, by way of preparing them. "It was a fair exchange for them taking Willow." I put the ledger book on the table.

It's Ezekiel who touches it first and he draws it towards him. "His ledger book?!" he says to me in wonder. "You took his *ledger book?*" I shrug my shoulders but deep inside me my heart does a few leaps with worry. Ezekiel understands that Mr. Cooper's anger over this would be a great and deadly thing towards me.

He opens up to the page that says, "West, Ezekiel/Jane" at the top and scans down the columns. He frowns and turns the pages and looks at other entries of other customers. "Why that bastard ..." he finally mutters under his breath.

"Ezekiel!" Jane says shocked.

"He has us buying more seed than we bought, for prices higher than he's charged others. He's charged you," he looks at me, "ridiculous amounts for the cost of your clothes and for your room and board. And the amount he sold Willow for," he shakes his head in disgust, "you should have gotten twice that."

"Does it say who the buyer was?" Jane asks and I think with excitement, *Good question.*

But Ezekiel shakes his head 'no'. "What's this?" he says at the piece of loose paper that has slipped out from the back. He opens the paper and Jane and I both peer over his shoulder to read:

Land Property Deed

29 Dec. 1815

Homestead Property Sale to Daniel and Francis Hobson, 320 acres Wards Mill, Virginia, west side of Reedy River, northern line between said John Benson and his father Charles Benson's old tract mentioned in said Charles Benson's will, south side by Bridges and Sammon's corner, Robert Duncan's old corner and line, Brock's corner.

Witnessed Isaac Bradley, signature, Dennis Chairis, signature;

Daniel Hobson signature

Francis Hobson signature

Received and acknowledged 22 April 1816.

"Old Man Hobson's deed to his property," Ezekiel says in wonder. He searches in the back of the ledger and finds more papers including the deed to the mill and the general store property. The third piece of paper which he opens we see:

Land Property Deed

15 March 1817

Homestead Property Sale to Andrew Graves and Elizabeth Graves, 320 acres Wards Mill, Virginia, west side of Buckhorn corner, on south bank of Weirs Creek, to Bruce's line.

Witnessed John W. Wood signature, Jeremiah Forrest his mark (X).

Received and acknowledged 3 August 1817.

Andrew Graves signature

Elizabeth Graves signature

Looking at the paper with my Ma and Pa's names written with their own hands causes me to sit down with a thump in the chair. "Are you alright, Elle?" I hear Jane say from far away. I can't imagine that Ma or Pa could have ever imagined what could happen to our family in just a few short years.

Ezekiel says in an excited voice, "Elle! Do you realize what these papers mean?"

I look at him in silence because I don't.

"Once a Land Title Deed is made, that piece of land can travel through many different hands. But the Land Title Deed just gets longer and longer with the additions and changes written on it. There is nothing added to these! That means that Cooper never went to the trouble to have the deeds officially changed over into his name! He would have had to travel to the nearest land office." He stops and thinks. "Why, that's probably all the way back to Richmond! He couldn't be bothered. Must of figured he had plenty of time to do all that." He waves the deed at me. "*Forget the ledger, Elle. Here is your revenge.*" He hands me the deed to my parent's land. "It belongs to Henry or you as the surviving children."

I take the paper in my hand and think, *What good is this to me? What could I ever do with this land?* And then the little voice in my head says, *No, that's not the point. Cornelius Cooper doesn't have it anymore. That's the point.* I reach into my basket and pull out my Isaac Watts book of hymns. I touch the faded leather cover, open the book and carefully put the deed inside. *Who knows what I will ever do with it?* I wonder to myself.

The last piece of paper we draw out is the Promissory Note that Henry signed for Cornelius Cooper. It promises to pay all bills *incurred by Miss Elle Graves while housed at Cornelius and Naomi Cooper's on the event of her return.* It is signed *Henry Graves, Esq. April 10, 1828.* I reach over and pick up the ledger and the Promissory Note and walk to the fire with it. Just as I go to throw them in, Jane shouts, "WAIT!"

I turn and look at her and all of a sudden I'm tired again and look forward to my quilt bed on the floor. I feel as if many ghosts are surrounding us in this tiny cabin all of them unhappy. They pound at my head and my heart and I feel like I am not much use to anyone at all. What good am I? I can not even keep my own self safe and out of danger. She walks towards me and takes the ledger from my hands. "Maybe it wouldn't be wise to burn that just yet," she says. Ezekiel looks at her and so do I.

"I can't take it with me," I say and look at them. "It's too dangerous for you to be caught with it."

She shrugs her shoulders. "Who'd suspect us to have it?" She walks over to the bed. She kneels down on the floor and wrestles with the bedclothes for a moment. We hear a brief tearing sound and then a crunching of hay and corn husks as she shoves the book deep inside the mattress. "A few quick stitches and no one will be the wiser. We can always burn it later if it seems the smart thing to do." She walks back over to me and takes the Promissory Note from my hand and tosses it in the fire. "*That* should have been burned long ago, though."

Moments later we're all in our beds. I've only a few brief moments wondering if I'll be able to sleep after having slept the day away before I collapse with exhaustion.

The morning dawns bright, clear and crispy cold with the sun casting a blinding glare on the snow. I eat a hearty breakfast and joke that I better leave before I eat their pantry bare. Ezekiel listens to the directions I remember George Maw giving me and agrees with the path. He adds important details like where he thinks will be safe places for me to stop and sleep for the night: a cave he knows at the top of the one ridge that he found hunting one day, Old Man Hobson's barn, and two other barns along the way that he knows of that he figures I can sleep in without being detected. We're unsure what Cornelius Cooper'll do but want my trail away to be as cold and hard to follow as possible. As a result, though it's possible I could request the hospitality of people along the way, we decide it'd not be wise to have anyone see me if possible. "Our greatest hope is that he thinks you froze to death and are buried somewhere under the latest snowfall," Ezekiel says. Neither of us discuss the possibility of that still happening over the next few days to come as I travel on foot through some mighty dangerous circumstances.

Getting word to Deer seems nigh on to impossible until I reach Major Everett and winter has ended. "I'll keep an eye out should someone come into town and is traveling south but until the snow stops and winter breaks there'll be little opportunity," Ezekiel says. "Even with the spring rains, there's the struggle with muddy roads that get so terrible that wagons can sink all the way up over their wheels." I know that if the opportunity arises, he'll send word and I must be satisfied with that.

"I promised Bright Feather I would return by the start of spring," I say. All three of us are silent, realizing that by then I'll be far along with my pregnancy and rough travel probably will be unwise for both me and the baby. "I tried to get him to promise not to put himself in danger by coming this far into white territory …"

Ezekiel snorts his disbelief. "I'm sure he refused," he says.

"He did," I say and I sigh a deep sigh of frustration.

Jane adds some foodstuffs to my basket even though I try to tell her no. "It's not open for discussion," she says firmly and embraces me. "I'm sorry it's only some tea and cheese … I'll keep you in my prayers," she says quietly in my ear. I remember my prayer of help and my request to find someone to cook with and I smile. "I prayed for someone just like you two just the other night." I look at the remains of breakfast still around the room. "Even down to the cooking," I hold my split lip together as I laugh at my own joke. I look at them and say, "I've been told that God loves us greatly and can hear even our most quietest whisper. You two are proof of that." I must remember, as I look at their worried faces, that even when things seem so dark and bleak, when you look careful, you can always find a shiny, good spot.

I leave by way of the footsteps that Ezekiel makes to their barn and hen house not wishing a trail of lone Indian footprints to shout any clues. He walks me as far as the forest edge and dumps a load of refuse to attract further footprints and confusion. "Until we meet again," he says to me with a smile. "Both *families* probably by that time."

"I look forward to that," I say in all seriousness. "Thank you for seeing the inside of me instead of just the outside."

The going's far more slow and difficult than I ever imagined. Sometimes the snow's over my knees and I'm ready to drop by the time I reach the crest of the ridge that Ezekiel has said to follow. I watch for the cave he's described and fight down times of tiredness that go into real fear. Can I do this? If I can't make it to the first stop, how can I make it the rest of the way? I talk to myself and the baby at the same time about what it's like to be a powerful woman, why I am one, and how tough things were to help me earn the title. That makes me keep going. At last I see the three large boulders that Ezekiel said hides the mouth of the cave and I begin to breathe slower and a little easier. I must work on this worry thing and right quick for I've a long way to go and have no spare energy to waste on foolishness.

Sure enough, it's a cave large enough for a full size man to crawl into so just perfect for me and my baby. *Isn't it amazing*, my head thinks. *I never feel alone anymore.* I put my basket down and take a moment to sit and look at my surroundings. My first order of business is to start a fire. I carry bits of kindling and dry straw to start a fire, although I'll need to find some wood that's close to dry to keep the fire going. Inside the cave are some small branches that look like they were washed inside by an old rainstorm. Every little bit helps I think. With my bow and arrow ready, but my pack safe in the cave, I stomp through the snow in search of sticks and food. I find a good supply of almost dry wood in the hollow of some more boulders. No sign of anything to eat though and I'm thankful for what I have in my basket.

As I work at starting the fire, I think about Beaver, for it is from him that I learned this skill. As I feel myself begin to warm up with the energy of the work, I think about how serious Beaver was when he taught me. "Being able to light a fire can mean the difference between life and death," he explained to me. "Always carry a hearthstone, always carry some small kindling or dried grass, and always carry your drill and fire bow." He had looked at me and said, "Those things are as important as your bow and your knife." I believed him when he spoke those words. Now, as I crouch in my cave and work up a sweat starting the fire I feel a rush of thankfulness for him.

Where is he now? I wonder to myself. The last I saw him he was stalking off into the night angry with the decisions that Great Elk and the rest of the council members had made regarding The Maple Forest. Beaver did not agree with joining the village with the United States Government and accepting their offer of citizenship while at the same time separating from The Nation of The Real People and all of the changes it was embracing. As I work at the starting of my fire, I remember Beaver and his passion for his people. A passion that was strong enough to make him leave all he knew and loved to fight for what he believed was the right thing to do. *Just like I have done*, my head feels inclined to point out. I snort out loud in my little cave. "I sure hope he's a sight more successful with what he's doing than I am," I say to me and my baby.

Learning to start a fire was almost as difficult as learning to ride Willow or learning to shoot my bow. Raccoon always made a point to be around when I began to practice all of those things so that he could be insured a laugh or two or ten. A wave of loneliness washes over me for all of those I hold dear and I put my head down and concentrate on the task at hand.

The hearthstone is a small flat rock with a small dip in the center. The drill is a stick that fits in the dip and the bow is just like a bow except the deer sinew is wrapped once around the drill. You pile a small bit of dried grass (I had straw with me) at the place where the drill meets the hearthstone and then you start the work. It's funny how much body heat you can work up just by trying to start a fire! Beaver explained that starting a fire was just like riding a horse. Everyone does it just about the same way, but everyone has their own special style that works just right for them. "I can only tell you what you need to have and do and show you how to put it all together. Whether you ever learn to start a fire on your own, though, will depend on if you practice and find your own special way of doing it."

As I squat, tired and hungry in the cave, working on my style of fire lighting I'm never so happy for Beaver and all those times he made me practice and finally master the art of lighting a fire. The smell of the smoke and the final glow of the small flame does more for my spirits that first night than I can put into words. In my basket I find some tea leaves carefully wrapped in cloth and placed in a battered tin cup. I think of Jane and drinking tea in her cozy little cottage. I melt some snow and float some precious tea leaves in the hot water. Sitting warm and snug in the cave sipping hot tea as I chew on the cold pork and the dry, hard biscuit I've taken from the Coopers by the light of my crackling fire, I catch myself almost smiling. *I will be okay*, I think. *I am a powerful woman on her own.*

The dawn of the next morning, I'm sore from leg, shoulder and back muscles that say to me, *Are you sure you know what you are doing?* But what concerns me more is the slight cramping I feel which reminds me of what I sometimes have when my monthly flows. I put my hand on my belly and hear myself say out loud to my baby, "Hush now, it will be just fine. You rest today and so will I." *What is the rush?* I think. I hurry to another white place that'll look at me with curious eyes. I can only guess at my welcome and am quite happy to take my time receiving it. I spend the day checking out the area by the cave. I stay alert. If Ezekiel found this place hunting, then that tells me I might be lucky with my bow and arrow. I finally shoot a rabbit, but it takes me two tries. I'm out of practice and am glad to be certain that Raccoon's not spying on me to tease me about my poor aim.

That night I dream of Bright Feather. He never speaks but he searches my face with fierce eyes that will me to tell him the truth, *Are you okay?* In my dreams I smile back at him, so glad to see him and to touch him and to smell him. *Yes I am okay,* I tell him although in my dream my mouth never speaks either. *I am warm and safe and dry and am remembering all the things I have learned that have made me a powerful woman. And I have wonderful news,* I tell him as he searches my face and touches my cheek gentle like he does, and I so much want the fierce look to go away. *We are to have a baby! I guess the wanting a baby finally got stronger than the fear of having one for both of us...* In my dream I kiss him deep and long and I delight in watching the fierceness fade away and the look of relief and joy replace it. *Come, I say to him, get warm with me in the furs and love me for it has been too long since I have known you that way ...* He kisses me fierce and it reminds me that I'm his and he's mine and the powerful love that there is between us that has made this baby in my belly.

I wake that second morning in the cave and I turn to look at Bright Feather's face to see it once again. I can't understand why he is not here with me and search the tiny cave with my eyes and my senses to find him. As I realize that it was a dream, I try with all my might to go back to sleep to find it, but it's no use. It's powerful hard to dwell on the delight of the dream rather than the reality of the day.

I'm anxious to move all of a sudden. I remember as Bright Feather and I traveled from Dark Cloud's village this past summer and the happy decisions we made between us to join. My muscles are still sore. *Let's get moving,* my body says. I let my remembrys of my pink horse keep me company as my baby and me get on the way.

The first thing I notice is that the snow is different as I work through it along the ridge, following the path of George Maw, with added bits from Ezekiel West. It seems heavier, damper and I realize that the air is slightly warmer, too. So spring is fighting the battle with winter to arrive at last. It'll be a tough battle I think for Winter has enjoyed her time here this year.

My next stop is Old Man Hobson's place. I think about *Life is what you make of it*, as Pa has told me. I think about all the pieces to the puzzle of my life and wonder if they ever will connect and make one great picture that makes sense *and* show more joy than sorrow. For the time being it seems that there is a bit more sorrow than I'd care to put up with. I worry about the pieces that connect my white life with my red. What will the picture show?

I stop on the ridge that overlooks Old Man Hobson's place in the late afternoon and look at the tiny cabin and small barn in the back. I study the place for a while to be certain that the only person at Old Man Hobson's is Old Man Hobson. I'm glad I wait for who do I see step out of the cabin but Cornelius Cooper followed by Old Man Hobson. Mr. Cooper seems to do most of the talking, as is the custom with everyone I realize. Except maybe Mrs. Cooper, I think after a time though. He points and has what seems to be angry gestures. Then he mounts up on his horse and rides away. Old Man Hobson stands in front of his cabin for a space of time and then finally walks back toward the barn and disappears inside. A few minutes later I see him go back into his small cabin and all is quiet.

I look at the sun. It's low on the horizon and soon it'll be more dark then light. I decide to wait until full darkness before I decide to settle down in the barn for the night. I chew on some of Jane West's cheese and the last of the bread and biscuits from the Coopers which is just as well for if I wait another day to eat them I'm sure I'll break some teeth. As the sun sets, I walk along the ridge until I'm directly behind the barn and I study the best way to walk down and leave the least amount of tracks in the snow. I decide to come down nearer to the necessary house for it's closer to the wood's edge than the barn. Then I'll just walk from there to the barn and hope that no one will notice two kinds of tracks rather than one.

It's a slight fingernail moon to enjoy once the sun sets that lights up the nighttime world a bit, reflecting off the snow and making things twinkly. I open the barn door just wide enough to slip in and give my eyes a moment to adjust. I hear the snort and stomp of horses and the familiar smell of hay and dung.

The first horse I recognize is Old Man Hobson's battered old mare. So old and so battered that I bet that it's the only thing that Old Man Hobson still owns since it's worthless to even Cornelius Cooper. I pat her muzzle and say quiet like, "Hello. Can I sleep here with you tonight in your barn?" She nods her head and snorts her welcome. But it's the second horse that gives me the greatest welcome, for it's none other than Willow! The rush of pleasure I feel as I stand there looking at her warms me from head to toe and I cannot help myself and I start to cry.

"Willow!" I say as I sniffle and touch her muzzle in wonder and she knickers her greeting to me that says, "And just where have you been all these days?"

My head thinks and I realize that of course Mr. Cornelius Cooper would have kept my horse and of course he would have hid her at Old Man Hobson's. How can a brain be quick one moment and slow another? *Some things just make more sense viewed from behind,* I hear Pa say. Willow's happy to share her stall with me and I bed down in the not so fresh straw while I think the choices I now face.

I am only here, free of Cornelius and Naomi Cooper because my debts with them were paid by Willow's sale. Before that time I feared for Henry should I have left with a large debt written in Mr. Cooper's ledger book. I think about the thing he called a *Promissory Note* and it even sounds bad just saying it in my head. But now I know things that I didn't know before. I know that besides being ruthless and heartless, Mr. Cooper is also a liar, a cheat, and a thief. I think about my working done at Cooper's General Store and how I never got paid for any of that. There's not one note recorded in the ledger book of all the *morning, afternoon, and evening* chores I did *every single day I was there*. I think how Ezekiel West said that the amount Cornelius Cooper charged me was much more than was fair for room and board of both my horse and me. And I think about the Promissory Note burning in the West's fire. I look at Willow standing over me munching on some hay and she looks at me. "I think," I say to her in the quiet of the barn, "that just like the land Ma and Pa originally had was still mine and Henry's, you are still mine, too." The choice is made. Willow leaves with me in the morning.

A soft horse muzzle shoves me awake the following morning and I open my eyes to the barrel of a shotgun aimed at my head. "Morning," Old Man Hobson says to me in a neighborly like tone despite the tone the gun speaks with.

"Good morning, Mr. Hobson," I say as I struggle to sit up and clear my foggy brain.

"Cornelius said I was to watch out for you. Seems he hopes you're dead but isn't foolish to believe it until he sees it. My visit to the necessary house this mornin' showed an odd set of tracks. Got my shotgun and followed them right to you."

I stare at him at a loss for words. *Now what?* my head says to me.

"I travel to Fort Winston to find Major Everett," I say.

"Cornelius says you stole goods – a whole side of pork - from the store and that you attacked him and Naomi with a knife you keep strapped to your leg. He's says that the time you've spent with the Injuns has made you crazy and that you should not be trusted for a minute. He says Naomi's so terrified by your attack that he's not sure she'll ever recover and that she's insisting that he keep the doors and windows to the house and store barred at all times." While he's telling me all these things he's watching me closely to see my reaction.

"He told me that you're a fool drunk and that your worthless mare has more brains then you do," I say back at him sitting there in the straw and leaning against the wall.

He snorts. "I'm sure he did." He gestures with his gun, "Git up." When I stand he says, "Make your way to the house." I pick up my basket and things and he follows behind me.

The hut's dark and glum and smells of unwashed body, dirty clothes and filthy bed linen. There is a tin mug and plate and spoon on the table with the last evening's meal still sitting cold and clotted on the plate. My stomach remembers it's empty, it *was* hungry, and how it's been mighty temperamental these past months. I swallow and try not to breath too deep. Mr. Hobson enters into the cabin behind me and shuts the door. He seems to see the place for a moment with my eyes.

"At one time, it was a right cozy place," he says almost to himself. He nudges me in the back gentle with the gun. "Have a seat."

I sit in the chair closest to me and farthest away from the plate of old food. "I want my horse back," I finally say as he walks over and settles himself in the other chair. He lays the rifle across his lap and before my disbelieving eyes picks up a bone from the plate and chews some of the old meat and grizzle off of the end. I swallow again.

"I suspect you do," he says. "However, Cornelius made it quite clear that the horse belongs to *him* now, in payment of the debts you owe." He looks at me intently for a moment. "Cornelius Cooper is not my favorite person, but I would take his word over the word of an *Injun lover* any day."

My head says, *Oh, so that's the way it will be.* My mouth says, "Just like this farm belongs to Cornelius Cooper in payment of the debts *you owed him.*"

"How is it you know of that?" he says, alert now like a rattler thinking about a strike.

I think and am careful how much I say for I don't want to get the Wests into any trouble of any kind. "I've heard talk about these things."

"Gossiping sons a bitches," he mumbles under his breath as he searches the plate in front him for something else to eat.

"How about we make a deal?" I say to him. He looks at me with eyes that tell me he'd just as soon eat horse manure. *Stop thinking of food and eating!,* my stomach says firmly as it flips and flops as Old Man Hobson crunches on the bone and grizzle off the second bone on the plate. I swallow and try not to breathe.

"Just what do you have to make a deal with?" he says and his look says there's absolutely nothing he sees that he could possibly want from me.

"I can get you your farm back," I say with a voice I hope sounds strong and sure.

He stops crunching on the bone and finally sets it down on the plate in front of him. He wipes his greasy fingers on his shirt front and very carefully and slowly picks up the shotgun and levels it again at my face. "What the hell do you mean?" he says at last.

"You gave Cornelius Cooper the deed to this farm as payment of your debts. I don't know how long ago that was but I know you did it because I've seen your deed. Only here's the important part. Mr. Cooper never traveled to Richmond to formally change the claim title. You're still legal owner. And there's more. Cornelius Cooper was dishonest in his business dealings with you. You probably never were in as great debt as you thought you were. You probably never had to give him the farm in the first place had he been fair about things."

He looks at me and I see him struggle to hear and understand and finally sort through what he thinks is true and what he thinks is not. "You're a lying Injun lover," he finally spits out making his decision plain as day.

I'm calm. I'm not frightened. I'm a powerful woman on her own. I know for a fact that he may have a shotgun but he's not going to shoot me when he's still not exactly sure what he should believe. I look him right in the eye when I say, "I'm an Indian lover who knows that your wife's name is Frances, yours is Daniel, and an Isaac Bradley was one of the witnesses who signed the deed."

He looks at me over the long barrel of the shotgun. "Isaac Bradley was my brother in law," he says almost to himself. "Francis' older brother …" He looks at me and takes aim with the gun. "Where's the deed now?"

I say absolutely nothing. My eyes though say to him, *Maybe it's time to put the gun away.* We sit like that for a good few long minutes until finally he lowers the gun. He gets up and walks to the window and peers out through the grimy pane of glass. In putting his back to me, he's saying he's giving up this game. I relax a might.

Without turning around to look at me he says in a voice filled with defeat, "The day a teeny tiny Injun lovin' girl terrorizes Cornelius and Naomi Cooper is the day that pigs will fly. Take your goddamn horse. I've no use for it."

I look at him and feel a great wave of pity. He's not as old as I first thought. He's old because he acts old and defeated and he's given up trying to live anymore. I stand and swing my basket on my back. I'll leave quickly before he changes his mind or Cornelius Cooper stops by to pay another visit.

"Thank you," I say as I stand at the door.

"Git out," he says low still without looking at me.

"If you're ever in the area, Mr. and Mrs. Ezekiel West make a powerful good cup of tea," I say just before I step out into the bright morning sun. "It would be worth your wile to make the effort to stop by for a visit." I stand there looking at him for one beat, then for two. He never once looks at me.

It's wonderful to be back on Willow again and I munch the last of the salt pork from the Coopers and the last of the cheese from the Wests as I ride as fast and as far as I can. Willow and I even ride for a time into the night for the moonlight reflected off the snow is bright enough to make the traveling safe. Late into the night, after the moon has traveled most of it's path across the evening sky, Willow and I bed down for the night in a natural shelter made by a huge fallen oak. If I am right with my directions, I hope to be at Fort Winston by noon time tomorrow. I make no fire for I'm too tired and sleep wrapped in my bearskin with the sounds of Willow only an arm's reach away.

Fort Winston is nothing like I expected. *What did you expect?* my brain asks me and I snort to myself. *I expected to never have to come here and see it so I never even thought of it. I expected to be on my way back to Bright Feather to see him before the first flowers of spring. I expected to ...* But I get distracted from my thoughts as I look at the sight before me.

Fort Winston's not a fort yet. I see two walls, standing tall and sturdy amidst the cleared forest. Walls made of huge tree trunks straight and tall, cleared of their branches sunk deep into the ground and lashed together with rope. One sentry tower rises above the highest part of the wall and I can see a lone soldier watching the business below him. Along the shelter of the two standing walls are a number of buildings that show all kinds of activity from the smoke that pours from some of their chimneys to the dirty snow and mud I see trampled all around them. Willow and I watch from the shelter of trees and I'm able to gradually figure out the stable, the long low building that must be sleeping quarters for the soldiers and then three other buildings that must be officer quarters or homes. I see two women, no children, and about twenty-five soldiers during the time I sit and watch. I'm too far away to see if one of the soldiers is Major Everett or George Maw.

It's hunger that finally makes me venture down into this new white world. I've not eaten since the pork and cheese the day before and have been unsuccessful at hunting. My stomach rumbles with its need to be fed and I feel dizzy and lightheaded from tiredness. I cannot see where is the best place to enter, through the door that stands open on one of the standing walls or just right down into the open living place of the fort. I choose to follow what appears to be the most traveled route; right up and to the main open door.

Willow and I ride slow and steady out of the forest and join the well traveled path of mud and snow towards the fort. The walls and the tower are much higher standing looking up, I think. I see the soldier in the tower look and then look again at me and then finally shout to someone down below. It's at that point that Willow and I just stop and wait and watch to see what happens next.

A mounted patrol of cavalry soldiers, four in all, ride out almost immediately from the fort at the shout from the tower soldier. They're too prepared and equipped to have been sent out just for me I think as they ride toward me with great purpose. It's almost fun to watch the expressions on the faces of the four men as they get close enough to me to see that I'm white and I'm a woman. At least two of the men scan the surrounding forests with nervous eyes to make certain I really am alone. I choose to be silent and just wait.

"Do you have business at the fort?" one of the soldiers finally asks me as we five sit silent and examining of each other.

"I seek Major Alexander Everett or Mr. George Maw," I say.

"Both of those men have traveled to Washington. They're not expected back for another few week's time." He looks up at the sky trying to determine the way of the weather. "Especially with the way the weather's been this past winter."

I'm at a loss and my face must show it. It had not occurred to me that neither man would be at the fort once I made my way there! *Now what?* my head cries in despair.

"Lieutenant Foster's who you should see," the same soldier says to me. "Follow me. I'll take you to him."

You would think that I would get used to being stared at. It seems that everywhere I go, white or red, I cause the same reaction; people stop, their mouth sometimes drops open in surprise, they stare ... I'm never more happy to be back on Willow. Somehow being high up on the back of a horse is always better than looking people eye to eye. We stop at one of the three buildings, and up close I can see that one indeed has more of a business look to it while the other two appear to be more of the home type.

The soldier knocks and we hear, "Enter!" shouted from inside. I think as an afterthought he would have liked me to wait, for he turns to say something to me and seems right startled to find me standing directly behind him. He wipes his heavy boots as best he can clean of mud and wet and walks inside. I stand behind him as he salutes. "Lieutenant Foster, sir," he begins, "as the patrol was riding out this morning the sentry informed us that there was a lone Indian rider approaching."

"Lone rider?" I hear. "Are you sure?"

"Yes, sir," he says, "here she is."

The soldier stands aside and Lieutenant Foster stares at me with surprised eyes, taking in all there is to see about me. I wonder how much of the bruising has faded from my face and neck and know that there is just a small scab on my lip. I know I could use a good wash and when was the last time I combed my hair? I think about my bear skin cape, my permanent marks on my chin and my Indian clothes and I stand a little bit taller. I think it'll work in my favor to look as savage and strong as possible. Shouldn't it?

Lieutenant Foster does the stare and the stop but he keeps his mouth from dropping open in surprise. I wait and let his brain catch up with what his eyes are telling him. He's older, I think as I study him, but not very old. I see lines by his eyes and mouth and gray in his hair. As I look at him I notice that his right hand's missing three fingers and his face has a long puckered scar down the right side. *How did he get his scars I wonder?* I think of my eleven scars on my chest from Weasel's teeth and knife and the rope burn scars on both my wrists. *Does he have memories locked far away that he never, ever opens, too?*

"Thank you, Private Watson, that will be all," he finally manages to say to the solider in front of him while he's still staring at me. I continue to stare back at him as Private Watson leaves and shuts the door.

Lieutenant Foster finally stands and he's one of the tallest men I have ever seen. He just keeps growing and growing and growing from behind his desk and then extends his hand to me. "How do you do, Miss...."

"My name is Elle Graves, late of Ward's Mill, Virginia," I tell him.

His eyes flicker and I know he knows the name. He gives me a formal bow from behind his desk and says, "Lieutenant George Foster, Commander of Fort Winston, Virginia, Second United States Cavalry, Company A, and Ninth Virginia Cavalry, Company D.

"Please Miss Graves," he says and I notice his mouth on the side with the scar moves funny as he talks sometimes, "do sit down," and he gestures toward a seat that faces his small desk. As I sit down he says, "You look a little road weary, can I offer you something?"

"I'd be most obliged for something to eat," I must tell him over the loud rumbling of my stomach, "as I've not had anything since I finished the last of my food yesterday morning."

He studies me again and then finally walks around his desk with the help of a cane, goes to the door and opens it. "Private Russell!" he shouts. "Bring up a tray of hot food and something to drink!" then shuts the door and goes back to his desk and sits down.

I decide to speak first. "You'd think that I'd get used to all the looks I get whether I'm in white or Indian Territory but it never seems to quite stop bothering me."

He absently rubs the scar on his cheek with his maimed hand and says, "I know a little of what you say. Someone always wants to hear the story of my scar and hand." He looks at me then with a pointed look. "I think I'll let you go first, though."

"What have Major Everett and George Maw told you of me?" I ask.

"They provided me with a very detailed account of your rescue and return as well as their perception of your welcome at Ward's Mill, Virginia." He searches through the draws of his desk and draws out a file that I assume must contain information about me. "I do not think either of them will be surprised to find you here when they return from Washington," he says as an afterthought.

So I tell him honestly about my situation with the Coopers. I tell him about Henry and what I thought had happened to him and now what I know about him. I tell him about what Mr. Cooper said he'd do to Henry or me if the debts were not paid and how he talked of something called a *Promissory Note.* I'm honest and tell him about taking the ledger and the discovery of Mr. Cooper's dishonesty and thievery after they'd taken Willow from me. I tell him of Old Man Hobson and taking Willow back and why I felt it was right and not stealing. I even tell him about the deeds we found and how I now hold the deed to my family's property in Ward's Mill although I admit that I don't know what I'd do with it. I don't tell him anything about my time with The Real People of the Maple Forest or where Mr. Cooper's ledger book is. And I don't tell him about my baby.

There's a knock at the door and a soldier brings in a steaming tray of hot stew that smells wonderful. Beside it is a hot steaming mug of coffee. He's surprised to see me but Lieutenant Foster hustles him out before he can stare too long. Lieutenant Foster pours himself a cup of coffee from a pot that sits behind him on the small stove and then gestures to the bowl of steaming food in front of me. "Please, go ahead. Don't wait another minute."

It's venison stew with potatoes and carrots and I don't stop until the bowl's empty. "Thank you," I finally manage to say.

"More?" he asks, but I shake my head 'no'. My stomach's happy for a bit now. "What are your plans now that you're here?" he finally asks me.

"Well, I am hoping that Major Everett would be willing to escort me back to the trading post of William Holland Thomas in Forest City, North Carolina."

Lieutenant Foster wrinkles his brow and looks confused. He looks down at my file and searches through the pages.   Finally he asks in puzzlement, "What does William Thomas of Forest City, North Carolina, and you have in common?"

"William Thomas is a good friend of mine and of the Indian people that I consider my family. Once I get to the trading post, it'll be a simple matter for me to be reunited with my husband," and I smile a real smile, the first one in months and months at the thought that I'm finally a small bit closer to getting back to Bright Feather and my life with him.

"HUSBAND?" Lieutenant Foster says.   "You claim to have an *Indian* husband?"

I feel the smile slip from my face like butter off a roll hot from the oven as I nod my head ever so slightly, 'yes'.

He looks down at the file and scans through what I can see to be neat tidy script. "This report says nothing of a husband, nothing of any type of family connection.   It refers to," he scans the writing carefully, "New Echota, Georgia, Major Everett's aunt and uncle in their capacity as missionaries down there, his offer to escort you home as he was headed back to Fort Winston anyway …"

He looks at me and I can see an anger that causes his face to get a shade of red that his scar does not. "What *Indian family* do you speak of that he has failed to report about?"

I swallow and take a deep breath and think, *oh no, Oh No, OH NO,* for I've opened up something that was obvious even Major Everett felt was quite wiser to be left closed. I can't close this thing I've opened any more than I can wash the permanent marks off my chin. I try hard to explain, "I didn't return to Ward's Mill, Virginia, because I wanted to. I returned to Ward's Mill, Virginia, to assure that the people I love and now consider my family were not blamed for my abduction. I returned to Ward's Mill to put out any fires that might be burning and cause danger or problem for My People."

Lieutenant Foster, reaches up to massage his scar, a gesture that seems to be a habit he is unaware of. "And who are these people that you love so dearly and you consider your family and," he looks at me and struggles to remain calm, "*your people?*"

"I am Bear," I say, "daughter of One Who Knows of the Elk Clan, mate of Bright Feather of the Wolf Clan, son of War Woman and Great Elk chief of The Real People of the Maple Forest."

"The Real People," he mutters to himself, "The Real People," like he's familiar with the sound of the Indian name but can't place where. At last he seems to remember, "You mean The Cherokee," he finally says.

I nod my head, "That's what the whites call them, yes," I say.

He folds his hands in front of him across the folder on his desk that tells things about me, but I now know *not everything.* "Do you know that the Cherokee are one of only five remaining Indian tribes east of the Mississippi?" he asks me. I shake my head 'no' for I didn't know that.

"Do you know that the government of the United States of America has been tremendously *generous* and *patient* and *fair* with these Indians and despite that they continue to grumble and complain about what they need, what they don't have but should have, what they're entitled to, how they're being constantly put upon by the white settlers?" I don't shake my head this time for I really don't think Lieutenant Foster cares what I know or don't know at this point.

"Do you know what the purpose of Fort Winston is to be? As well as the five forts currently being built in Alabama, the thirteen forts currently being built in Georgia, the eight forts currently being built in Tennessee and the five forts currently being built in North Carolina?" I stare at him waiting for him to continue and fearful at the same time of what I'll hear. He keeps asking me questions that I'm sure he knows I have no answers to.

"Do you know what our new President of the United States, the esteemed President Andrew Jackson's policy is towards the Cherokees east of the Mississippi? Do you know why he was able to win the election primarily from the overwhelming support of the south eastern states of Virginia, Tennessee, North Carolina, South Carolina, Georgia, and Alabama?" I feel a terrible chill all of a sudden like cold water has been poured down the inside of my warm furs and I shiver slightly waiting for Lieutenant Foster to finish talking so that I can go away and hide somewhere, *anywhere.*

He looks at me and I wait for him to tell me the answers to all these questions. He stands and reaches for his hat that's hanging carefully on the peg behind his desk which he settles on his head. "You must rethink your plans, *Miss Graves,*" he says pointedly using my white name, "for the policy of President Andrew Jackson and the platform on which he was elected promises *Removal Of All Indians* from *all* lands east of the Mississippi either by their *consent and willingness* or," he gestures around him grandly and smiles broadly and I can see that besides the scar and the fingers, he is missing all the teeth on the top right side of his jaw as well, "*by force* with the aid of thirty newly built forts to assist those Indians who think they'd rather fight. For you see, the United States of America *will* succeed in this endeavor to eliminate all red savages east of the Mississippi. It's just a matter of time to prepare and then follow through on our well laid plans."

He smiles what he tries to be a friendly smile at me. "I'm so happy that you're such an *adaptable* young woman and that with the death of your first family you were able to *adapt* and find comfort with the Indians. That'll set you in good stead now for unfortunately, *you soon will have no Indian family to go home to.*"

He comes around the desk and ever so politely supports me under the elbow to help me stand. "Let's see if we can find you suitable accommodations while you stay here with us, shall we?" and I allow him to lead me out into the fading afternoon twilight. I realize with the greatest of despair that I'm farther away from Bright Feather than I've ever been in my whole life.

In the end, I stay with Lieutenant Foster and his wife Joan and their three children, Lydia, Nate, and Paul. Lieutenant Foster is the only one to have his family present at this early stage of the fort's existence. I'm told by Joan that eventually other wives will come but for this first winter she's the only one. Lydia's younger than me by only two years but towers over me and her mother already. She's the other woman I thought I saw as I watched the fort. Nate and Paul at twelve and ten are as close to being cavalry soldiers as a body can without actually joining. They drill, ride, and work at the fort's continued construction along side the other soldiers. They're tall like their father, too, and aside from being told their true ages cannot be told apart from the other soldiers.

I know that both Joan and Lydia find me and my choice of life style dreadful but they are so starved for the company of another woman that they swallow their disgust and tolerate my company. Lydia must also tolerate sharing her small bed with me and spends each night pressed as tightly to the wall as a body can get. I told all of them that I was more than happy to sleep on the floor with my bearskin but they would not hear of it.

Talk of my Indian life and family is never discussed. Should I mention my time with The Real People in passing to make an observation or correct a misconception it seems as if the entire world stops stock still for a moment, cleans its ears of the filth, and then moves on as if I've not spoken a word. I learn to talk careful like. I can say, "Down south the spring comes much quicker," and that receives a conversational response. Should I say, "In the Maple Forest the winters do not seem so harsh," the world cannot seem to hear.

I'm allowed to send Deer a letter informing him of my change in location *due to unforeseen circumstances* and am encouraged to write another letter to the Department of the Army in Washington requesting the whereabouts of one *Henry Graves*. The second letter, Lieutenant Foster takes an active interest in, instructing me as to the proper wording, telling me what details I should tell and what details I should avoid (yes to former homesteader of Ward's Mill, Virginia, no to being the mate of a Cherokee brave). He tells me who and where to address it to. I'm encouraged to see both letters leave almost immediately with patrols; one that's headed south and one that is headed north. It's somewhat reassuring to me to know that soon those that love and care for me *in the south* will know where I am and how I'm faring. The letter that goes south is a brief note that offers no details other than to say where I am and what date it is. I've no great hope for locating Henry and establishing any kind of life with him. What would an enlisted army soldier do with a long lost sister pregnant with an Indian's child?

After a few weeks as winter slips into spring and the snow is replaced by rain and rivers of mud, talk turns to providing me with some "suitable" clothes. I'm agreeable to this for much to my dismay I find my Indian clothes becoming snug with my growing belly. I don't think that anyone suspects as of yet for I've been careful but I can feel the tightness of the space around my middle and I know that I don't have much time left in these clothes. It's almost the beginning of April and I think of Jane West's small stomach. In private moments I gaze down at the growing mound and I think, *What am I growing in there that I am so much bigger?* There's no doubt in my mind that come the end of May, anyone who doesn't know my secret is either blind or powerful stupid. I'm startled one morning as I lie in bed next to Lydia, trying not to think how much I need to pee for I will wake her with the movement and I feel the strangest feeling in my stomach. I gasp for it feels just like the touch that Bright Feather does on my cheek to give a tender sign only this time *it's in my belly.* I put my hand on my growing stomach and I think, *Hello little one. How are you this morning?*

Miss Joan and Lydia are thrilled when I don't fight the idea of a new wardrobe. There are bolts of cloth in the stock house (the other cabin that eventually will be another home should a family arrive) and in between the pile of chores that are a typical part of running a household with three children, we work on sewing me a new set of clothes. When the time for measurements comes, I put on a grand show of being powerful shy about things. I manage to whisper, "scars from my time down south", and "difficulties I'd rather not have to remember" and I'm afforded great understanding and courtesy. I learn to bat my eyes and look downcast whenever talk involves something that might reveal the true state of me and the baby and Miss Joan and Lydia are happy to cooperate. In the end we sew two petticoats, a camisole, a corset (which I agree to for it may help with the hiding of The Belly), two full over skirts and two over blouses. It's with great sorrow for Miss Joan and Lydia that they do not have extra materials for making proper stockings and there are no extra materials for shoes and I'm barely able to hide my delight. All in all, if I can ignore the agony of the corset, I'm quite happy to at least still be in my silent and comfortable moccasins.

This family's a puzzle to me. I struggle with the two different sides they show to me over the course of my time with them. In some ways, with their obvious hatred of the Indians they are no better than the Coopers and even Old Mr. Hobson and others I have heard speak at Cooper's store who see with their eyes and nothing more. They seem unable to even consider the idea that a 'red savage' is anything but greedy, stupid, and in general, downright evil. *My* only fault seems to be that I'm unable to understand and agree with this. How can a body hate another body just for the way they look? How can a body wish another body *dead or gone* just because they live their life in a different way? Am I so very odd in the way I think? Is there truly no one else like me? Have my experiences over these past few years changed me so much that I can now look at a body and assume *nothing* based on how a body looks? And is hard experience the only teacher to make a person wise?

I do my best to smile and be polite and cooperative. I try extra hard to do all the chores expected of me plus any extra ones I can find. As a result, the other side they show me is always kind and friendly. They don't mind my questions about their family history or life at the fort. Nor do they seem bothered by the additional hassle my presence has brought. They work to include me in all aspects of their family and show a general love and kindness towards each other. When I talk of repaying them for the clothing they've helped me make Miss Joan is stunned by the idea. "Do you realize how much work you save Lydia and me around the house? You're more than deserving of a new set of clothes." In those instances they're so far different from the Coopers that I scarce can see how I would consider such a thing.

I have no one to talk to about all this. But one thing is right certain: every single word and action I feel I must guard. I can't ever be the person I am; the powerful woman I've become. I feel just like I am being pushed backwards instead of forward. I am no longer a blooming plant but instead I am being stuffed back into the seed pod. For the Fosters like me, but only so long as I be the young woman they want me to be. I can't be Bear except in my most smallest snatches of privacy and there are never enough of those. I miss Bright Feather but I miss someone else even more. I miss myself.

On the morning that I see Major Everett and George Maw ride into Fort Winston at the beginning of May as the first flowers bloom, I've once again adjusted, as best as I can, to life in a new place. I worry as Major Everett and George Maw make their way into Lieutenant Foster's office to give their report of their travels. I stand out in the bright sun so they can see me. The fact that Major Everett stops, says something quick like to George Maw and then both men look at me tells me that *one surprise* – that of my presence – is no longer a problem. I hope they see the message that I try to communicate to them with my eyes. *Lieutenant Foster knows more than you told him about me now and it is all my fault. I'm sorry.* For a brief moment the three of us stare at each other across the muddy ground and then they both turn and make their way into their meeting.

They're in there a long time and it's not until the next day that I hear my name from behind as I am working on a pile of laundry in the bright May sun. I turn and see Major Everett standing watching me.

I straighten up and massage the crick in my back. "Welcome home, Major Everett," I say. "I've been waiting a powerful long time for your arrival." I know that Miss Joan and Lydia are just a stone's throw away working on the next load of laundry for me to hang up and I glance in their general direction.

"So I understand, Miss Graves. Would it be suitable for you to go for a walk and talk and finish your chores in a bit?" *Let's talk private where no ears will hear,* his eyes say to me from under the brim of his hat.

"Just a moment and let me tell Miss Joan." Moments later we walk across the wide open area that'll one day be the center of the fort, doing our best to avoid the mud and puddles from the rain the night before.

"I'm sorry," I say in a rush before he can speak. "I hope that I didn't cause you problems with saying things that I didn't know I should've kept quiet."

"You had no way of knowing," he says in response. "I tried to keep my word to you and not let *anyone* know the location of your village. I wrote a very detailed report, but I simply left a few bits out." He shrugs his shoulders. "Until you said something, no one noticed.

"I think it's really just as well," he says after we walk for a bit. "The truth's out there now, no deception and now we must just work on getting you where you should be."

I stop and look at him. "And where's that?"

He smiles and puts his hand under my elbow to keep me walking and to steer me around a massive puddle. "You're not stupid, Miss Graves." He sighs and looks at me quick. "That makes some things easier and some things harder.

"I argued that you should be returned to William Holland Thomas. I know that's what you wish and should you ever be reunited with Bright Feather, that's the place we need to get you to."

I stop walking and interrupt him. "What Lieutenant Foster has told me is true then about the removal of The Real People east of the Mississippi?"

He makes me keep walking. "You must keep moving, you must look cheerful, you must make this look like a polite social call. There are many eyes watching us at this very minute."

I walk again and take some moments to gather my thoughts. I sigh a deep sigh, make myself laugh out loud at nothing in particular and then finally flash him a bright smile. "I'm just about five months pregnant and any day now everyone will know. I want to go back to my husband and my people, Major Everett."

Now it's his turn to stumble, but he recovers quickly and throws back his head pretending to laugh at the funny thing I've told him. "Holy

Christ," he says with a smile to match mine although his eyes look full of panic, "Who knows about the baby?"

"Just the two idiots standing in the middle of this half finished fort," I whisper and laugh again, this time a little more quietly.

He tucks my hand in the crook of his arm and steers me out past the sentry up in the tower out down the road that leads into the forest. We walk only a short distance until we come to a log that can serve as a bench for a seat for the two of us. It's a good spot for we're in view of the sentry and seem to be hiding nothing.

Major Everett takes quite a few moments to gather his thoughts before he begins to speak. "In answer to your earlier question," he says with a sigh, "yes, President Andrew Jackson will propose The Indian Removal Act to the Senate and House of Representatives of the United States of America at the end of this month. He will request the authority to exchange lands with all Indians currently residing in any states or territories east of the Mississippi with lands west of the Mississippi with *or without* their consent or agreement." He looks at me with sad eyes and says, "And as sure as I'm sitting here with you, he will be given that authority. There is no doubt."

"Does that include The Real People of The Maple Forest?" I ask quiet like.

He nods. "They're Indian," he says, "so they'll be removed. The authority given the President will allow him to nullify any existing treaty agreements that are currently in place."

"They're United States Citizens, too," I say to him and watch the look of amazement grow in his eyes.

"What foolishness are you talking about?" he says to me.

"From what I understand, The Real People of the Maple Forest are part of a small group that broke from The Nation of The Real People and accepted the offer of citizenship that was offered to them in the Treaty of 1819."

Major Everett looks at me with stunned eyes and then turns to stare off into the forest and think. "Well, I'll be damned," he finally says after a time, "I'll be damned ..."

But finally he shakes his head. "That won't help you too much at the moment, though," he says after a bit. "Lieutenant Foster is dead set against sending you *south*, but is more inclined to let you wait until you hear from Washington regarding the inquiry you sent about your brother. He has a," he pauses for a moment searching for the right word, "*history* with the Indians that would make it powerful unusual for him to allow you to be returned to them."

I look at him without speaking. *You know,* I think, *I am getting powerful tired of having my life made more difficult by all of these people with stories from their past that seem to interfere with my life right now.* I look at Major Everett and give him a mighty fed up glare. *Go ahead, let's hear it,* my look says to him.

Glancing at the fort, Major Everett takes off his cap and runs his fingers through his hair. "I'll make it a quick story. Lieutenant Foster was captured by the Creek Indians when he was leading a battalion. He was in the army fighting during the Battle of 1812. I don't know exactly all the specifics. He was held prisoner and they tortured him. He'd been knocked unconscious by a rifle butt to the face, that's where the scar and the loss of the teeth happened. But from what I understand they gradually cut his fingers and toes off, bit by bit. He was rescued before they could kill him. When he's in his cups," he looks at me serious like, "which isn't often mind you, he likes to joke that the Injuns thought so highly of him that he was forced to leave a few bits of him behind to keep them company." Major Everett looks at me. "He's a good leader to the men but it's not by chance that the army put him in charge of *this fort* for the purpose it's being constructed for. I can think of few military officers who would be more than happy to oversee the removal of the Indians from this area.

"He told me that you are welcome to stay here at the fort for as long as it takes to find your brother and bring him here to claim you." He looks at me for a moment as though deciding if he should say something else. "He even hinted broadly that perhaps you'd find a man here at the fort and be happy to settle down."

He reaches over and puts his hand on my tightly clasped ones, staring into my eyes that are filled with worry. "I tell you that only so you understand how much he does not understand of what and where you want to be."

"What do I do?" I say to him. This circumstance I am in is getting messier and messier with each passing day!

"Well, in a few more weeks, according to you, you won't have to worry about any more hints of you finding a man here at the fort," he says in an effort to bring a little humor into our conversation I suspect. The exasperated look I give him makes him apologize. "I'm sorry.

"Look, let's wait a few more weeks and see if we do get a quick response from Washington about your brother. In the mean time, I will talk with George Maw and see if he has any suggestions. Is it alright that I tell him of your *situation?*"

Calling it a *situation* doesn't make things sound any better.

A few weeks later as we sit at the breakfast table, me and the Fosters, Paul Foster sees fit to tease me as I bring fresh biscuits to the table. "Miss Elle, you better skip these biscuits, you're getting quite a belly on you!" He laughs and laughs at his joke. I laugh too, to cover the blush that blooms across my face. The conversation continues to swirl around the table and I resume eating my breakfast but as I look up and meet Miss Joan's eyes the look on her face tells me that my secret is out. We clear the breakfast dishes and I do my best to act like everything's normal but my brain works powerful overtime as I consider all the options. It could almost be funny I think. I may not be able to mention my time with the Indians, but how are we going to avoid *this?*

My thoughts are interrupted by the shouts of my name outside. "Miss Elle!" I hear shouted with great excitement. "MISS ELLE! MISS ELLE!! COME QUICK! YOU'R BROTHER IS HERE!" My heart begins to pound and my fingers go numb as one of Miss Joan's good china platters drops to the floor and smashes into a mess of pieces.

Remember the sky that you were born under,

Know each of the star's stories.[7]

~Jo Harjo

Sister

I stand frozen for a long series of moments, my heart hammering in my chest like it's just going to explode. I bend over to start picking up the broken pieces of china that are scattered all over the floor. *"Go,"* I hear said firm and forceful behind me and I look up to meet Miss Joan's eyes. She can't wait to get me and my dirty secret out of her house her looks says. "GO." I stand up and walk out the door.

It's Major Everett who's calling to me still as I walk out the door, shouting his excitement over the good news that's walking right next to him. "Miss Elle, look who's here! Your brother Henry's just arrived from Washington! Can you believe it, Miss Elle? He's here! HE'S HERE!"

I look at the face grinning with delight standing in front of me and I can't believe what my eyes tell me they see. There he stands, done up in his Sunday best with a suit and tie looking nothing like I last saw him and nothing at all like I remember him to be. For standing in front of me is *not* my brother Henry at all, but William Holland Thomas, eyes twinkling with delight and mischief. "Sister dear!" he shouts for all to hear, "What an answer to my prayers it is to see you standing in front of me well and healthy after all this time." He steps forward to embrace me as I collapse into his arms.

I never fade to blackness, really. I'm aware of strong arms lifting me up and bustling me in to sit on the chair at the table still filled with the remains of breakfast. I hear the crunch of Deer's boots as it breaks the china into smaller bits. I hear conversation swirl around me, "Been on business in Washington," "Came as soon as I received the letter," "Can't wait to get her home to our new family home in North Carolina," "All the excitement seems to be too much for her," "Always was a fragile child even when she was little". At that last comment I start to stir and I see him give me a teasing glance. Major Everett hovers on the fringes of the excitement obviously terrified I'll say the wrong thing and cause him even more problems.

I put my hand up to touch his face. "Let me have a look at you, Henry," I say.

Deer squats down grinning broadly in front of me enjoying every moment. "Elle, my sister, after all this time ..." He makes a show of wiping the corners of his eyes as if to catch the tear or two he's shed from pure happiness and joy.

I touch his face and a wave of emotion hits me as I realize all of a sudden that I'm closer to Bright Feather than I have been in more than five months and I begin to cry. Great gulping sobs as I touch his face and hair and finally rest my hands on his broad shoulders. "She always was an emotional mess over things," Deer says to our surrounding audience, reaching into his pocket for a scrap of linen. "Here my dear sister, use this."

He hands me his handkerchief and I can't resist. I blow my nose noisily in it. Pulling myself together I decide to join in on the joke. "It is so good to see you, Henry," I finally manage to say wiping my eyes and blowing my nose again. "Our separation has been hard on you I can see. You look so much *older* and more *tired* it seems." I grin at him, now having as much fun as him. "I hope that you've been able to control that horrible twitch you get in excitable situations."

"We'll have to see, dear sister," he says, "We'll have to see," and I'm crushed in a bone breaking hug as I begin to sob again.

Deer's in his element, talking with Lieutenant Foster, complimenting Miss Joan, and teasing Lydia about her beautiful eyes. The more he talks the more I come to realize that he really *has* been in Washington for he knows even more current information about President Andrew Jackson's Removal Act than Major Everett did. "President Jackson presented the Indian Removal Act before the Senate and the House of Representatives on May 28th, and it was well received by all," he reports.

Lieutenant Foster's in fine spirits over this news and whiskey's shared by him and Deer and Major Everett. He talks about his grand plans of completing Fort Winston by the end of the summer and having it fully manned and operational by fall.

"How long will you be staying here with us, Mr. Graves?" Miss Joan finally asks. She looks at me and I can see her struggle mightily to contain her disgust. "I imagine that Miss Graves is eager to move on with her life and get back to something more settled than this temporary situation."

"First, before I answer your question, I must thank you from the bottom of my heart for the hospitality and kindness you have shown my sister," Deer begins and Miss Joan blushes her acceptance. "I hope you'll not think me terribly rude if I make plans to leave at first light with her though. I've been away from the homestead far too long and must return as soon as possible to see to my crops."

Miss Joan's so pleased by his answer that she insists I help her pack my things right away. I find it most funny that she's just as happy for me to leave as I am.

I cannot sleep. My mind and body are so full of excitement that the thought of going to sleep seems inconceivable for the rest of my life. I lie next to Lydia as she twitches and jumps and mumbles in her sleep and I keep thinking over and over and over again, *I am going home! I will soon see Bright Feather! All this is over at last!*   I don't care what situation or circumstances I return to, alls I care about is that I'll be with Bright Feather. At last I think I see a lightening of the night sky and I ease myself out of Lydia's bed and make my way to the necessary house. Knowing it's useless to go back inside, I sit out on the front porch steps and wait for dawn's full light to come.

I hear stirring inside and footsteps and I'm surprised to see Miss Joan sit down next to me with one of the bed quilts wrapped around her. "Will your brother be understanding of the child do you think?" she asks. She looks tired and worried, her eyes red from lack of sleep. Seems as if she's not had much sleep this past night either. I think, once again, about the puzzle of this family. While she can't abide the thought of me having a child by an Indian brave she still worries about me and what the future holds. I think of Henry and wonder if I ever will truly see him in this lifetime and what he will think of me should that happen. Then I look at Miss Joan.

"This child was brought about through great love and was something I wanted very much with my husband, Bright Feather. I long for my husband still, just as I have longed to see my brother. I would hope that both parts of my life will be able to live with the choices I have made so far." I look up to see Deer emerge from Lieutenant Foster's office, stretch and greet the morning and us. "When I last knew my brother he was a hard working, loving ... man. I cannot see how he would reject this child of mine."

I reach over and touch her and I feel her stiffen, working hard to not pull away from me. I do not remove my hand and wait until she raises her eyes to meet mine. "I know that you don't approve of the choices I've made and yet you and your family have made every effort to make me feel welcome here in this place. I thank you, my brother thanks you, and my family thanks you." Then I remove my hand and stand up to prepare to leave.

We eat a hearty breakfast and it's funny how fast both Deer and I eat. We're given generous supplies of grain and meat for the trip we take *south* to North Carolina. Major Everett's waiting as we mount up on our horses and comes to bid me good-bye. "I thank you once again for your kindnesses to me," I say to him. "If you're ever in the area, I hope you'll stop by."

"If I'm ever in the area, I hope you'll still be there," Major Everett says back to me very serious like. He looks at Deer as he is checking the supplies on the back of the two pack horses then as he mounts up his own horse. Deer's talking and laughing with Lieutenant Foster and some of the other men all the while he works. "He's a good man to have on your side," Major Everett says, "I have heard things about him in Washington and all of it is good."

"My brother's an amazing man," I say with a smile that's big enough to split my face in two.

We leave finally and once on the trail I can't contain my happiness and excitement. Deer laughs at me for every time he turns around I have a broad smile on my face. Even the baby jumps with delight over the thought of going home. We must make more stops than usual for me to have private moments in the woods and after the third stop, as I return to mount Willow, I find Deer standing silent next to his horse chewing a blade of grass. "How far along are you?" he asks quiet and watches my face closely.

I can't help myself as I smile another big smile, turn sideways and press my skirts close against me to show my growing belly. "Nigh onto five months," I say.

He thinks for a bit and then says, "So you didn't know before you left," almost to himself.

"No," I say puzzled, "why do you think that?"

"One Who Knows told Bright Feather that you were with child when he returned from his first trip to me after you had left." He stares off into the woods, "It always puzzles me how that old woman knows stuff sometimes before everyone else." He mounts his horse and I mount up on Willow. "I'd thought perhaps you'd told One Who Knows before you'd left but didn't tell Bright Feather to keep him from worrying."

I think of One Who Knows' last words to me, *I've filled it with important herbs that will be no good to you if your thick skull can't remember what to do with them. At least most of them will smell good when you are sick.* I think about the herbs the basket contained: figwort root (good for fevers *and* anxiety and sleeplessness in pregnant women), red raspberry leaves to brew for tea (good for sore throat *and* used to strengthen pregnant women and aid in childbirth), wild yam ground up for tea (good for stomach upsets, *in particular* morning sickness), and minty perilla leaves (good for colds and fevers and *also* for relief of morning sickness and irritability during pregnancy)[8]. Each and every herb particularly good *I remember now* for morning sickness, stomach upsets, tiredness and pregnancy woes in general. I shake my head at my thick skull and sigh. *I didn't even remember to try smelling them.* "Seems she knew even before me," I say to Deer.

"Won't be the last time, either, I suspect," he says. We travel in silence for part of the day, careful I'm sure of where we are and the trickery we have used to get there. We do not speak in the language of The Real People. We behave just as we have pretended to be at Fort Winston: a business man and his long lost sister traveling home.

"I was in Ward's Mill quite a few weeks back," Deer says at last. "On my way to Washington, I promised Bright Feather that I'd stop there. Seems like I missed you by just a few weeks."

"What did you find?" I ask almost afraid to hear what he has to say.

"Those Coopers are a right friendly couple, I must say," he says and I wish I can see his face to see if he's teasing me. "We had a right neighborly conversation until I asked them where Elle Graves was and if I could speak to her."

He turns to look back at me so I can get a good look at his face when he says, "You can imagine my reaction when they told me you were *dead.*"

"Oh ..." I say.

He turns forward. "They went on at length about how you were a thieving, plum crazy, Injun lover and that after you attacked both of them at knife point you ran off into a raging blizzard stark naked."

I have to chuckle at the story that they tell. A wave of pure joy at where I am, who I'm with, and where I'm heading hits me and I know I'm grinning again. "You know," I say casual like, "many parts of that story are quite true."

I see Deer's shoulders shake like he is chuckling and he shakes his head back and forth. "Well, then," he says after a moment, "I'm glad that I said what I said then."

"What did you say?" I ask and I can only just imagine.

"I might have said something along the lines of how I'd hoped that you'd caused them great injury and pain during the attack and that should I find out what they say is true about your death that they'd better be miles and miles away from here for you were not a lover of *one* Injun, but of an entire *village* of blood thirsty, revenge loving Injuns who would like nothing more than to eat a hearty dinner of their cold unfeeling hearts and their big fat asses. I assured them that at my earliest convenience I would inform this village of blood thirsty, revenge - loving Injuns of the story that they had seen fit to tell me. I promised them that they would be hearing from me and or some other not - so - civilized as me in the near future and they should make every effort to prepare." Deer shrugs. "Course, I also pointed out that being prepared and fortified for attack only makes the Injuns angrier and more determined and as far as I was concerned the two of them best get their affairs in order because there wasn't much time left for either of them. Then, I *think* I said I was much obliged for the information, tipped my hat and left.

"I was followed out of the store by some sorry old man who'd heard the whole exchange while soaking up some liquor over in the corner. He volunteered that while it was best to let the Cooper's think what they think, the last time *he* saw you, you were in fine health, in full Injun gear, and heading out on your horse north."

"Old Man Hobson ..." I say quiet to myself.

He looks back at me and winks. "I *had* to get to Washington, Bear, and I liked the sound of the old man's story better than the Cooper's so I went with that one. Nothing prepared me for the letter I was shown by a friend of mine in the Department of the Army though once I got to Washington from one *Elle Graves, late of Ward's Mill, Virginia* inquiring of the whereabouts of her brother Henry Graves currently enlisted in the United States Army." He shrugs, "At least I knew you were alive."

"I discovered many things while I was in Ward's Mill these past months," I say quiet like. "Including the fact that Bear John's surname seems to have been *Cooper.*"

Deer turns once again to look at me and I suspect my sorrowful face convinces him how true my words are. "I'll be damned," he says for lack of anything else.

We stop early that first day out as I am unaccustomed to a full day in the saddle and I am a bit sore from the riding. But when Deer says something about my 'delicate' condition I have to laugh at him.

"Where did you hear something silly like that?" I ask him as I help set up camp and care for the horses. "You should know that I *did* leave the Coopers stark naked in a blizzard and that I *walked* the first part of the way to Fort Winston in that same blizzard. I didn't have Willow until Old Man Hobson put his shotgun away and let me take her back."

As we prepare our meal by the light of the fire, Deer finally says, "Tell me of your time," and so I do. It all comes pouring out and I realize just how hungry I have been to be able to speak freely and just be Bear. I tell him of the Coopers and the Wests and even Old Man Hobson. I tell him of the discovery of Henry being alive and of Bear John being known as "precious Johnny". I tell him of the promissory note that I burned, the ledger that Jane and Ezekiel West have hidden in their straw mattress and of the deed to the Graves homestead I have in my book of hymns.

When I am at last quiet and finished telling my story, Deer says, "Seems trouble, mystery, and disasters follow you in the white world just like they do in the red." He ducks when I throw a rabbit bone at his head.

"Did you know of Lieutenant Foster?" I ask him finally. "You seemed right comfortable with him."

Deer snorts. "There are few people who travel in military circles that do *not* know of Lieutenant George Foster. He is a bit of a legend in some circles: whispered about and spoken of with great awe. As for me seeming comfortable with him, that's one thing that's good about me and the life that I've led. I can be right comfortable in most any situation if it suits me."

I think about Lieutenant Foster and my time spent with him and his family. I think about the different faces he and his family showed. "He reminded me of a dog that has been sorely mistreated by its owners and then rescued," I say as I stare into the fire and remember flashes of my time at the fort. "When the dog gets to his new family, he adjusts well and gets on fine with them but should a stranger come that looks or smells like the first family, the dog is inclined to rip the stranger's throat out as soon as look at him."

Deer hands me a cup of hot tea in my battered tin mug. "You continue to be a good judge of people, Bear," and I think *how good it feels* to hear my name *Bear* spoken. "Foster was a soldier during the War of 1812. I was just a boy then, just adapting to my time in Great Elk's village." He looks at me. "Bright Feather has told you of me."

It is a statement, not a question and I just look at him over the fire. I sense he wants me to tell him what I know so I swallow my sip of tea and say, "I know that you are an orphan like me and that you were adopted into Great Elk's village like me. I know that you were brought in by a hunting party that found you wandering in the woods but that you were never able to remember how you got there or what happened to your family. I know that after a time you struggled with who you were and where you belonged and that you traveled back to the white world on your own. You found some family but never learned the story of how you became an orphan. You chose to live in the white world, get schooling in the white world, and you have ever been a friend of The Real People of The Maple Forest from then until this very moment and beyond."

He studies me for a moment and I can hear the hoot of an owl somewhere out in the dark shadows. It's a beautiful spring evening although a bit chilly and I've my bearskin wrapped around me. He looks at the fire, picks up a stick and pokes the flames to life a bit. "Well, that's the general story, but it isn't exactly accurate." He looks at me, wanting to see my face, I suspect, and says quietly, "Actually, my mother's still alive but she's been insane for almost her entire adult life from what my aunt has told me. It never seemed necessary to say anything different once I found her and saw her condition. She never recognizes me. She lives on the family estate that my aunt and uncle still run and that I'm technically still owner of. Seeing her and the condition she's in is one of the many powerful reasons that made me choose a life other than that of a plantation owner. I couldn't have lived out the rest of my life with her near."

He stirs up the fire again with a stick, sending sparks flying high while I sit there so shocked that I have no voice to speak. He shrugs, "It's true that I never remembered *how* I actually got to be where I was the day the hunting party found me, but I did eventually remember *why*.

"My parents did *not* have a good marriage. Oh, I think my Pa tried, but even the small memories I have of my time at home with the both of them are filled with tension and fear. I think my Pa spent much of his time away, traveling to stay as far away from my Ma as possible." He looks at me then and says, "He was a fine businessman and trader. I think I take after him in that respect."

He takes a sip of his tea. "He left me with my mother and the slaves that ran the estate. I wonder sometimes if he knew just how terribly ill she was or if he thought that she was just unhappy with him and that things were better when he was away." He shakes his head. "I'll never know.

"When he was away, things were definitely *not* better and probably they were worse. I remember hiding under beds and far in the woods to escape her crazy ranting and her anger. She would get so furious …" He smiles a sad smile at me. "She never called me William, I remember that. She called me 'Martin', my father's name, and any anger she had for him she directed at me when he was away. If she caught me, she would beat me something fierce, I remember that, too. The slaves were as good to me as they could be, especially the big cook, Elishebah. She hid me in the pantry or even under her skirts a time or two, I recall.

"My Pa came home one time as my mother was chasing me across the front lawn, screaming threats at me. I was never so glad to see him in all my life. I remember hiding behind him as he dismounted from his horse as she continued to charge at both of us never once stopping her shouting and yelling." He stops almost seeming to regret the picture he's making in my mind of his mother.

"Sometimes she was peaceful, you know. Sometimes she was quiet and kind and would take me on walks or tell me stories or laugh at my playing. It was just so unpredictable. One minute things would be fine and the next moment the world would be in chaos."

He makes eye contact with me again across the fire as I sit there with my tea going cold in my hands. "She marched right across the lawn that day, eyes blazing. She never hesitated or seemed to register that Pa was standing there now, not me and that was when I truly knew that she was crazy.

"I can remember him talking quiet and low to her. 'Now Amanda, no need to carry on so ...'" Deer's quiet for a minute and he swallows with difficulty and then looks past me into the woods and stares for a bit. "She pulled a knife from her apron pocket and before he could even raise his hand to defend himself she plunged it into his throat. He dropped like a stone. I did eventually remember how I stood there in those first few moments staring at the both of them frozen in place with disbelief. Had I really just watched my mother kill my father?

"She looked at me standing there in shock and as angry as ever said 'Martin ...' then bent over and pulled the knife out of my father's throat."

He makes an effort to smile. "I'm dumb, but I'm not stupid. I ran like hell and kept on running. I got my name 'Deer' for being a fast runner. When I arrived at Great Elk's village with the hunting party I'd been running practically my whole life." He takes his hat off and runs his hands through his hair. "I didn't remember any of what I just told you until I traveled back to the whites, met my aunt and finally saw my mother again." He laughs a bitter laugh. "The first time she saw me after all those years, she said how good it was to see me and called me 'Martin'." He shook his head. "Some things never change it seems."

"It was in Great Elk's village that I learned the meaning of love, security, family, honor, ..." He grows silent. "I did all of my healing and growing to be a man in that place. I owe them my life."

"Why did you ever go back? Why didn't you just stay with The Real People?" I finally have to ask. I think about his mate Possum who struggled with learning to live in the white world as a trader's wife named Mary Thomas. I think about Bright Feather, Beaver, Great Elk and War Woman who are as much a family to Deer as One Who Knows is to me.

Deer gives me a sad smile. "Don't forget, I didn't remember a lot of this until I saw my mother once again. All through my childhood in The Maple Forest I had the same dream over and over and over again of my father calling me, pleading with me to help." He snorts and shakes his head. "I still have it now and then." He tosses the remains of his cold tea into the fire. "I worried maybe, *just maybe*, my father needed me and that's why I finally went back.

"I'm sure One Who Knows knew a big part of the whole situation. She was the one who encouraged me to go back but she cautioned me before I left about preparing myself to face whatever horrors I originally ran away from. She said, 'You are Deer now, of the Real People of the Maple Forest. You must face your past and understand it before you can go on with your future. No matter how dark your past is, remember it is what pushes you towards future greatness.'" He studies me for a moment and then winks at me. "I bet she's said things like that to you, too, hasn't she?" and I nod my head.

"I came back after a season to the village and I just wanted to hide there and never face that darkness again. But my aunt and uncle were kind and eager to help me. They offered to send me to school. My uncle is a lawyer and offered me all the resources and opportunities that were available to him. They were not thrilled with my love of Indians and yet they were appreciative of what they had done for their nephew. It was my uncle who pointed out that equipping me *in the white world* would make me more powerful to help those I loved *in the red*. For a while there I wondered if I'd ever have peace *anywhere.*"

He grins at me. "Possum helped me find my place in life. She helped me understand that I could not abandon either part of me and that I had to find a happy place right in the middle. She was the only one who could show me that, because she struggled, in some ways, harder than I did between both worlds for no other reason than *just for the love of me.*

"I feel a tremendous responsibility towards The Real People of The Maple Forest, Bear. There is nothing I can make right in my white life, but there is *everything* I can make right in my red one."

He chuckles, "We were talking about Lieutenant Foster, weren't we?" he says and he catches me hiding a yawn. "How about I tell you *that story* tomorrow on the trail?"

As we bed down by the fire, it is my turn to chuckle as I hear his quiet snores even before I can fall asleep. I look at Deer fast asleep curled up in his bedroll looking everything like the typical white homesteader. I think about what brought him here and how every single one of us is so much more than what we show on the outside.

As Deer tells me Lieutenant Foster's story the next day, I realize that if what you are on the *inside* is so scarred that it shows on the *outside* then that makes for an even more complicated individual. And a more dangerous one as well, I think.

"Lieutenant Foster's story is best started at The War of 1812. And The War of 1812," Deer begins as we ride out bright and early the next morning after a quick breakfast consisting of the leftover remains of the meal the night before, "was a war unlike any other. Depending on where you were, you fought for totally different things, against totally different enemies." He shrugs his shoulders. "You even fought against ghosts from the past." He's quiet for a minute as he gets his thoughts together.

"Just remember this rule that never, *ever* changes: the French have always hated the English, the English have always hated the French, and the *Americans,* by the early 1800's have big issues with the French *and* the English but cannot openly declare a hatred for either of them for they are busy establishing a new country that needs their trade business." He turns back and looks at me over the two packhorses. "Got that so far?" I smile and nod my head 'yes'.

"Have you heard of the five civilized tribes?" He asks me still staring back at me.

"Lieutenant Foster mentioned them my first day at Fort Winston but I don't rightly remember much at all about that day ..." I say.

He turns forward. "Well the five civilized tribes," Deer continues, "consisted of The Cherokee – our Real People, the Choctaw, the Creek, the Seminole and the Chickasaw. They were called the five *civilized* tribes because these Indians tribes had made some attempts to accept the white ways and it was a back handed compliment to differentiate between tribes out west that had done no such thing and were still actively involved in warfare. Through treaty negotiations with *the five civilized tribes*, the white language, religion, and customs had gradually begun to seep into these tribes making them *civilized*." The tone he uses as he speaks to me says he thinks little of this opinion. He shouts back to me. "Got that so far?" but he doesn't wait for my answer.

"Now remember this rule: the Cherokee have always hated the Creek, the Creek have always hated the Choctaw, the Choctaw have always hated the Chickasaw, and *all of them* have always hated the Seminole." He turns around again to look at me and I can see laughter in his eyes, "Got that so far?" I smile at him and nod my head even as I try to keep all of these rules of hatred straight.

He sighs, turns forward again and says, "Okay, so here's where the problems begin. There were some Americans that felt that some British were helping some Indian tribes for the purpose of war. Then there were some British who felt that some French were helping some Indian tribes for the purpose of war. Then there were some Indians that felt that some whites were helping certain other Indian tribes for the purpose of war ..." Deer waits while all this sinks in. "These problems grew and grew until it got big enough for war to be considered as the only solution.

"America declared war on Britain in June of 1812, just two summers after my arrival at Great Elk's village. I was, near as I can figure, about seven years old by then. I, of course, was unaware of most of the political intrigue between the white governments, but became well aware of the existing hatred between The Real People and the Creeks in the south.

So *my* understanding of the War of 1812 had little to do with much beyond the Indian perspective." He hesitates for a moment and then laughs. "Here I'm afraid to tell you, it gets a little complicated, for you see the Creeks within their tribe were divided and fighting amongst themselves, too. Tensions were so bad that there was already a formal distinction between the two groups. There were the Upper Creeks, who called themselves the Red Sticks after the custom of casting red sticks in their council circle to determine when, where, and how to go to war. The Red Sticks believed that anything white was evil. They sought in all ways to maintain the ancient way of their people and rejected anything the whites had to offer.

"There were about one thousand Red Sticks, or Upper Creek warriors plus women and children. They settled at the Tallapoosa River in the state of Alabama along a stretch that the white's called Horseshoe Bend because of its shape. They built, from what I'm told, a massive barricade of dirt and logs that sealed off the bend of the river as a defense. I've heard soldiers who were there and actually saw it, speak of it still with awe to this day.

"Now opposing the Red Sticks, were the Lower Creeks who had managed to put aside their differences with the Cherokee – The Real People. The Lower Creeks, The Real People and more than three thousand United States Army troops commanded by then General Andrew Jackson assembled to fight the Red Sticks." He looks back at me, but now his look is sad. "Got that?" he says. I nod 'yes'.

We ride for a while in silence and I ponder all the different forces: men, women, children, red, white … all meeting up at Horseshoe Bend on the Tallapoosa River in Alabama that day. Every single one of them fighting for what they thought was right and true and for so many different reasons.

"It was a brutal fight," Deer says. "There was tremendous bravery on both sides, both red and white from what I was told. The barricade is so strong that the cannons that Jackson has brought along cannot penetrate it. Some Lower Creek and Cherokee braves actually swam *up the Tallapoosa River* and began the attack from behind. Others, including many American soldiers, led by a tall, wild and crazy *Corporal* George Foster scaled the barricade and attacked from the front.   Foster managed to scale the barricade in the heat of the battle and kill many Red Sticks before he was wounded and taken prisoner. The Creek women," he looks at me with a serious face, "as was the custom of the Cherokee women you should know, tortured many of the prisoners as the battle continued around them. I've heard different stories of how he eventually escaped. Some stories say he was rescued by the victorious army. But one I heard, claimed that as he was being tortured - they were cutting his fingers and toes off one by one – he got a hold of one of the women and literally tore her head off with his bare hands. Despite his injuries, he established himself as a fearless leader and continued with great success in his military career – primarily in the constant battle to suppress Indian uprisings. He was a *very good* friend of Andrew Jackson's and his command of Fort Winston is his crowning military achievement, I would think.

"In the end over eight hundred Red Sticks were killed as well as many women and children and they were defeated. The Creeks as a nation signed a treaty with the United States after the battle – Upper *and Lower* – and were forced to give away *all* of their land, over *twenty million acres.* It was a lesson for many to learn as both the losers of the battle *and the victors of the battle,* both the enemies of the United States of America *and the allies of the United States of America* ended up homeless."

We stop for me to have a private moment and drink from a nearby stream. "The Battle of Horseshoe Bend made a tremendous impact for many of those that were there. The *victory* at Horseshoe Bend was a great accomplishment for General Andrew Jackson and a primary reason why he is *President* Jackson today." He looks at me pointedly. "Always remember that we are *all* products of our past, even Presidents and Fort Commanders." He looks at the water flowing past in the stream and says quietly, "And Indian Chiefs as well.

"Great Elk and Dark Cloud fought in the battle of Horseshoe Bend, too, Bear. For the Real People, it was the start of a division that we live with today. Great Elk and Dark Cloud looked at the battle and the results with very different eyes and as a result took their villages in very different directions. For Great Elk, he saw the deception and trickery that he and War Woman had seen before with the whites and their government during the Great War with Britain. He witnessed the unfairness that the Lower Creeks were forced to endure in losing their land all the while they called themselves victors and the United States continued to call them their allies and friends. He saw the treatment of the Lower Creeks and rightly thought, *What will make The Real People different in the future?* He knew that the friendship between *any Indian tribe* and the government of the United States lasted only until more land would be needed.

"Dark Cloud saw the opportunity to advance in prominence within the white culture. He gained the attention of General Andrew Jackson in his fierce and brave fighting. In fact, Jackson told Dark Cloud, 'As long as the sun shines and the grass grows there shall be friendship between us, and the feet of the Cherokee shall be toward the East.'" It is a promise that Great Elk remembers in particular each time more land of the Real People is taken away in treaties. Dark Cloud has risen to a level of leadership that with the Old Way of doing things he never could have achieved. And Dark Cloud and Great Elk both came to realize that warfare was no longer the way to succeed against the might of the white army, no matter *what* you believe."

That night as we make camp for the night, Deer makes one more observation about the lasting changes the War of 1812 brought about as we both fall asleep for the night. "There are some things about war and betrayal and the truth of life that can only be experienced first hand and not with just telling words. That's something that Great Elk could not explain to Beaver that night when they disagreed. Sometimes words are not enough to understand the way of things. Sometimes you must experience the fear and sorrow and defeat first hand. It is unfortunate that Beaver will most certainly have to discover much of this for himself."

The days pass and I get comfortable with the rhythm of travel and seem to become happier and happier with each passing day as each step brings us closer to home. Deer explains that we travel to Forest City first for he *has* been away a long time and at the pace we are traveling, he suspects we should be there in ten days or so. From there, he will take me to the Maple Forest and Bright Feather. He chuckles, "I suspect, though, he will be waiting for you in Forest City. Before I left for Washington he and I calculated the time it would take me to travel to Washington, with a stop at Ward's Mill, of course, the time I knew I was going to have to spend there and then the journey back. I am late already by our calculations so I can just imagine his impatience to hear news of you."

"How has he faired while I was away?" I ask at last.

"It's been a hard winter for him," is all Deer will volunteer at first about him when I ask. Yes, he is well. Yes, he has stayed close to the village. "He was packed and ready to travel north to see you and make sure you were safe when the first major winter storm hit." I remember that night, too, when I found out from the Coopers that Henry was alive and looking for me. "Bright Feather told me that was when One Who Knows told him that you were carrying his child and that he could not subject you to travel in the dead of winter or the upset of him getting hurt, jailed or even killed should he be found in white territory. One Who Knows convinced him to wait the season out and that no matter how difficult things may be for you, you were better off *there* dealing with things that needed to be dealt with." He looks at me, shakes his head and chuckles. "She's scary sometimes that old woman, I tell you."

I grin back, "You better be really scared if she ever hears you calling her 'old woman', that's for sure."

He looks around like she may be lurking in the dark shadows somewhere. "You're right, I better be careful."

On the seventh night of the journey I dream of Bright Feather. He cuddles with me in my sleep and places his big warm hand on my belly and delights in the feel of the baby kicking. I feel safe and secure and loved cradled in his arms. It's a wonderful dream. I wake in the morning cold on my pallet to the sound of Deer stirring up the coals of the fire to eat our usual breakfast of leftovers. I try hard to slip back into the dream for just a few moments more but it disappears from my head like the smoke above a fire. At last I open my eyes. I'm surprised at how bright the sun is and I think how Deer will tease me all day about sleeping so late. Then I puzzle at the cluster of late spring flowers I see tied in a bunch just an arm's length from my face. *I'm just a little bit late in returning,* I think to Bright Feather as I look at the flowers, *just a little bit late past the first spring bud.* And then my sleepy mind asks, *Why has Deer brought me flowers?*

There's a sudden wave of hope that's so strong it's painful as I think, *Was the dream real?* There's a length of time that I can't look for the disappointment would be more than I could possibly stand. I reach out and touch the flowers and see hidden in the cluster three feathers: one yellow goldfinch, one red cardinal, and one blue jay and I sit up and pick them up. I turn to look at who is tending the fire and it's Bright Feather and he looks *so beautiful.* He smiles his precious smile at me and I have a moment's panic as I think, *Am I still asleep?*

"Are you real?" I finally ask him. He stands and comes by me and touches my cheek and then his hand reaches down and covers my belly.

"What must I do to convince you that I am?" he asks back.

I search his face and I see relief and worry and tiredness and delight all rolled into one. "Don't disappear," I say thinking of the dreams I've had over the past months and disappointment of realizing the actual way of things. I can't help myself and I touch his face to feel it warm and alive and *real.*

His hand comes up to grasp mine and he brings my palm to his lips and he kisses it and I feel the slightest touch of his tongue. I feel like a body feels when it touches a hot ember by accident and the shock of the pain shoots through your whole body, making your heart pump and your muscles jump, only this feeling is *nothing but delight.* "Never again," I hear him say finally. "Never, ever again will we be separated like this. We will travel together and face our challenges together. Never again will we let life break us apart." It's a promise that I'm happy to make.

I start to laugh and I touch his hair and his arms and his broad chest and finally throw myself into his arms. I kiss his mouth and smell his smell and I taste salty tears, too, and I don't know if they are mine or his. I end up in his lap cradled there and he holds me close while I concentrate on the sights and sounds and smells and feel of him near me again *at last.*

I find we are to spend the day together, just the two of us. Deer has 'gone off to hunt a bit' although he will rejoin us tonight at a point agreed upon by him and Bright Feather. "I have traveled too far into white territory to his liking," Bright Feather says to me while at the same time putting a finger to my lips to quiet any comments I might wish to add about the matter, "and he does not feel it wise that we should be without his help should it be needed." He shrugs, "I can always disappear quickly into the woods should the need arise and you could still just travel with Deer and no one would be the wiser."

The first thing he makes me do is take off all my white clothes so that he can see my belly. He asks me many questions, Have I been well? Have I had much tiredness? Have I been eating enough? How do I feel? Is the baby active? It feels so wonderful to talk about the baby with him and watch the looks of delight on his face. I tell him that I'm quite certain that the baby will be born sometime at the very end of the summer and explain to him the friendship I had with Jane West and her thoughts on babies and such. He examines me all over and I realize he looks for scars or marks of misuse. I assure him with words although he seems to need to be assured with his own eyes more. When I reach for my clothes he makes a noise of disgust and throws them in the fire while I stand helpless and naked watching them burn.

"Great Elk's village will think little of me arriving naked, but I can promise you that any white folk we meet on the way back will be mighty put out," I feel a need to explain to him as I sit back in his lap.

He wraps one arm tight around me while he leans far over to reach for a parcel. "From One Who Knows and Otter," he says by way of explanation and drops it in my lap. "One Who Knows said that *if* you still had your old clothes, and *if* you could still fit in them, no matter what I was to burn anything you were wearing so that you could start fresh." Inside the package is a short summer top, wrap around skirt and moccasins, simply but finely made. The skirt, I can see, is cut fuller for my growing belly. I also find special herbs that Otter uses to clean her hair and body as well as new ties for my hair. "Otter sent those," he murmurs close to my ear. I feel him begin to undo my hair from it's wrapping. He works slow and steady undoing the ties and finally winding them up careful for they are still good to use again. I've wrapped some old strips of cloth close around my braided hair and those he unwinds and finally throws in the fire. Lastly he works at undoing my braid and I feel his fingers touch my back starting lower and then going higher and higher up as the braid becomes undone. Between sitting in the warmth of his lap naked, the tickling of my unbraided hair and the warmth of his breath against my neck, my body is tingling inside and out.

I start to giggle. "I have to pee," I finally confess. "It happens a lot with me lately," I say. We untangle ourselves and he takes my hand and walks me into the woods. We walk for only a short ways and I can hear the river. I go one way into the woods and he heads towards the water carrying my parcel of bits from One Who Knows and Otter.

I find him standing at the edge of the river and he is as naked as me now. Again I must think, *He is so beautiful.* I come up behind him and wrap my arms around his waist and rest my face against his warm back. "I think," I say after a time, "that I can stay like this forever," feeling the warmth of his body against my cheek and breasts and my sticking out belly. I feel the baby kick and I giggle again. He turns around and looks at me. "Not that often I hope," he says thinking I need to pee again. I must tell him about the baby kicking for it is too soon for him to feel those things yet.

The water is cold, cold, cold! I yelp and shout as we wade in but it feels so glorious to wash and be washed. He sits patiently on a rock while I soap up his hair and help him rinse it clean. As he does mine I think, *Who ever would have thought that hair washing could make someone think so much of mating?* I puzzle over this out loud to Bright Feather as we work on rinsing my hair and as I work to control my shivering from the cold I feel his hot breath on my neck as he kisses it. I sit up and swing my heavy wet hair over my shoulder and feel the icy trickles of the water running down my back and I can see that I am not the only one that thinks of mating when hair washing is done. *That is a good thing I know.*

It's high noon before we break camp and travel on and that's only because we know we must get to the meeting place and find Deer. We are clean and dressed and our hair has been carefully combed and braided each by the other. It seems that there are many odd things that make us think of mating over the course of the morning. I point this out to Bright Feather as we are readying the horses to leave and he grabs me and swings me high and then hugs me tight to him in a fierce hug. "In a lifetime I will not get enough of you," he says and kisses me firmly on the mouth.

Deer has left us the pack horses to bring along and we set off in high spirits. "I must tell Deer that I much prefer watching your back to his," I tell Bright Feather.

I ask of those in the village and he tells me bits and pieces. Otter is well and far along in her pregnancy. Raccoon is well, too, and anxious to begin his teasing of me again. Little Bird is speaking many words and Raccoon has already begun to teach him how to hold a bow and arrow. One Who Knows looks forward to my return to resume teaching me about the herbs.

I think of her giving me the basket and how she knew of my pregnancy even before Bright Feather and I. I ask him what he thought when she told him the news.

He is quiet for a moment and then he says, "I was terrified."

I think of his first mate Black Fox and the baby she died trying to give birth to. I think of my mother, too, and how I was the only mother that Eli ever knew. *Childbirth is the war that women fight*, I think. "I did not realize I was to have a baby for almost three months I guess because I was just too busy trying to not die from missing you," I tell Bright Feather. "By the time I realized, I was so glad for the company of your baby."

"When I argued that I was going to see you in Ward's Mill, One Who Knows told me I had two choices to consider. I could let you be the powerful, capable woman we all knew you could be or I could go off into the dead of winter, drag you and the baby back with me, leave a pile of unfinished business and probably kill all three of us in the process." He shrugs, shakes his head, and finally grunts. "Believe it or not, it was a difficult decision for me."

I can't help it, I have to laugh. "She has a way about her, doesn't she?" I ask. After a few moments, I say, "It was a hard, hard time being away from you and feeling so alone. It was lonelier than even my first time at Great Elk's when I didn't even understand the language." I tell him some of the hardest bits. When I get to Willow's sale I say, "That moment, was the worst time for me, I think. That was when things seemed the very darkest. But all of a sudden I thought of you and the baby and I realized that sometimes when things are the very darkest *maybe, just maybe*, it is because I am just in the shadow of something because things are really *so bright*."

He turns and looks at me with such a tender face it feels almost as if he touches me. "You are good for me for you force me to believe that this life is worth living even when we are in those dark shadows, my mate."

We endure Deer's teasing the entire evening once we finally meet up.

"Could have built an entire white man's cabin in the time you two have been gone."

"I'm glad to see you remember the pack horses since the two of you seem so oblivious to anything but each other."

Deer bends over, at one point and looks close at Bright Feather's neck. "Is that a bite, my brother?" he asks in mock concern. "You seem to have some fresh wounds ..."

It's hard to not giggle which only encourages him. Deer has gone out of his way to prove how long he has been waiting in the planned spot and we eat an enormous dinner of squirrel (three), biscuits (two each), fresh coffee, and some cheese which he insists he had time to prepare right there in the forest while he waited.

"I hope you had time to bake one of Possum's apple pies," I say with my best try at a straight face.

"It's in the oven I had time to build as well," he says.

As we sip our coffee and I snuggle against Bright Feather's side and stare in wonder every now and then that he is *really right there where I can touch him*, Bright Feather says to Deer, "Tell me of Washington."

Deer sighs, deep and low. "I am trying to think of some good news to tell before I tell you all the bad," he says at last and then shakes his head as if to give up. "There isn't very much I'm afraid."

"Major Everett spoke of the removal of all Indian tribes that live east of the Mississippi ..." I say in the silence of the evening.

Deer looks at me with great sorrow. "That is now a *law*," he says to both of us. "The Congress of the United States of America, the part of the government that makes up the laws that give one group of people power over other groups of people, has passed a law that gives President Andrew Jackson the right to move every single Indian west of the Mississippi whether they want to go or not. The law is very specific for I have spent the time in Washington reading it carefully. If you are in a state or just a territory of the United States east of the Mississippi, even if you have a treaty that has made promises to the contrary, and you are part of an Indian tribe or nation, *you will be required to move west of the Mississippi*. They make all the same promises that have been given before: like quality of land, cash for improvements you may have made that will be lost as a result of the move, and free assistance in transport during the removal." Deer puts his head in his hands and his despair can almost be seen rising off of him like hot steam.

He can't look at us it seems as he continues to speak without lifting his head. "Their arguments are amazing. 'It will separate the Indians from immediate contact with white settlements.' 'It will free the Indians from the oppressive power of the states.' 'It will enable the Indians to pursue happiness in their own way and under their styles of governing.' They have even said, 'It will help *save* the Indian who has suffered greatly from the white encroachment and will slow down the lessening of their numbers.' They say they hope that this move will help the Indian Nation gradually, with the help of the United States Government and other *good counsels*, become a less *savage* place and more *civilized* community." Deer then looks at Bright Feather and me and shakes his head in disbelief. "They can even be heard to say that they are not only being *open minded and fair*, they are being down right *generous*.

"They were so confident about the passing of this law," Deer says, "that they have people like Lieutenant Foster *already building forts* specifically for the removal *and containment* process that they plan to begin as soon as possible. I understand that there are *thirty* forts being built across all states that currently have existing Indian populations."

"You said that you had *very little good news*," I finally say in the silence that follows all of Deer's bad news, "but you did not say you had *no* good news. So I think I would like to hear what little good news you *do* have."

"There is only one small thing that seems to offer The Real People of The Maple Forest any hope at all," Deer says quiet like and I see Bright Feather wrinkle his forehead in puzzlement, but like a bright flash of lightning on a hot, dark summer night, I know what it is and I sit up fast.

"The Real People of the Maple Forest are *not* part of an Indian tribe or nation," I say softly and Deer looks at me across the fire sitting suddenly stiff and alert by Bright Feather. "They are citizens of the United States of America..." I say in wonder.

"That's it," Deer says grimly. "Now if I can get anyone important enough to listen to me tell them that." He looks at both of us and says, "It is our only hope."

It is good to see Possum and the children when we arrive at Forest City and the trading post but I'm tired from traveling for over two weeks and eager to get home to the Maple Forest. We spend just two days recovering and then head out bright and early, just Bright Feather and I, for home.

Deer will spend some time getting things in order at the trading post and then travel out, too, to The Maple Forest to talk with Great Elk, War Woman, One Who Knows and the others that regularly sit in the council circle. "We must move fast," is all he will say but we know what he means. I worry that nothing will be fast enough.

As with every visitor to The Real People of the Maple Forest the first to announce them is always the dogs. I think about the first time I arrived here, with Weasel and my fear of them as they barked and barked at me. I remember my worry about being so strange and looking so different. Now I grin at the barking dogs and smiling faces that hurry to add their shouts of greetings to the animal noise and I think, *my family.* I am a daughter here, I am a mate here, I am a sister here and I cannot help myself as the happy tears fall. I can hear Deer saying to me, *It was in Great Elk's village that I learned the meaning of love, security, family, honor ... "* I realize how fortunate I am for I *knew* of love and family and security and honor before I arrived here but to be able to find it again, having lost it all, is still a wonderful and amazing thing.

The crowd that surrounds us is full of welcoming faces and even though my eyes are filled with tears, I'm able to shout greetings to those who call to me. Bright Feather's surrounded by well – wishers, too, and it's Raccoon who comes and lifts me off Willow and gives me a big hug. He holds me at arms length, then and looks down at my belly, acting surprised at it. "Oh NO! Not *another one* like you!" he says in mock horror.

I laugh through my happy tears and wipe my eyes and nose on the end of my saddle blanket. "I plan to teach this baby as many ways as possible to bother Uncle Raccoon."

"I would not have it any other way!" he shouts, eyes dancing with delight.

Heavy with the very soon to be birth of her baby, it takes Otter more time than the others to make her way to greet me. We laugh as we bump bellies and try to find a good way to hug each other tight. We put our hands on each other's stomachs and both say, "Sister," to the other at the same time. That causes us to laugh and cry some more. Raccoon shakes his head and rolls his eyes at us and then reaches to put an arm around his mate for comfort and support.

"Make room for a nasty old lady!" we hear shouted from somewhere in back of the crowd and the crush of people parts to allow One Who Knows to make her way over to me. She looks approvingly at my clothes and touches my belly and nods her head a few times. Gradually the crowd gets silent as she examines and pokes and prods me.

"Don't suppose you even remembered to *sniff* those herbs I sent you," she snarls under her breath. I decide not to answer since we both obviously know the truth of things. She looks me in the eyes then. "You seem healthy enough, eh?" and I nod and smile.

"The great fool told you how he wanted to rush off into the storm just to come and catch a kiss?" and I hear Raccoon stifle a laugh with a quick cough. I glance over at Bright Feather across Willow's back and he has his blank Indian face on.

I smile at One Who Knows. "Ahh, Mother, how I missed your loving and tender words when I was away," and I lean forward and give her a kiss on her wrinkled and weathered cheek.

"Hrumpf," is the best that can be said for the sound she makes as she turns and walks slowly away, back into the crowd. She stops and looks around at everyone who seem to be just waiting for one last word from her. "And *I* missed someone to have around who knows how to show me proper love and respect," she says. "I look forward to a visit from my daughter when all of these *prying eyes* have had their fill of things," and she shuffles off without another word.

Otter and I link arms and waddle off to our huts. We are both filled with news and questions and stories to tell and ask each other and we bump words just like we have bumped bellies as we try to talk at the same times. I look over at Bright Feather as I walk away and he's following me with his eyes. I smile back and his look says, *We are home, my mate, really home!*

Within those first few hours in the village, aside from Little Bird, who's no longer the Little Bird I remember, but an active toddler running around and talking almost as much as Otter and I, it seems little has changed in the village for me to see and I say so.

"Well," says Otter with a delighted grin, "Red Fox and Turtle have joined just this past spring and I think she is already with child! One Who Knows has claimed her for a daughter, too, since she has pointed out that her other worthless daughter is never around to help and care for her anyway." She looks at me and laughs.

I laugh, too, and shake my head. "Turtle has been in her hut longer than I was. At first I thought that I should speak with her and give her some advice, but perhaps it should be the other way around."

It's high summer when I arrive and I fall right back into the rhythm of the work of the village, gardening and gathering. Hunting's no longer on my list, because much to my frustration, the shape of my belly and the way I now stand to support its weight, has made it impossible for me to aim and shoot with any accuracy. "That's as good an excuse as any," Raccoon observes as I speak of my frustrations over dinner one night and I hear Bright Feather grunt.

Deer's expected before summer's end, for those in the council are anxious to question him, having heard all that Bright Feather and I can tell. It's decided in council to send some messengers down to Dark Cloud's village to find out their understanding of the way things are, too. "It cannot hurt," Great Elk says, "to hear their impression of the United States Government's policies as well." Red Fox and two other braves from the village make the trip. I wonder if they will see the same things that I saw when I was there. And then I have a greater worry. Maybe things will be even worse.

In the two months or so that I have been home in The Maple Forest, the idea of hiding my pregnancy is now a joke. While I'm not as big and uncomfortable as Otter, I'm obviously very pregnant to anyone with eyes to see.

Sigh. Or ears to hear me walk, it seems, according to Raccoon. One morning as I'm walking over to their hut to begin morning chores with Otter, I look up to see that Raccoon has his bow and arrow drawn and aimed right at me. "What are you doing?!" I ask in shocked tones.

"Oh, it's just you," he says, putting his bow away. "I thought a buffalo was coming and I was going to be able to feed the village for the rest of the summer and maybe even into the fall ..." Bright Feather shows just how wise he truly is for he knows not to grunt when I tell him of the story.

On one of the hottest days I have known since I have been in The Maple Forest, when the air is so heavy you feel you cannot breath it and when your skin feels permanently sticky and sweaty and when you struggle to remember whether you were really ever, ever truly cool, Otter's baby decides to be born. Both of us, miserable in the heat, have gone down to the river to just sit on the edge and try to stay cool.

As we both sit in the coolness of the stream and let the water flow past us, Otter sighs in contentment. "I am not moving from here," she says with force. "No one can make me and I am too heavy to be lifted by even the strongest of men. I'm staying here until it snows." I giggle at her while Little Bird runs around and splashes on the edge of the water just as delighted as we are to be wet.

"Snow?" I say, pretending to be puzzled and confused. "Snow? What's that?"

In the midst of our talking - Raccoon says he has never known two bodies that can never stop talking about nothing in particular - she gasps and clutches her stomach. "Bear ..." she says. Then she laughs, "I'm going to give birth in this river," she says firmly, "because *nothing* and *no one* is going to make me go back up to that hot, sticky hut!" I stand – with great difficulty mind you! *What a pair we are,* I think to myself, and begin to waddle quickly into the village to get some help. I can still hear her shouting, "Tell them I'm not leaving the water! Tell them I mean it!" I chuckle to myself as I make my way to find Bright Feather or Raccoon.

Raccoon looks startled as I puff into view and with one look at my face, he seems to know. "Otter's time?" he says.

I nod and try to catch my breath as the sweat trickles down the sides of my face and I feel it make rivulets down between my breasts and my back. "She says to tell you that she's going to give birth in the river," I manage to gasp out. "She says that she's not moving and no one is strong enough to lift her."

He snorts and looks at a loss for what to do first. "I think," I say to him as I feel my breath slow and my heart begin to go back to an even rhythm, "you should go to her and wait with her and Little Bird. I can make my way to One Who Knows or at least find someone who will go for me."

He looks grateful at me and then smiles. "I will wait until One Who Knows comes before I try to move her. I'd rather have someone meaner than me do the telling if she needs to be brought to a different place."

He heads off to the river and I make my way towards the center of the village and the hut of One Who Knows. Bright Feather's sitting at War Woman and Great Elk's hut and I'm happy that that's the farthest I need to travel in the heat. I tell them the when and where and who and Bright Feather runs off to find One Who Knows.

"Sit, for a moment," War Woman says and she hands me a gourd full of not too cool water, which tastes good just the same. I tell her how Otter says she plans to give birth in the river and she smiles. "Little Bird was a very quick birth and that is unusual for a first baby. It is very possible that she *will* give birth in the river unless everyone hurries."

Bright Feather soon appears with One Who Knows and her gathering bag that I have given her and a rolled bundle under her arm. She takes one look at me struggling to stand and join them. "If we wait for *her* the baby will be on her second name by the time we get there," and she walks right past me. Bright Feather looks torn as to who he should go with.

"Go," I tell him and wave him away. "I'll make my way at my own pace." One Who Knows is traveling at a good speed and he touches my arm before hurrying after her.

It's War Woman who helps me to stand and walks with me in the end. "Men are useless during births, I'll come along in case another pair of hands is needed." She's in no rush though and her quiet, unhurried manner calms my head and my heart a bit.

"You both will be fine," she says almost reading my thoughts. "Both of you are strong and healthy and have had easy times throughout these pregnancies. Some women are just made for having children and I think that both of you are in that category." I think of my Ma and how she had two babies before the final one killed her. *I hope you are right*, I think and then I push the worries away for *what good will it do me?*

I smile at her in thanks for her kind words.

Everyone's *in* the river by the time we get there, although they have moved to the quieter shallows at the edge. It seems that Otter has gotten her wish and will not be moved to the *hot hut*. Raccoon's now squatting behind Otter in the cool of the water bracing her as she too, squats, while straining and pushing. One Who Knows squats in front of Otter and is talking quietly and firmly giving her instructions. I can see Otter, eyes closed as she thinks, breathing and panting in between the pushes. Bright Feather stands next to One Who Knows, obviously frightened and uncomfortable. He seems to be the official gathering bag holder for he holds it carefully above the water so it will not get wet. Even Little Bird's quiet, his hand in Bright Feather's quietly watching the action.

To me, War Woman says quietly under her breath as we both look at Bright Feather, "See? What did I tell you? Men are no use when babies are born." To One Who Knows she says loudly, "We are here, One Who Knows, is there anything you need?"

For a moment I think that One Who Knows has not heard her but finally she says, "It is good you are here for the only help I have seems to be no better than the furniture we sit on and walls we hang our things on. Quickly pass me the new deer skin that is rolled over there!" she points to the bundle I saw her carrying before. I watch in amazement as I see Otter give another great push and a small dark head emerge at exactly the spot where One Who Knows has her hand. Another quick push and the head is followed quickly by the rest of the baby and a rush of liquid. War Woman's moved swiftly and is now standing ready next to One Who Knows who cleans the baby's face and airways with fresh river water. It begins to wail, a loud angry shout, partly I'm sure because of the cool water being splashed all over it.

One Who Knows hands the baby over to War Woman who bends down to receive it, kneeling in the river, too. One Who Knows works quickly tying the cord with bits of sinew and finally cutting the cord with her knife. War Woman finally stands with the baby and wraps it carefully in the soft deerskin. "Well done," I hear One Who Knows say to Otter over the baby's wails, "your daughter is happy to finally be out in this world."

One Who Knows sits down in the water to rest and Raccoon gradually lowers himself and his mate into the cool of the river, too. Otter leans against him, eyes closed in exhaustion, and Raccoon takes his cool, wet hand and wipes her sweat-streaked face.

Raccoon leans over and whispers something private in Otter's ear and she reaches up and wraps her dripping arm around the back of his neck. She's still exhausted, her eyes are still closed, but now she smiles, too.

That night, Bright Feather and I decide to sleep outside under the stars for the hut is just too hot to bear even with the sides open as is done in the summer months. As we make preparations for our beds, Little Bird's curled up asleep close by, exhausted from his busy day and the fun of sleeping at our hut for a change.

"I cannot do it," Bright Feather all of a sudden says to me and I give him a puzzled look.

"Do what?" I say back to him.

"I cannot watch you go through that kind of pain and be unable to help you *and* know that I am the cause." He shakes his head full of despair. "It will drive me mad."

I'm quiet for a bit for I *know* that things with Otter were *very quick* and *very easy* compared to what I've heard and seen before. I don't think that this is the best thing to tell Bright Feather, though. I know he thinks of Black Fox and the baby that never was.

"What does your quiet voice tell you?" I ask him and he looks at me at last.

He snorts, "It tells me you will be fine, but I don't know if it is just my head insisting and shouting louder to be heard."

"War Woman had good words to say to me about how she thought Otter and I were strong and healthy and the type of women that are just made for having children …" I begin but he interrupts me.

"She's been singing that song to me since the snow was still falling and I hadn't even had a chance to see your belly," he says with surprising frustration.

"Oh," I say at last.

"Losing you is the only thing that I fear in this world," he finally says to me and I feel my heart just about stop to look at him.

I go and sit next to him and finally rest my head on his lap as we sit and enjoy the very brief night breezes. "When we were separated, I had great fear that each day I was away from you would make it harder and harder to get back here, until it would become impossible. The night I realized that I was to have your child, at first I was so happy to no longer be alone, but then I realized that it could be just another piece that would keep me from getting back here. I thought I was in a deep dark pit that I would never get out of. I was truly afraid then."

He sits quiet, listening to me talk. "I finally prayed. I remembered Ma's verse that Henry and I liked, *Thou preparest a table before me in the presence of mine enemies*[10]: and I prayed that God would send me someone to cook with. The next day I rode on Willow to Jane and Ezekiel West's house and found not one friend, but two.

"I watched my mother die in childbirth, Bright Feather. Part of the powerful woman that I am is because of that. I didn't understand or know that then, but I sure do know that *now*. I've had moments when the fear of having this baby makes me want to curl up and die rather than face it." I shrug my shoulders. "But what good would that do, I think?" I reach up and touch his face and smile a gentle smile and whisper into his worried face, "*Teach me the measure of my days, Thou Maker of my frame; I would survey life's narrow space, and learn how frail I am. A span is all that we can boast, an inch or two of time; man is but vanity and dust in all his flower and prime.*[11] "

I sit up and put my hand on his arm and he looks at me and I look at him. "Would I have come to this village on my own without Weasel? Would I have been able to withstand some of these hard things in my life so far had my Ma not died and I'd been made to grow up faster than I should have? Would Deer have chosen the way of life that brought him to be alone and lost in the woods that day the hunters found him and brought him back here? The answers to all of those questions is 'no'. One Who Knows says that *Joy never comes without a bit of work to get it.* I think it's even a little more. I think great hardship causes great joy. How can you tell day without night? How can you tell pleasure without pain? How can you know fullness without having felt emptiness?"

I take his face in my hands and I kiss him as I start to cry. "Would I risk my life to have a life with you however brief or however long and know all the joys that go with it? How much sorrow can a person say is worth how much joy? I *cannot* live each day worrying about what bad thing lurks around the next bend. I *can* enjoy each and every moment I have with you and be thankful for just that. I carry *your baby* inside me and just the making and the carrying and the knowing and the sharing with you has been joy enough for me *already*. When the worrying does come and I cannot seem to escape it, I just put it in a place in my head that I leave for when I have someone to cook dinner with – be it enemy or friend or husband."

I kiss him deep and long. I kiss his forehead and he sighs and closes his eyes and I kiss each eyelid, gently like a butterfly's touch. I kiss his strong, tan cheeks and finally his mouth again. "We travel on this path together you and I. There are those that love us and wait ahead, there are those that walk beside us and even those that walk behind us. What joy it has been for me to live in this *garden walled around, chosen and made peculiar ground; a little spot enclosed by grace, out of the world's wide wilderness*[12] ... *with you.* But there was great sorrow and heartache for both of us before we got to this place."

I take his big warm hand and I place it on my very busy belly that is jumping and hopping like a puppy in a sack. "I will whisper to God and talk about all these things and you will listen to the voice in your head that continues to talk loud and clear and tell you that things will be all right. And then we will have this baby and face all the many other things that we must face *together.*"

We walk to the river in the faint moonlight and sit naked in the rushing water, enjoying what has to be the only cool spot in this garden we call home. I think of another verse from my book of Isaac Watts hymns that I have read many times, for it's another one of my favorites and I say it to Bright Feather over the sound of the river's passing; *Let my Beloved come and taste, His pleasant fruits at his own feast, I come, my spouse, I come! he cries, With love and pleasure in his eyes[13].*

There's a point, as the summer tries to melt me with its last burst of burning heat and stickiness, that I decide I'm so uncomfortable with this baby, I would rather go through the pain and trial of the birth than go *one more moment* with this baby inside of me. When I tell this to One Who Knows she snorts and says, "So now you are ready to give birth then." She looks at me with a twinkle in her eye. My back aches whether I'm standing, sitting or lying down. My feet are swollen and painful to walk on. The weight of the baby in my belly seems so great at times that I find it more comfortable to hold my belly in place as if were I to let it go it would just rip right off and fall to the ground. I know things are bad when even Raccoon stops teasing me and looks away as if it is painful to even look at me.

Bright Feather seems delighted with the whole process despite the fear I know hides just below the surface. More than once I have awakened in the night to pee to find him wide awake and watching the movements of my belly. "How can you sleep with all that going on?" he asks me one night in wonder.

As I struggle to get up, like a turtle turned on its back, I grumble, "What choice do I have?"

In the final weeks as we wait for the baby to be born, he seems unconcerned with my moodiness and general lack of good humor. He's patient and kind and loving and a day does not go by that he does not tell me how beautiful I am. Sometimes his cheerful self is almost too much for me to take and I think to myself, *It is a good thing that my knife does not fit around my great big waist now for he has no idea how much danger he is in.* Somehow I manage to keep thoughts of that nature quiet and I just give him pale, tired smiles instead.

Since the birth of Otter and Raccoon's daughter, whom they have been calling Squirrel for the cute little face that she has, the heat has not let up, not one bit. For almost an entire month each day begins hot and sticky and ends hot and sticky, followed by nights that are hot and sticky, too. I have no appetite, just a desire to drink as much water as I can get my hands on. The river develops an appeal for more than just it's cooling ability; I drink it and I pee in it, too.

Finally a morning dawns with a different feel to it, but as I make my way slowly out of the hut, it is not necessarily better. The sky is full of dark gray clouds and there is no sign of the sun. The air still feels heavy and muggy, yet it does seem a shade cooler, although that's probably from the cloud cover. Bright Feather follows me out and gazes at the sky and frowns a bit. "Storm coming," he finally says and as an afterthought it seems he adds, "big one." As if to confirm his prediction a breeze blows up suddenly from the east that sends a blast of dust and leaves flying. Storm or no, the breeze feels *wonderful* and I stand there letting it dry the sticky sweat that seems to be permanently dripping from all parts of my very big body.

Raccoon wanders over and he and Bright Feather make observations about the gathering clouds while I am fully engrossed in *enjoying the breeze.*

"Bear? Are you listening, Bear?" I turn to look at Bright Feather who's purposefully moving about the hearth and walking in and out of the hut. "Raccoon thinks that this is a *very bad* storm and that we should move to better shelter."

"Better shelter?" I ask. "Where's better shelter?"

"There are a series of caves up along the ridge," he says and he tips his head to show the direction because his hands are filled with his preparations. "Just a little way further up from your thinking rock. I'm surprised you never found them in your exploring. Some here in the village wish to stay, but others feel it would be wiser to go. I think we should go."

I feel a slight start of panic. "I can hardly walk to the river let alone climb up higher than my thinking rock! I've never gone any farther than that spot because the climb was so steep just to get there! How do you plan on getting me up there? Will you carry me?" I put my hands on my hips and my enormous belly thrusts out at him making my point. *When was the last time I saw my feet?* I think and I stifle an almost hysterical giggle.

"We'll ride the horses as far as possible and then walk the rest of the way. I'll help you, then, and so will Raccoon." He comes and stands in front of me placing both hands on my shoulders, serious and tall. I look up at him and feel the baby give a hearty kick. *Great,* I think. *I have to pee again.* "One Who Knows will *not* come with us. She cannot make the climb and refuses to be carried," he says slowly to me. "She's chosen to stay with a number of others here. But she agrees that *we* should go to the caves."

We stand staring at each other for a few moments as the breeze blows up again and a wisp of his hair blows across his face. I reach up to catch it and put it behind his ear. I sigh. Another choice that seems to be no choice at all. "I have to pee," I finally say to him, "and then it will only take me a minute to get ready."

He kisses me on the mouth. "Good," he says and goes back to packing our carry baskets.

One Who Knows is waiting by our hut when I return from the woods. She holds a bundle just like the bundle she brought when Otter gave birth as well as a baby board. "Just in case," she says and it's my turn to snort at her.

"I cannot see this time," she says and her face shows her frustration. "I truly do not know if your time will come to have the baby during this storm. I told you once before this special sight is a blessing *and* a curse for it does not always tell me what I want to know. I *do know* that should I travel to the caves it will mean my death, I know that for certainty. I think I will take the risk and stay here with the hopes of seeing my," she hesitates and grins, "*grandchild* in the near future."

She sets the bundle down and now it's her turn to put both hands on my shoulders and look serious at me. Only this time I look *down.* "I am not worried about you during the birth should I be unable to be there with you. *It is not your time, you will not die.* Otter has helped me many times in the village and will know what must be done should you need that kind of help. Remember, *stay calm and listen to your body.* It will tell you most of what you need to know." She embraces me quickly and says, "See you in a few days," before heading off back to her hut.

Bright Feather has the horses packed and ready and helps me up onto Willow's back. He adds One Who Knows' bundle to his saddle and mounts up onto Companion. I insist on wearing my own pack basket on my back and even am able to joke a bit, "It helps balance me with a great weight in the back *and* the front." For a while it feels good to be moving, good to be cool, good to be doing something other than waddling around growing bigger and bigger with each passing moment, but gradually the ache returns to my back and it becomes so uncomfortable that even Bright Feather can see the strain of it as I keep trying to shift to make it easier.

I learn that there are many caves up in the hills. Some are closer but with steeper paths, some are farther but with easier paths. Some are larger and some are smaller, too. Some are well hidden and some are wide open and easy to find. Raccoon, with Little Bird, Otter, with Squirrel in her cradle board, Turtle without Red Fox for he is still south at Dark Cloud's village, Bright Feather and I travel to one cave that from what I can understand is *somewhere in the middle of all of these things*.

As I ride on Willow's back behind Turtle and in front of Bright Feather it becomes increasingly plain to me that these back pains are different than the back pains I have been suffering for the past month or so. They are low and when they grip me, seem to travel all the way around to the front of my stomach, causing the pain to grow in a terrible wave that if I concentrate enough makes them gradually fade away. I push my fear of giving birth back over and over again as it works hard to burst out from the spot in my head where I have it tightly stored. *You cannot have the baby ... now, ... here, ... yet,* I say over and over again as each pain arrives and works its misery on me. I gradually become so focused on the passing of each pain I'm no longer aware of the moving or the coolness, just the *not now, not here, not yet*.

I feel Bright Feather's hand on my arm and look down surprised to see him standing next to me his face a miserable mask of worry and fear. "The baby is coming, isn't it?" he says to me at last and I can't help myself as I nod my head in misery and start to cry. He grips my hand tightly for a moment and then reaches up to lift me down and I am caught off guard to be standing instead of sitting when the next pain hits. I stand with Willow

behind me and Bright Feather in front of me, him holding me up with my arms around his neck and his arms around me and my great belly.

Otter comes into view, her face very similar to Bright Feather's. I'm conscious of the wind now, no longer a breeze and the faint patter of rain drops splattering every now and then on my face and bare arms. "Bear," Otter says, "tell me what you feel."

I describe the pain to her and we wait, the group of us, for the next pain to come to see how long apart they are. When it comes, I rock myself in Bright Feather's arms and think, *Where can I go to get away from this?*

Otter says to Bright Feather, "The good news is that I do not think that she will be long in bringing this baby into this world, but that is also the bad news, too. She has still some time before she will want to push, but I do not think it will be enough time to get to the cave." She looks at me with sympathy, and brushes escaping bits of hair from my face. She manages a small smile, "You asked for cooler weather, but I bet you never thought to be more specific as to what was sent!" I manage a small smile for her. "You might feel better walking for a bit. It sometimes lessens the pains a small way."

"Let's go," I hear myself say. "We can't have this baby here." It's Turtle who steps forward and takes my basket with a shy but determined smile.

In between the pains, I walk as fast as possible. As far as I can tell, walking does not make them hurt less, but I *am* more comfortable in between them than sitting on Willow. When we get to my thinking rock, I must wait again as another pain comes and this time I feel a great rush of wetness pour down my legs. I shout with anger when Bright Feather picks me up and begins to carry me. "Hush," he says fiercely as I try to argue. "You have done all you can. I can carry you the rest of the way now *and I will.*"

I loop my arms around his neck and we actually move more quickly for he carries me through the pains now and we no longer stop. I hear him mutter in amazement when the first pain rides through for he can feel the pressure I feel now as he holds me tightly against him.

The rains come. It's as if one moment you are standing looking at a waterfall and listening to its roar and the next moment you are under it. It comes in great sheets of wet that soaks us to the skin just like *that*. I hide my face against Bright Feather's shoulder so that I can still breath and not be drowned. I hear One Who Knows say, *Listen to your body, it will tell you most of what you need to know* and I concentrate on the *Stay calm* part for I all of a sudden have a powerful urge to push. I can hear Raccoon shouting something up ahead and I feel Bright Feather's arms tighten around me as he says loudly in my ear over the downpour, "We are here. The cave has been found."

The cave's not large, but it's big enough to fit all of us plus our belongings. I hear the wind and the rain and the murmurs of those around me getting things set. As Bright Feather lowers my feet to the ground I'm gripped by another pain and I cannot help myself as I hold onto him and squat and push, push, *push*. I can hear the panic in his voice as he calls, "Otter!"

What a sight we must be, all of us soaked to the skin, except baby Squirrel who for some unbelievable reason is fast asleep cradled in her babyboard, pretty much dry from the little awning that protects her *usually from the sun*. Bright Feather braces his back against the wall of the cave and I squat and brace myself between his legs. Otter's in front of me, just as One Who Knows was in front of her less than a month ago. She talks loudly over the wind and the crashing rain, "Breath in between the pains, Bear! Slow, easy ..." Another pain comes and she says, "Now take one deep breath and push! Push with all your might!" She yells at me, "GET THAT BABY OUT!!" I push and push and I can't help myself and I yell my war cry for it makes me feel just a tiny bit stronger.

"Good!" Otter says and I feel her reach down. "Feel, Bear! Feel your baby!"

I reach down and am amazed what I feel with my hand. It is hard and damp and *it feels enormous!*

"One more push and we should have the head out! That is the hard part," I hear Otter say and the pain comes. "Deep breath!" she reminds me, "Now PUSH!" and that she *does not* need to remind me about.

I feel a burning, hot but not hot pain and some release of the pressure and I can feel Bright Feather grow even tenser than he already is as we hear the crying of a baby, *and it is not Squirrel.* Turtle, without being told, has a gourd full of rainwater and a soft piece of deer skin and as I wait for the next pain, I know they clean the baby's face, as I saw One Who Knows do with Squirrel. Otter looks at me with a great big smile on her face, "*Last time*," she says as I feel the pain begin to build again. "War Woman was right, you and I are made for making babies!" And the last pain comes and I push and I feel a rush of relief as the baby leaves my body.

Even over the sound of the storm outside, the baby's cries are loud and I hear Bright Feather laugh low in my ear. "Someone is *very angry* it seems." He lowers us both slowly and carefully to the floor and I sag against him unable to even lift my head it seems to look at the baby. "You did well, little mother," he says and uses his hand to wipe the wetness that is still trickling down my face from the rain and maybe from some sweat, too.

Otter brings me the baby wrapped in soft deerskin and says, "Here, feed this son of yours before we all go deaf!" Bright Feather helps me lift my wet top up over my head and Otter guides the baby to my breast. I jump as his hungry mouth latches on and look at her with shocked eyes at the pain of it as he starts to eat.

She laughs at the look on my face. "They always seem to forget to tell us about that until it's too late. You will adjust and it will become a pleasurable time for both of you very soon."

The baby nurses hungrily, making funny slurping and grunting noises and I shift a little more to get as comfortable as I can having just given birth on the dirt floor of a cave in the midst of a terrible storm. Although I'm soaking wet and sore, I'm at a comfortable temperature for the first time in weeks and weeks and *the baby is born.* I feel a wonderful rush of relief to realize that *I did it, it's done.* Bright Feather's long legs surround us on both sides and his arms encircle us, too. I see his hand reach out and tentatively touch the top of the baby's dark, wet head.

"He has a lot of hair," he finally says in wonder.

"I guess the storm was one way to keep you from worrying about me too much during the birth," I say with a tired smile.

I hear and feel him grunt behind me. "Did you pray about the weather change *and* that I would not fear for you during the birth? You must be careful how you ask these things, I am thinking!" I can hear the relief in his voice about it being done, too.

"Rest," he says to me. "Go to sleep if you can. I will keep you both safe here in my arms." It's the last thing I remember for a while.

I wake up some time later curled on my side, still between Bright Feather's legs. I feel his warm hand on my back and as I sit up I see the baby nestled in his other arm. The look he gives me, wrapped in a smile of wonderment says, *Look what I've got!!* A fire's burning in the center of the cave and the storm is still raging outside. I can see the rain coming down so hard it makes only the closest things something you can barely see. The few trees I see are being whipped back and forth in a wild dance. *How are those in the village?*, I wonder.

Otter's there, and Turtle, too. "Do you think you can stand?" Otter says. "It would be good to try to get you cleaned and cared for now …"

She and Turtle help me to stand, carefully though for the ceiling of the cave's not high enough for even me to stand upright. I can feel the rush of blood and fluids down my legs. We go to the opening of the cave and stand under an overhang and they help me wash as best as I can with the help of the raging storm and a soft deerskin cloth. We lay my skirt out in the rain to be rinsed and I put on a breech cloth - just like the men - wear between my legs and anchor it around my waist. I have brought another skirt that I put on and a short, cool top like the one that still lies wet beside Bright Feather. I smile at them, "I feel better already!" Otter gives me a hug. "You did well, my sister," she says with a big grin. "*You did well!!*"

Turtle looks at us both. "It seems I will be next," and puts her hand on her tiny stomach. "It is good to have sisters to watch and learn from."

Remember your birth, how your mother struggled
To give you form and breath. You are evidence of
Her life, and her mother's, and hers.[14]

~Jo Harjo

Mother

Our son is hungry all the time and impatient with even the slightest wait. He makes his wishes known loudly and with such force that it causes everyone to scurry and get him to me and my breasts fast. Raccoon observes within the first day of his arrival, as the rains and winds make a powerful sound outside the cave, "Which storm is louder, the one outside or the one inside?" and we all laugh. It seems our son has his first name.

"Storm, son of Bear, daughter of One Who Knows, of the Elk Clan, and Bright Feather, son of War Woman of the Wolf clan and Great Elk, chief of The Real People of the Maple Forest," Bright Feather says to him over my shoulder as he wrestles and slurps and gulps his meal, "It seems you are in control of the situation already."

I look down at him nestled in my arms over the course of those first few hours and days in the cave; sleeping, burping, yawning, screaming, and just staring and I fly back in time to when I cared for Eli as a baby in those early times so many years ago. I've always loved babies. I remember being *so excited* when I realized Ma was to have one, and her saying to me more than once, *You are going to be such a great help to me, Elle.* I think, *Little did we both know.* I remember that Eli was a loud baby, too, just like Storm. I can still hear Pa saying, *Hush now, little man, we're all doing the very best we can!* as he yelled and screamed his fury. Pa, Henry and I took turns juggling, rocking, singing and just holding that screaming mass of tears and stink and as I look down at Storm howling at me to *Hurry up and get me fed!* I catch myself getting teary at all the remembrys.

"What's wrong?" Bright Feather asks and I shake my head and sniffle. "Are you in pain? Is there something I can do?"

He looks so worried that I tell him through my quiet sobs about Eli and my remembrances of a time long gone. "Storm has Eli's eyes," I tell him and I must giggle a little through my tears as I add, "and his scream."

Bright Feather smiles and hugs me tight. I tell all of them in the cave how when Eli was first born I remember trying to deal with all the terrible changes in the midst of having a screaming, always hungry, never happy little one to deal with. "Once he settled down with life," I tell them, "he was the sweetest, most loving little one you ever would want to meet. But those first few months just about did us in, Pa and Henry and I." I think about the process of Ma's death and how that has a very shadowy, hard to remember quality about it, compared to all the bright details I remember about Eli: his vivid blue eyes, his stickin' up black hair, how he'd curl his legs up tight to his stomach just before he let loose with screams that would rattle the windows, how at the height of his fury even his fingers would turn bright red but his knuckles would stay white. They all sit there quiet listening to me talk and sniffle.

"I have only one thing I remember when Beaver was born," Bright Feather says finally. "Otter was born when I was about four or five summers I think," he looks at her and she smiles and shrugs, "so that is not clear, but when Beaver was born I think I was close to nine. I remember, after the first few weeks of his crying and settling in, I offered to return him if they could figure out just where to take him." He grunts. "Great Elk told me that I was more trouble than Beaver was and did I think I should have been returned, too?" He reaches down to stroke Storm's hair as he nurses. "That kept me quiet after that, I will tell you."

I sniffle and wipe my nose on my sleeve and manage a tiny smile. "I am glad they didn't return you."

"Me too," he says.

"I have a memory of *you*," Otter says, smiling at Bright Feather, having listened to our talking and remembering. "I was very little and I'd had a terrible dream that really scared me. I remember lying on my mat and whimpering, too afraid to call out even or ask for help. You must have heard me," she says with great tenderness, "for all of a sudden you reached out your hand and I took it. You never said a word, that I remember, you just held my hand and I fell back to sleep at last."

Raccoon speaks up. "I have a memory of Great Elk and War Woman that still haunts me to this day." He glances at Bright Feather. "Do you remember the time with the horses?" and Bright Feather looks very much like he wishes that he could not but does.

"Yes, I remember," he says at last with much regret.

Raccoon looks at all of us seated with him in the cave eager to hear his story that will fill the time. "Deer, Bright Feather and I were out in the woods." He shrugs. "We were *always* out in the woods, hunting, fishing, fighting, running, riding – if we could get ourselves a horse. There was more than one time that we got into a little bit of mischief."

Bright Feather interrupts, "I spent *all* my time trying to keep the two of you from getting *all* of us in trouble." He shakes his head. "Every single day there was some adventure, some plan, some *trouble,* they were planning ..."

Raccoon looks at all of us and then back at Bright Feather. "He was *no fun* I tell you. *Absolutely no fun.*" Bright Feather snorts and shakes his head again.

"We had been exploring in the forest and had traveled the better part of the day a pretty fair distance from the village," Raccoon begins with his story, "I cannot remember what we were originally doing, when we heard horses approach and we hid to see who was coming. It was soldiers of all things! Five of them, mounted on horses, in uniform, weapons shining … We could not believe our eyes! What were they doing in our part of the forest? Why had they invaded our territory? We were all in such a state of excitement."

"*You two* were in a state," Bright Feather feels a need to correct him. "*I* was of the opinion to fade away quiet and go back and tell the village of their presence."

Raccoon ignores Bright Feather and continues. "We followed them for a good mile or so, practicing our stalking. It was the same summer that Beaver was born, was it not?" He asks Bright Feather who nods his head 'yes'. "It was getting to be nightfall and it was Deer who finally suggests that when they set up camp for the night *perhaps* we could take a few of their horses for our own. The idea of having *our own horses* was more than we had ever imagined. We justified that they did not belong on our land, that they were the enemy."

I look at Bright Feather, amazed at the danger and foolhardiness of the idea. "What did you say to them *then?*" He doesn't answer me, but Raccoon does.

"*He* wanted a horse more than the two of us combined, for he saw himself as a great warrior and hunter. But he wasn't much of one *always on foot.*"

I look at Bright Feather and he makes a grand show of studying his son's sleeping form in his arms. When he finally looks up at me, he shrugs his shoulders and says, "Bad influence from bad company."

"We waited until cover of darkness," Raccoon said. "Taking the horses was easier than we imagined. We snuck up while the guard was taking a piss and before he could get his pants done up we were on the backs of three of the most magnificent horses you had ever seen and ridden off into the dark night." He shakes his head in remembrance. "It was a grand thrill, was it not my brother?"

Bright Feather looks at him across the glowing fire and is unable to deny it. "Yes, it was, my brother. It was a grand thrill."

"We had already planned out where we would hide the horses and we reached there before first light. We hobbled them, rubbed them down, fed them and then returned to the village like nothing had happened." He grins. "We had two days of the most glorious fun with those horses, did we not?" he says, his eyes dancing with wonderful memories, and I see that even Bright Feather cannot help himself and he nods his head with a dreamy look on his face. "And on the evening of the second day as we returned to the village you can all guess who was seated at the fire with Great Elk, War Woman, and many other leaders of the village."

"The five soldiers," I whisper, and Bright Feather and Raccoon both nod.

"They were on their way to our village all along, part of a regiment that was assigned with scouting out villages of The Real People and recruiting them to fight in another great war that was about to happen with the British. They were not our enemy, they were not trespassing on our land. They were there with the blessings of the leadership of the Real People and it turns out that one of the soldiers was an elected agent from The Real People. Great Elk and many other men from the village agree to join in the fighting for it was against our greatest Indian enemies the Upper Creeks." *Battle of Horseshoe Bend*, I think in wonder.

"They, of course, spoke of the theft of the horses and told of when and where. They had seen nothing specific but suspected that there were three culprits as only three of their five horses had been stolen."

Raccoon laughs. "I can just imagine the expressions on our faces when we see the soldiers as we enter the village. Deer and Bright Feather must return to their hearth," Raccoon gives a wide grin, "which is the *same hearth* where the soldiers are seated."

"I have never been so afraid in all my life," Bright Feather admits. "Poor Deer, had to step forward and converse with the soldiers, being a white boy in an Indian village. He stuttered and stammered and looked like he was ready to just die right there on the spot. War Woman studied us as we stood there. I could feel her eyes boring right into our brains and seeing all the things we had done in the past three days."

"The next morning," Raccoon continues, "we did not know what to do with ourselves. Do we leave like we always do? Do we go to the horses? Do we stay in the village? We are hovering by the river talking, arguing amongst ourselves as to where we should go and what we should do when Great Elk comes and sits on a rock near the river's edge a little ways away from us.

"Now he looks just as casual as could be sitting there in the morning sun on the rock, and yet the three of us knew that there was nothing casual about it."

Bright Feather looks at Raccoon in the dimness of the cave. "Tell them what your brilliant idea was," and Raccoon looks like he would much rather not.

After a pause, Raccoon says, "I went over after a few moments and told him clearly and with great seriousness that if he was wondering or at all worried that we had nothing to do with the theft of those three horses." Otter cannot help herself and collapses into disbelieving laughter.

Quiet Turtle finally speaks up and asks, "What did he say?"

Raccoon grins at her. "Great Elk looked right at me and said, 'Are you speaking of the three horses you have been hiding over the ridge that you've been riding for the past two days?'" Raccoon looks at Bright Feather. "Were we that obvious do you think?"

Bright Feather shrugs his shoulders. "I think that he did not suspect until the soldiers told him of the theft." I can see his eyes smile a bit. "I think he was absolutely sure only after you spoke to him and told him for sure that we had not done it." I see it is Turtle's turn to stifle a giggle.

Raccoon laughs. "It was Deer that comes forward and says, 'What do we do, Father?' and Great Elk looked at him and said, 'Why, tell the truth, son. Always tell the truth.'

"We went and got the horses and brought them into camp to the soldiers. They were busy sitting in council talking and making plans for the coming weeks. We walked the horses up to them and just stood there not knowing what to do. War Woman and Great Elk did not say a thing. The soldiers were very stern with us. They talked at length about the penalties for horse theft."

"What were they?" Otter asks, for Raccoon doesn't say.

"Hanging," Bright Feather says matter of fact. He looks at Raccoon. "War Woman and Great Elk must have spoken with the soldiers in preparation, do you not think?"

Raccoon shrugs. "All I know was that I never felt inclined to take anything that was not mine ever again.

"When the soldiers left, the three of us were summoned to council and we had to sit before all the village elders and explain ourselves. War Woman said to the three of us, 'Many unhappy shadows will happen in your life that will cause you trouble and strife. You should spend your days trying to *prevent* making unnecessary shadows, not causing more. Acquiring something through honest hard work will always mean more than acquiring something through theft and deception.'"

Bright Feather snorts. "Then we were told that we were responsible for *caring* for all of the horses in camp for the rest of the summer *but forbidden to ride any*."

"And *I*," Raccoon said, "was required to sit at council each night for the entire summer and listen to *wise and honest words* so that I would learn to speak them myself." He looks at Bright Feather. "Bright Feather and Deer escaped that one because I was the one who had lied to Great Elk."

As the storm outside continues with no sign of stopping, the Storm inside wakes and asks to be fed. Otter and Turtle begin making preparations for the brief evening meal we will share together from what we have carried in our baskets. As they work, we hear Turtle say very quietly, "I have no memories of the woman who gave birth to me nor do I even remember what my first tribe or village was." She looks at Otter, Raccoon and me. "Do you know how I came to be in this village?"

It's something I've puzzled over at times. I remember the night in which I stood in the council circle, *so long ago now it seems!*, unable to understand the language, battered and bruised from my treatment with Weasel, still a pitiful white girl slave. I remember Great Elk speaking with One Who Knows and Weasel and seeing Turtle for the first time and knowing just by the look in her eyes, that she was a slave captive just like me. "I remember the night that you were given to One Who Knows and I was given to Bright Feather," I say to her.

She looks at Bright Feather and he looks back at her. "I was part of the goods you brought back from Deer's trading post just that day, was I not?" He looks at her with his Indian face and I can't see anything.

"My earliest memories are of hunger and fear," she begins as we all settle down to eat our meal and the storm outside rages while the Storm inside gulps and gurgles contentedly. "I have been a slave most of my life and I have never known real freedom until these past few months since I have become the mate of Red Fox and the daughter of One Who Knows."

She looks at Raccoon and then Bright Feather, "The unhappy shadows that War Woman spoke to you of were so great at one point in my life that I did not know that there was such a thing as a sun." She includes all of us as she says, "The earliest family I remember that owned me, Indians like myself, told me that my birth mother gave me to them in trade for an amount of liquor." She looks at each of us, shrugs and says, "I believe that to be true for they had no reason to lie to me."

"Deer offered to take me in trade for some goods at the trading post from my last owners. I think he took pity on me." When he saw Turtle, I know Deer was thinking of Raven, One Who Knows' daughter that was sold into slavery by her husband Weasel. "Bright Feather was there trading and Deer had me travel back to this village with him when he left." She smiles a sweet, shy smile. "One Who Knows was easy to live with compared to some of the others I have had to suffer with in my past." She sighs. "And now look at me!" and she pats her growing belly. She looks at me for she knows that me - of all of us - can understand her next words. "Life can be *so strange*, can it not?"

"You were not brought back to this village as a purchased slave," Bright Feather says quietly but firmly. "I brought you back to this village at Deer's request for the trading post was certainly no place for you. He purchased you to gain your freedom from the family you were with, but you were *never* brought here to continue your slavery. It made sense for you to go and live with One Who Knows and help her and learn our ways as you were both in need of what the other had to give." *I never knew,* I think in wonder as I look first at Turtle and then at my husband.

"I owe Deer my life, I know," Turtle says so quietly you can barely hear her. "I owe One Who Knows my gratitude." She looks at all of us. "And I owe all of you my support and strength and love."

The storm's unlike anyone in the cave can remember. It rains and rains and rains for two full days and nights and all of us work to keep the worry out of the cave about those who have stayed in the village for there's nothing we can do. I worry for Willow, too, although Bright Feather assures me that the horses will be fine. On the morning of the third day as the rain slows down to just a drizzle, all of us cannot wait to get out of the cave and stand and stretch. Only Little Bird has had any fun with the adventure, playing with all of the adults and dancing in the mouth of the cave among the drips that fall from the overhang and in the puddles that collect there, too.

Having finally seen a glimpse of the sun peeking through the breaking clouds, everyone's more than ready to travel back to the village. Traveling down from the cave with our remaining supplies, and me with the comfortable weight of Storm in his cradleboard on my back, we're unprepared for the destruction we see as we travel down out of the mouth of the cave. Massive trees are uprooted and lay on the forest floor as if some giant has come and had fun for the day tearing them up and dropping them where ever he chose. The horses are nowhere to be seen, however, all agree that they did not expect them to be where they had been hastily left. "They will have traveled back to the village, I suspect," Bright Feather tells me.

When we reach the place we call home, we stand at the edge of what was once Great Elk's village and there's not one hut standing. Turtle beside me whimpers in fear and we both take the other's hand for comfort.

Raccoon and Bright Feather begin searching the destruction looking for signs of those who stayed behind. We're unsure how many have truly stayed in the end and how many went to the caves. Bright Feather and Raccoon search each and every hearth and destroyed hut calling and searching but not one person is found dead or alive. Otter,

Turtle and I busy ourselves with starting a fire and then searching through our respective home sites looking for things worth salvaging.

Gradually people return and it's with shouts of relief and gladness that each is welcomed. Slowly, the village comes back to life with fires and sounds and smells. By nightfall, as the village gathers at the council circle, the only ones missing, besides Red Fox and the two braves who have traveled south to Dark Cloud's village are Great Elk, One Who Knows, and War Woman.

That night, as we sleep under the stars, Bright Feather, Storm and I, we worry about those that are missing even as we are thankful for what we do have. It's not until the following night after a full day of working to rebuild shelters, gather crops that can be saved and retrieve belongings scattered throughout the forest do Great Elk, One Who Knows, and War Woman walk casually into the midst of us.

They seem as glad to see us as we are to see them, but each within his or her own style. War Woman informs Otter and me that the moment we rode out for the caves, One Who Knows looked at her and said, "What are we waiting for, let us go!!"

War Woman said, "I looked at her puzzled and said, 'I thought you did not wish to go to the caves …' She looked at me with great impatience and said, 'I didn't want to go to a cave that had two tiny children, two crabby pregnant women, and two know-it-all men. If you had listened carefully, you would have known that I *never* said that I did not want to go to the shelter of a cave, it was just a specific one I refused.'" War Woman chuckles in remembrance. "At our hearth was her basket already packed, which she carried herself to a cave a fair hike from here. It was a bit wet but we managed just fine."

One Who Knows, after examining her hearth and inspecting the damage of her precious herbs, comes to examine her grandson. She holds him tenderly in her arms and over the course of long moments counts his toes and fingers, examines his belly for all the proper signs of healing and even touches and manipulates his privates. She looks up at Bright Feather and me with the same fierce look everyone's familiar with and opens her mouth to make a flip comment, but instead seems frozen for a moment unable to speak. Slowly her mouth closes and she takes a great swallow as we watch in great amazement as the tears fill her eyes and spill over her wrinkled old cheeks. When she finally finds words to speak, all she can manage is, "He is magnificent..." while she goes back to looking at him, touching the curve of his nose and the slope of his forehead.

"We will call him Storm *Eli*," I hear Bright Feather say to One Who Knows as he gives me a sweet look and it's my turn to join her at a little bit of crying.

At council that night, with a full village present, we discuss the damage of the storm and how it will affect us this winter. Crops were either already harvested or ready to be. Many have been working all day to salvage those that were damaged in storage and those that are still in the field and can be retrieved. We have lost much, but have managed to save much, too. Not all the horses have been found, including Companion and Willow, but many have been and all the dogs have returned. I try not to worry as no one else seems to. Tomorrow, Bright Feather promises me that he will search for the rest of the horses with the other men.

A new location is discussed for the village before all of the rebuilding is done. I discover that every seven years the village is relocated to give the land a chance to regenerate and recover from our presence. Another spot someone remembers from many years ago is talked about. In fact, this village that I have always known as my Indian home is the location that the village moved to only a few summers before my capture. It's decided that it makes wise sense to make the most of our circumstances and start fresh at an altogether new place.

The place where we will travel to I discover is where One Who Knows was actually born and many in the village call it "One Who Knows' Place". I'll always think of this spot I've known for these years as "Storm's Place" I realize as we pack the next day in preparation to leave. I look up to see Bright Feather coming out of the woods. He is leading Companion and one other horse and I am disappointed to see no Willow. My face must show my concern for as he comes close to me, he touches my cheek and says, "Can you whistle?"

I don't have time to though as Raccoon emerges from the woods behind him with Willow and three other horses. She has a great gash on her leg and is favoring it. One Who Knows comes and helps us as we clean it and dress it with herbs and salve that she carries in her bag. The smell of the ointment reminds me of the time after Dark Cloud's village. "You cannot ride her until this heals," One Who Knows says and I nod my head.

"Will she be all right?" I ask as I pet her muzzle and smell her good horse smell.

"She will be the first horse that Storm will ride on," she assures me.

The new village location's along the same river that I have always lived nearby since my time with The Real People, just a two days easy hike east and north a bit. I watch these people, *my people*, and realize as I watch them laughing and talking and singing as we travel why I have felt so quickly a part of them. In just a matter of days, the entire destruction of their village has been turned around as a new adventure and an exciting new beginning. I think about Bright Feather's words to me at a time that seems so long ago, *You are someone who despite all the things that have happened to you can still find joy in life.* And I realize, *my people are like that, too.*

We stretch out throughout the forest as we hike, an amazing mix of tall, short, young, old, loud, quiet, and I feel a wonderful sense of belonging and happiness as I feel Storm give a contented sigh behind me in his cradleboard. "Shadows only show when the sun is so bright," I say to myself and *of course* who's nearby to hear me talking to myself but Raccoon.

"Does motherhood make you talk to yourself?" he asks with a great grin on his face.

"No," I say flip like, "but the search for smart company does sometimes."

"Hmm," he says and we fall into easy step. He is carrying an enormous pack on his back as well as leading two horses piled high with things. No one rides, for the horses are too important to carry things.

"Do you know much of the place we travel to?" I ask him and he nods his head yes.

"I have never lived there, that I remember anyway, but it is an area that I have hunted and it is well known in our history."

"Tell me!" I say, eager to hear a story.

"This river," he points to the one that I have drunk from, bathed in, and that Otter has given birth in, "that we have lived by for so long we simply call '*The River That We Are Always By*' flows from *The Ambush Place* and it's beginning headwaters are called *Where The Spaniard Is In The Water*."

He grins at me when I laugh at the names. "We travel closer towards *The Ambush Place* and I think that is good for us, given what we fear is coming in the future." I feel the laughs grow quiet in my throat all of a sudden, well aware of where we have come from and where we head to.

"The Ambush Place is named in memory of a battle between The Real People and The Shawnee which took place long ago." I think of Deer and his naming of *the five civilized tribes* and I know that the *Shawnee* were not listed as one of them. "It was a tremendous battle. The Shawnee had sent a large party to invade our territory and The Real People had hidden along the gap which has many large rocks and caves as well as being heavily forested." He smiles at me, but it's a different smile from his teasing one and I feel the goose skin creep up my arms and through my scalp for its fierceness. "The Real People killed every single Shawnee *except one*."

"Why did one survive?" I ask, foolish in the ways of war.

"Why to go and tell his people of the defeat, the fear, and the massacre, of course," he says matter of fact and I think, *oh, of course.*

"What does the Spaniard in the water have to do with things?" I ask.

"Nothing, with this story," Raccoon says. "But The Ambush Place has been successful in more than one battle you see. The Spaniards were the first whites to arrive, before the British, before the French. Stories tell of them arriving in great ships, with great armor, and with great greed. They wanted nothing but *gold*, something that we did not have, but they did not believe us and they enslaved many unsuspecting Real People – and others I suspect – to look for this gold. They brought sickness and death with them in great numbers and the only good Spaniard I have ever heard of was *a dead one*."

We walk through the woods for a bit in silence and I think, *Is there any place and any people that has only happiness and joy in their lives?*

"The Ambush Place," Raccoon says, "was a place that the Spaniards found death from The Real People just as the Shawnees did. One Spaniard in particular found death in the water at the base of the gap where The River That We Are Always By finds its beginnings. *A good place for a Spaniard,"* he grins at me with his sinister smile and I think, *I am glad you consider me your sister!*

At the new spot, each family chooses a hearth spot that suits them. Great Elk and War Woman's hearth are at the center for it'll once again be the spot for council meetings and all other hearths fan out from there. I remember my first impression of the village, arriving as a captive slave with Weasel and thinking how the village looked like a great wagon wheel. It's decided that a large hut will be built with Raccoon, Otter, Little Bird, Squirrel, Bright Feather, Storm, Turtle, Red Fox, and myself in one as a true extended family. It makes much sense as Red Fox is still not back from his travels south to Dark Cloud's village and Bright Feather and Raccoon can work quickly and efficiently together to construct our new hut.

Otter, Turtle and I go to find One Who Knows. Both Bright Feather and Raccoon know that we go to ask her to set up her hearth with us, although I must stifle a giggle at the pained look that Raccoon wears as a result.

"You do the talking," Otter says to me and Turtle nods her head vigorously.

"But you have lived longer with her!" I say to Turtle, unwilling to bear the burden and suffer the probable scars of the conversation to come.

Turtle says as she shakes her head 'no', "You are the *only one in the village* that speaks to her as you do and that she seems to still tolerate in the process." "We did very well living together as long as we did because I am *quiet and cooperative and unassuming.*"

Otter giggles. "You are many things, Bear, but you are *not any of those.*"

One Who Knows is sitting at War Woman and Great Elk's hut tending the fire. She's calm and seemingly unconcerned with the noise and activity around her as trees are cut down and stripped of branches, as holes are dug for poles, as ground is cleared and hearth spots are staked out.

There's a peaceful, yet productive feeling throughout the area as everyone works hard to get things the way they need to be.

We sit with her and wait for her to look up and acknowledge us, none of us brave enough to start the fight. She gradually raises her eyes and looks at each one of us and then snorts in disgust at us. "What a group," we hear her murmur under her breath as she goes back to preparing a meal.

"You seem well from the traveling, Mother," I begin, deciding at some point that the silence around the fire has become more tense then the coming conversation. She ignores me and my foolish talking.

"We would have you live with us, Mother, in our hut. All three families plan to be together and your daughters would have their Mother live with them." She stops her meal preparations to look at each one of us for moments. She studies our faces and I feel her, as she stares into my eyes, probe into my head to read my thoughts. It's a most disturbing feeling.

"All right," she says, at last and now it's time for the three of us to sit there stunned at the ease of it all. I can't see the twinkle of mischief in her eyes, but I can just imagine it as she says, "But first, send Raccoon and Bright Feather to convince me as well," and then she looks up at us and she smiles her wicked smile and I have to laugh.

"Very well, Mother," I say as we stand to go. "We will send them to speak with you as well."

Bright Feather's silent at the prospect of going to see One Who Knows and invite her to live at our new hearth, but Raccoon is beside himself. "Why? Why must we go and invite her when you have already done that? She will take one look at my face and know that I am not excited about the prospect of living with her sharp tongue cutting me to pieces at every turn."

"Perhaps," I hear myself say, "she is not excited about the prospect of living with your teasing tongue and all it's joking comments at every turn. I, for one, think it will be quite fun to watch the two of you over the long winter that is to come."

"Me, too," says Turtle and Otter in between giggles. Bright Feather grunts.

In the end, a compromise of sorts is reached between One Who Knows and the men that pleases everyone. One Who Knows will have her single hut built right next to our large family one. That way she will not have to suffer the hands of curious children disturbing her herbs, the constant wit of Raccoon's tongue and yet will still be part of the everyday life of our hearth.

We find that we work well together as a group to establish a home hearth and begin the seemingly endless preparations for the winter that will come all too quickly.

Within those first two weeks after our arrival at our new village site of *One Who Knows' Place* in the Maple Forest, our village settles in and falls into the rhythm familiar to us all. As the second week comes to a close and we adjust to the changes of living in a large family hut, Bright Feather and Raccoon put the finishing touches on our shelter. Turtle, Otter with Squirrel on her back, me with Storm riding happily behind me and Little Bird running through the woods in front of us, head out into the forest to collect wood, late berries, nuts and herbs. We're talking and laughing and enjoying the beautiful early fall day when we all stop and listen to the oddest sound we have ever heard. Little Bird comes and holds Turtle's hand as the sound gets closer and closer to us and a real fear begins to go through the group.

"What is it? Do I hear *bells*?" says Otter to me at last as we listen and listen. It's a strange but oddly familiar sound and I look at Turtle who seems to mirror the same look that I think must be on my face.

"I think it is *cows*," I say at last, disbelieving even as I say it.

"I think *goats*, too," says Turtle more familiar with the ways of things outside this village than Otter is.

And out of the brush and through the trees burst not one, not two, but *five* large cows, mooing and clanking from the bells around their necks. The cows are followed by a grinning Deer, and his oldest son, James, *Red Bird*, and Eliza, *Sleeping Rabbit*, all mounted on horses. Behind Deer, roped, is an enormous bull, horns and nose ring included. Eliza and James have behind them six goats, five females and one male each with their own bells as well. Five more pack horses follow behind loaded down with all manner of things and I can hear the hysterical angry squawks from penned chickens. The sound's deafening in contrast to the earlier silence of the forest: animals, bells, shouts of greetings, Storm's inconvenient sudden screams of hunger, and over all of it, Eliza *Sleeping Rabbit's* questions. But it's wonderful just the same.

"What Ho!" Deer shouts, surprised to see us this far east and I can see the delight on his face as he sees the baby board strapped to my back. I'm not so sure he's pleased to hear the screams anymore then any of the rest of us are, but he's polite enough not to say. Over all the noise, he shouts to me, "It seems that there is a new mother in the village, eh?" And I nod, smile and turn my back so he can see the screaming mass of fury attached to my back. "Powerful voice," he says by way of a compliment, I suspect.

In the end, Turtle stays with me, Storm and Eliza, or *Sleeping Rabbit*, we are reminded to call her, while Otter, Squirrel, Little Bird – in front of Deer on his horse, James, and all the animals travel on to the village. I nurse Storm and answer Sleeping Rabbit's many questions and get answers to a few myself. Turtle, ever silent, smiles at me over Sleeping Rabbit's head, happy to listen to all the chatter.

I learn that the storm delayed their arrival by a good two weeks, but everyone recognizes how fortunate it is that the storm came *before* rather then *during* their trek here. The cows and goats were purchased with monies that Deer has secured from the tribal funds he has been able to get a share of.

"Pa thought that it might be a good source of food and income to the village and that was *before* the storm! We figure, if your supplies were destroyed in the storm, the worst thing you can do is eat all of the animals before the spring! Pa says that Red Bird and I can stay for a few weeks and help you care for the animals until you get accustomed to them in the village."

She asks questions about the baby and is thrilled with the offer of wearing the baby board on the side of her horse as we make our way back to the village. I attach it to her saddle and within moments, Storm's fast asleep with a full belly rocked to sleep by the motion of the horse's movements.

As we enter the village, noisy with shouted greetings and cows and goats and chicken's squawking and bells, I hear even more loud noise as Turtle screams and runs from my side. She throws herself into the arms of Red Fox and he lifts her high with shouts of delight and welcome. I think there will be a party tonight!

Red Fox, and the two braves he traveled with to Dark Cloud's village, Young Wolf and Spring Frog return with one more familiar face that I'm sure I'm not the only one surprised to see. It's Beaver, handsome and fierce, looking much the way he did when we last saw him except for the white man's rifle I see added to his collection of weapons on him and his horse. *It's powerful amazing,* I think to myself, *that they all arrive at the same time to talk about the same concerns. How different will their ideas be this time?*

It's decided that no difficult discussions will be spoken of this first night when *all sons* are present to celebrate the end of the summer and the start of the fall. A little bit late, and without the usual bounty of harvested crops, The Green Corn Ceremony is still one of the highlights of the year. As we gather around the fire, enjoying family and full bellies, War Woman rises to tell the story.

"Grandmother Selu was raising a small boy," she begins as the fire crackles and Storm and Squirrel slurp the last of the evening's food. "His parents were away on a long trip that took them far away from these smoky blue mountains for many moons. Each day, the Little Boy went into the planting field as Grandmother prepared the hard ground to plant corn, beans, and squash. She would rake the ground with a stick to soften it. Sometimes she would call to the worms in the earth to be helpers for the seeds to rest in soft soil for growing. Little Boy would watch her do the medicine magic as she sang an old song, one that had been lost with the passing of the moons. Each evening they went back to their hearth, where she boiled or roasted corn for the evening meal.

"Often Little Boy went to gather kindling for the fire while Grandmother Selu said that she had to go to the corn basket for corn to cook. She always said, 'Little Boy, you gather the wood for the fire, and I will collect the corn from the storage basket.' He was told to stay away from the basket where the corn was kept because of a snake that fed on fallen corn around the basket. It seemed strange to him that he never saw Grandmother Selu carry corn from the field to the storage basket, but she always had beans in a basket and squash from the planning field. She always brought the corn back to their hearth in a long apron, which she then wore over her dress while she prepared the food for their evening meal.

"One day, near the time when the Sun was at rest and darkness was near, Little Boy decided to follow Grandmother Selu and hid in the high bushes near the storage basket. To his amazement, she did not even open the basket but just rubbed her hands as she held the apron open. Golden yellow corn would appear in her apron! Little Boy was so surprised that he immediately said, 'Grandmother Selu, how did you do that?'

"Startled, she turned to him with a look of stars in her eyes and said that now she would have to go away forever. He suddenly felt sad. Grandmother Selu fixed the corn for their evening meal, and later she held him, explaining that some things are not to be seen. The next morning, when Little Boy awoke to the bright morning light, his aunt was there to stay with him. Grandmother Selu was never to be seen again, but in the fields were rows and rows of golden yellow corn ready to be picked from the large stalks.

"As Little Boy harvested the corn, he sang the song he remembered hearing her sing as she planted the corn, which The Real People call *Selu*.

"Corn is considered sacred by The Real People," War Woman says to those of us sitting silent and listening. "Life is focused on survival and this Green Corn Ceremony celebrates and gives thanks for this food of life. We remember Grandmother Selu, who gave her life for the sons and daughters of The Real People to have corn for survival, as long as they worked diligently to plant and grow corn in the fields each summer."

She raises her arms and sings,

"O Great One,

Thank you for the Spirit of the Wind,

It stirs our spirit and sends messages to our hearts.

I thank you for the spirit of Mother Earth,

As I listen to the drum beat,

I hear the heart beat that gives us life.

O Great One,

I thank you for the Ancestors and the teachings,

That guide our way of life here on Mother Earth.

I will forever hold sacred the pipe of peace,

And I will share the tobacco for prayer,

As I give thanks to the elders and the Ancient Fire.

O Great One,

I give thanks to the way of The Real People.''[15]

I look down at Storm sleeping in my arms, a dribble of milk caught in the pool of his mouth against his fat cheek, and I think, *I am a mother now.* Will I ever be a grandmother? I wonder. I look at One Who Knows and War Woman and Otter. I look at Turtle snuggled close to Red Fox, so happy to have him home. I look at the faces of the women that sit around this circle, young and old, and I am proud to be a part of this powerful group of women.

The next night around the Council fire, celebration takes a distant place as we must discuss the realities of the white and red worlds that press at our borders and remind me that *our garden walled round* has walls made of only words and paper.

Great Elk begins the discussions expressing pleasure to have all of his sons present and tells how all of us are eager to hear what news there is to hear, *good or bad.* He expresses his hope that we will gain strength from the different things we know and the different opinions we share and the different paths we walk. He asks Red Fox to speak first.

Red Fox smiles shyly at the group but speaks with confidence. "I was in Dark Cloud's village much longer than we thought I would be. When I first arrived, I was warmly welcomed and they were happy to hear the news that I brought." He smiles and looks at Deer, Bright Feather and me. "It is amazing that this small village, separated from so much of the world seems often to be at the front of the line when it comes to news and information from the outside world. That is a good thing, of that I am certain.

"My words were greatly doubted when I told them of Deer and Bear's discoveries north. Beaver will confirm their disbelief, just as he will confirm *his belief* in the truth of my words." It's a respectful and wise move, I see, that Red Fox has done, bringing Beaver into the discussion of the circle so early by the mention of his name.

"Red Fox speaks the truth," Beaver says, "his words were listened to, but not believed by anyone but me. At first."

Red Fox continued. "Within the first week, however, messengers from Washington, those who were present, I imagine, for the very vote that Deer was present for and that Bright Feather and Bear told us of, arrived at the village and reported things just as I had told them." He looks sad. "Then they believed me."

Red Fox looks at Great Elk, War Woman, and says with great concern in his voice, "There is great controversy within the leadership of The Nation of The Real People. This division has reached such a level of hatred that there are those of one position who wish the deaths of those who take the opposite position. It can only mean disaster for all of The Real People." He seems at a loss for words and looks at Beaver for help. "Again, Beaver will confirm my words and add to them."

Beaver speaks. "I have returned to this village with Red Fox, for many reasons. First, I am eager to see my brothers and sisters. I wish to see that you are all well and assure you that I, too, am in good health. I have taken a mate and am the proud father of a strong son born at the start of this summer." There are happy murmurs that float around the circle, in and out of the dark and light of the fire. I think, *I hope you have found happiness there, Beaver.*

"I have also returned to this village to share with you what I have learned and now know as fact about The Nation of The Real People. Red Fox has witnessed these things. I have *lived* with them." He looks at Red Fox and then Great Elk. "May I have permission to speak and tell you these things?" Both men nod.

"What Deer has told us in times past of The Nation of The Real People is all true. Dark Cloud, seeks very much to run his village and The Nation like the white government with red skin. I cannot discredit anything that Deer has said and I must give my apologies before this council for any insult I may have caused him in my anger and behavior at the last time I sat here in this council circle." Deer nods his head, Beaver's apology is accepted. I can see approval on Great Elk, War Woman, and One Who Knows' faces as well.

"What is interesting to know, however," Beaver continues, "is that Dark Cloud is not the *elected* leader of The Nation of The Real People. He holds great power and is well thought of by some, especially within the walls of the white government in Washington, but within the hearths of those who call themselves The Nation of The Real People, he is trusted and considered a leader by only a small few. Within the white world, he calls himself *Major Ridge* – a military title to commemorate his great past battle victories - and he has embraced so much of the white world and its ways and beliefs that few feel that he operates any longer for the *best interests of The Nation of The Real People.*

"Within The Nation of The Real People, the *chosen leader*, the one who has been elected within the accepted ways of the tribe now is *John Ross.*" He looks at War Woman and One Who Knows, "No women are allowed to be considered or to cast a vote. He is part white to look at but he has a passion for the welfare of The Real People that makes him full red. Between these two men - Major Ridge and John Ross - is such a fierce hatred that only death would be a satisfactory end. Both of these men, reside in this village, we have known to be Dark Cloud's for these many years, and what is now called, New Echota, Georgia by the whites." Beaver looks at me. "It would seem, during your time in Great Elk's village, that John Ross was in Washington trying to secure treaty promised monies, lands, and supplies. That is why you never met him." I nod. *Would John Ross' presence have made a difference for me during my time there?* I wonder. I will never know.

Great Elk speaks. "We know much of Dark Cloud, tell us of this John Ross."

Beaver looks across at Deer. "Do you know of him?"

Deer nods, "I have met him," is all he will say and I think that he waits carefully for his turn and also to hear what Beaver will say.

"He is a good leader," Beaver finally says. "I respect him, too, and feel that if The Real People are going to survive and keep *any* of their Old Ways and tribal lands, it is only John Ross who will make sure it happens. It is difficult to fight a battle *and win* when you have two powerful enemies to watch, however, and the United States Government and *Major Ridge* are about as powerful as they can be."

Beaver looks at me again. "You were right about the village. It is nothing like it is here. I remember you saying that *nothing is as it seems* and that is a good description." He looks at the rest of the council. "No one's words are to be taken as they are said, no one's actions are to be accepted as they appear."

"Have you come home to us here in The Maple Forest, then?" War Woman asks him.

"My mother," he says with great respect, "it is good to see you and hear your voice these past two days. But I must tell you no, that I will return to New Echota. I feel a responsibility there. I believe that my purpose still lies with The Nation of The Real People and the struggles they face.

"I hope that my presence will help John Ross and will hinder Dark Cloud. I have left my mate and family to travel here to make certain that The Real People of The Maple Forest know the truth of things.

"I wish that the difficulties you have heard spoken here in this circle - between the United States Government and two men who would be leaders of The Real People - were the only problems that we face, but that is not true. Besides this United States Government law that seeks to force all of us west, that I am sure Deer will tell us of in detail, there is another battle that must be fought that causes just as great concern. You must understand that this is as great a threat as any other. The whites of the state of Georgia, on which some of The Real People's land rests, have become greedy. Many of these whites are in positions to make laws of their own that also greatly affect us. Already they have passed laws that make it illegal for The Real People to make agreements with whites and speak in their council meetings concerning grievances. The Real People are helpless against their greed and violence.

"Things that have been promised in past treaties regarding land rights and protection have already been revoked. White settlers have invaded hearths and villages of The Real People and stolen their land and their homes and possessions. With these new laws there is *nothing* that can be done by The Nation of The Real People. Although the state, North Carolina, that The Maple Forest rests in does not have laws such as those that Georgia has made, I fear that soon it will.

"I return to New Echota because I must protect my family. I return because I must fight for the rights of my people. I return because *it is my duty.*"

Bright Feather asks Beaver, "Do you still intend to fight with weapons other than words?"

Beaver does not answer his brother right away. The two men stare at each other across the council fire's flickering flames for long moments. Finally, Beaver says very carefully, "I will fight with *everything I can*. There are many who think the same as I do."

When will things change? I think about the greedy whites and I think about the rifle I saw strapped to Beaver's saddle. The battle for land and things never, ever seems to end.

It is Beaver who looks at Deer. "Tell us what you agree with and disagree with in regard to what I have said."

Deer shrugs. "That is easy to do. I agree with everything you have said up until your last statement. I still cannot agree with you that The Real People will ever be able to succeed with violence. The time for guns and battles and killing is long past. You may kill a few whites and have a moment's glory in the feel of sweet revenge, but you have not been to Washington, you have not been to some of the forts that I have been to and seen the might and strength that sits lazily in the summer sun like a sleeping panther. Any white blood you shed will cause more sorrow, death, and destruction than you could ever imagine for all of those who call themselves The Real People."

Deer looks at Beaver and then at those around the council circle. "May I speak now?"

"We have waited many weeks to hear what you have to tell us, Deer," War Woman says with one of her fierce, unblinking looks.

"I assume that Bright Feather and Bear have told you what I have told them about Washington. I know that Bear will have described to you Fort Winston that is being built." Those around the council nod their heads.

Deer sighs. "I agree with Beaver about John Ross. He is a good man and The Nation of The Real People could have no better leader. Unfortunately, it is the thoughts and beliefs of Dark Cloud, also known as Major Ridge, that are the way of things in Washington and what they want to hear.

"Washington is an interesting place," he says slowly, seeming to struggle to find the right words to paint the best picture. "It is a place that, like it or not, holds great power even right here in this council circle. To travel there and walk the wide streets and see the grand buildings, you begin to understand the forces that came together to create it. Here is what you must understand about the white world in general and Washington in particular: you are only powerful in Washington if you can find someone who will listen to you who is a little bit more powerful than you are. And *that* someone's power is simply measured by who with more power will listen to them. John Ross and Major Ridge are both powerful within The Real People. But it is Major Ridge, I fear, who in the end will find the open doors into the President's office; the place that holds the greatest authority.

He makes eye contact with many of those around the council circle. "Over eleven years ago you made the decision to separate yourselves from The Nation of The Real People and request citizenship with the United States of America in the state of North Carolina. You did this not to choose a side, but to achieve the right to remain *separate and apart* and live the way you have always wanted to live. *I still think it was the right decision.* Now, more than ever, you must seek to separate yourselves from The Real People who look to John Ross *or* Dark Cloud as leaders."

Deer looks at Beaver across the fire with great sadness. "I fear that you will get your fight and that many lives will be lost. And after the fight is over, those of you that are left alive will be picked up and carted across the Mississippi River to the new lands you are to live on *whether you like it or not.* There is not any doubt in my mind that those of you that claim to be an Indian tribe east of the Mississippi River, whether you are Cherokee, Choctaw, Chickasaw, Creek or Seminole will not have a tree to claim your own in a few short years time.

"For those of you here in the Maple Forest, you too must prepare as if for war. You must live your life as you have always done, preparing for winter and hunting and surviving. But in addition, I must encourage you to begin to make preparations to go into hiding. Gather supplies, stock up on things that may be stored and kept for future needs. I fear that as the hostilities grow between The Nation of The Real People and The United States Government, many will be unable to distinguish – at first glance – the differences within this village and any other Indian village. *That is my job to do* as your agent and your son. There is a time coming of great danger and fear and hardship that I will do my best to ease as much as I possibly can."

He laughs a laugh that holds no humor. "That is why I have brought you these animals. We cannot always rely on the success of your hunts anymore. You cannot risk a lean winter that will weaken you and put you at any further risk. You must embrace some of these white customs for the sake of survival as an investment in the future. You must learn to care for these cattle, chickens and goats as they will help you survive. Butcher them if you must for food or raise them to sell for profit."

Deer looks at me. "Bear will know how to care for them." He smiles at me. "Do you still remember?" And I nod. "She will show you how to get products from them and how to prepare them should you decide to eat them for survival. You must begin to stock pile supplies should you need to leave this village in haste and you must choose and prepare safe places to hide." He looks so fearful for a moment. "I know that time will come, I just cannot tell how soon.

"I have heard of the laws that Georgia has passed." He looks at Beaver. "I heard of those laws when I was in *Washington*, and I know for a fact that they will not be stopped by the President or the United States Government there. The mind of the State of Georgia is the same mind that is in Washington."

To all of us around the circle, he says, "I am hopeful that North Carolina, who recognized the promises made in the Treaty of 1819, acknowledged their mistakes in not keeping the designated land available for you, honored their responsibilities and have paid out real cash money in reparation will not follow in those sorry footsteps made by the state of Georgia. But we cannot be careless, even for a moment.

"There are important meetings to come. Those that are held in Washington, I will be a part of. But those that are held in Dark Cloud's village in New Echota, Georgia, at the place that is considered the capital of The Nation of The Real People you must attend." He looks directly at Great Elk and War Woman. "Not all of you, but a strong representation of this village. There are some that sit around this council circle," he looks at me and, briefly, at Bright Feather, that speak the languages of both the white and the red world. Those people are your strongest warriors now. You must establish your presence; do not let *anyone* make decisions about this village without your say so."

Deer looks at each and every face around the council fire and then says, "I have finished speaking."

Finally, Beaver speaks. "Deer and I may disagree over the course of action that is best taken, however, we are both unified in our concern over the welfare of this village. When I last spoke in this council, it was with anger that I now regret. It was important for me to return to you and establish once and for all with this council that whatever we both decide and whatever direction that we both travel, our goals will always be identical: the safety and preservation of The Real People of The Maple Forest. Perhaps between both of these different paths, we may be successful in the end. I wish only harmony between us and will not leave again until I am certain that I have achieved that."

Deer leaves within a few days needing to get back to the trading post but, as Sleeping Rabbit has told us, leaves both of his children behind to help with the care of the new animals for those first few weeks. Things get busier still as work has begun on a pen to corral the bull, while the cows are left to wander the village and the nearby forest and fields. We grow accustomed to the clank of the bells, although One Who Knows has some choice words about the racket on more than one occasion. The goats must also be penned for they seem inclined to eat just about anything and James worries that they'll not see the end of the first week before they are all killed one after another by the furious villagers. The chickens set up roost in all manner of places throughout the village.

Beaver stays in the village with us for two full weeks, well into the start of fall. He visits each hearth and helps build shelters and hunt to replenish our winter's stock. He's as serious and strong about what's the right path for The Real People as he always has been and yet he seems to carry a new purpose as well. It's almost as if, I tell Bright Feather in the privacy of the night as we snuggle together in our corner of our new large hut, that he's been searching all his life for something he knows he *must find* and he's finally found it. While he still talks of battles and weapons and violence, and seems committed to achieve the path he feels is right *at all costs,* he seems more content with the way of things. I wonder out loud if it's maybe because he has found more like-minded people like him for support. Maybe it's because he's closer to the action and can see more clearly what must be done. Maybe it's because he's finally decided just what course of action he must take and is actually doing it.

Bright Feather nuzzles my neck and offers another reason. "Maybe," he says as he causes shivers to run up and down my spine, "he has found a good woman to love at last."

I'm not inclined to disagree with him at the moment.

Fall rolls into winter and I'm happy for the fierce breath of the season that will slow down white man and red man alike in all this talk of land and laws and who's right and who's wrong. Winter rolls into spring and I'm pressed down by the heavy rains that are like tears of a worried mother about her children. The harmony that's so precious to us here in this center of the world of The Real People of The Maple Forest believe their village to be isn't as smooth or certain as it once was. Spring rolls into summer again and I watch riders travel out to gather the latest news from Dark Cloud's village and Deer's trading post. We'll do as Deer tells us and work to not be caught by surprise.

I watch Storm go from an infant to a baby to an active crawling mass of delightful trouble. I watch Red Fox and Turtle welcome a baby daughter, Laughs Much, and finally enjoy an early summer visit with Sleeping Rabbit and we sew her an Indian tunic with real rabbit fur just as I promised her so long ago. I wander the woods with One Who Knows and work hard to remember all she can pack into my thick skull about herbs and such. When the heat of the summer wraps itself around all of us, I remember the time a year ago when I was *not* a mother, *but almost.* I look down at the sturdy little man at my feet, clinging to my skirt and taking his first steps to the delight of the extended family around him.

I think of the fears that all of us have just close below the surface; fears of soldiers and broken promises and worries of the future. I know of the preparations we've worked hard to do and still continue to work hard toward; of caves well supplied and provisions carefully stored. The puzzle of my life that I once thought, so foolishly, was all finished is now, I realize, just a small part of a huge, never ending scene. There's The Maple Forest part that's almost complete thanks to my listening at council fires and Deer and Bright Feather's patience with my many, many questions.

The Ward's Mill part has many parts filled in, but so many pieces are still missing. What of the Wests? Are they safe and well? Do they still have Mr. Cooper's ledger book hidden in their mattress? What of the Coopers? Do they still hold power over so many of the farmers in the area like a rabid dog guarding its pile of bones? A big part of me hopes they tremble with fear as often as possible of me and my village of 'red savage' friends.

My heart skips a beat and my stomach clenches as I think *What of my brother Henry?* Is he well? Is he safe? Does he worry for me? Miss me? Is he part of this battle to remove all Indian tribes east of the Mississippi? For the truth of things is, if he's still in the army, *how could he not be?* Which makes me sigh and think of Miss Joan's question, *"Will your brother be understanding of the child do you think?"* I snort to myself as I work to wash a struggling toddler boy and think a better question is, What will your brother think of your pink skin? Will I someday find my brother only to loose him once again simply because of the choices I've made about the course of my life?

I sigh as I watch Storm wrestle from my grasp and run on fat toddler legs to Bright Feather who's walking slowly towards us. I battle with the big wave of worry that threatens to pull me down about all my missing puzzle pieces. What of this village that's my home? And my people? What of my husband and son? And mother and friends? Do I have what I need to go to a council circle filled with white and red faces who'll hate me just because of the way I look? Will I be able to speak my mind and heart in such a way to keep all those I love and care for safe?

For I am just a ...

But I stop my self. I'll not finish that sentence for it's not true. I'm not a "just" anything. I am many things. I am Bear, daughter of One Who Knows of Elk Clan of The Real People of The Maple Forest. I am also known by some as Elle Graves, late of Ward's Mill, Virginia. I am a powerful woman who has survived a mighty big pile of difficult surprises and heart - breaking sorrows so far. I am a mate of a man who encourages my many questions, listens to my thoughts and concerns, and loves me with an abiding love. I am a mother of a fine son and I will work hard to grow him into a fine man. I am a sister to many who are inclined to tolerate my pink self. And I am many more things I suspect ... But I remind myself with firm words that I am *not* nor will I ever be "just" anything. For to use that word about myself only serves to make me less that I can be.

My two men approach me; one with a serious face full of love and one with twinkling eyes filled with mischief. My husband and I have survived fear, worry, death, separation, hatred, and sorrows no body should have to ever face. I sigh a deep sigh. I suspect that there are still a pile of shadows we still are yet to fight our way through. But we'll do it together, side by side and hand in hand.

I step forward and Bright Feather wraps me in a warm embrace as Storm tangles himself between our legs. I take a deep breath and make myself squint my eyes towards the sun rather then the shadows, *for that is the way it must always be.*

My friend is one who takes me for what I am.[16]

~Henry David Thoreau

Actual Facts: Book II

Situated by the *Oconaluftee River*, (from the Cherokee work *egwanul'ti* meaning "by the river") is the Qualla Boundary, or Indiantown. The Oconaluftee Indians or the Eastern Band of the Cherokee Nation were described by an author who visited them in 1848. "About three-fourths of the entire population can read in their own language, and though the majority of them understand English, a very few can speak the language. They practice, to a considerable extent, the science of agriculture, and have acquired such a knowledge of the mechanic arts as answers them for all ordinary purposes, for they manufacture their own clothing, their own ploughs, and other farm utensils, their own axes, and even their own guns.

"Their women are no longer treated as slaves, but as equals; the men labor in the fields and their views are devoted entirely to household employment. They keep the same domestic animals that are kept by their white neighbors, and cultivate all the common grains of the country. They are probably as temperate as any other class of people on the face of the earth, honest in their business intercourse, moral in their thoughts, words, and deeds, and distinguished for their faithfulness in performing the duties of religion.

"They are chiefly Methodists and Baptists, and have regularly ordained ministers, who preach to them on every Sabbath, and they have also abandoned many of their more senseless superstitions. They have their own court and try their criminals themselves. They keep in order the public roads leading through their settlement. By a law of the state they have the right to vote, but seldom exercise that right, as they do not like the idea of being identified with any of the political parties. Except on festive days, they dress after the manner of the white man, but far more picturesquely. The live in small log houses of their own construction, and have everything they need or desire in the way of food.

"They are in fact, the happiest community that I have yet met within this southern country."[17]

The above description was the real world that the fictional Bear chose to live in. The band of Eastern Cherokee honored the Old Ways; respecting the wisdom and insight of women, promoting the opinion that internal peace and goodness was projected outward into the world you lived in, and recognizing values in family and loyalty to others over material gain. The freedoms and recognition she received as a woman within the Indian world made her choice, to leave the white world, seem easy and sensible. No one should be held back from doing something simply because of their race, sex, or religious belief. No one.

I tried very hard as the author of this story not to make any one type of person "bad", but rather point out that goodness comes from within and is directly influenced by those things we value most. Furthermore, I so wanted to make it clear that God can work goodness into even the darkest of circumstances. We need not be educated, ordained ministers, we need not even be solid, church going folks, we need simply to be trusting and faithful to God's design in our lives. Elle did that. It didn't help her escape the "sorrowful, hard parts of life" but it did help her survive them and find her way out of the shadows. Anyone can do that.

As for William Holland Thomas, I found at least one reference that puzzled over his insistence of calling himself an orphan, despite the fact that his mother lived on family property and was a "continual influence". I never discovered the true reason why he did this, however, so I made up the whole interaction and murder between his mother and father. My choice to have his mother be insane, is based on factual information that will be better explained more thoroughly in the next book in this series ...

It would be so nice to say that Elle and Bright Feather's story ends on this happy note and that all the hardships are behind them. But, though fictional characters, the reality of the circumstances that the Cherokee Nation endured dictates that the difficult times have not begun yet ...

When you were born,
you cried and the world rejoiced.
Live your life so that when you die,
the world cries and you rejoice.[18]

Acknowledgements

Personally, the entire process of this book, from the initial idea (a very vivid image of a frightened white girl being very gently touched on the cheek by a fierce Indian brave) to the final, *real* possibility that this could be published has been nothing short of a miracle. I could write pages about all the wonderful coincidences (some that gave me goose bumps) that occurred during the writing, but the book is too long already. Suffice it to say that I could *not* have done this on my own.

There is a strong Christian message in this story and that is not by chance. Had the book arrived, packaged with a nice neat bow on my front step, God could not have shown me more clearly what He wanted to do. While I did not want to cram any of this "God stuff" down reluctant throats, I cannot escape the very essence of what I strive to be; "a woman after God's own heart". No one's life is perfect; there is great sorrow we must face, things rarely work out just as we'd hoped they would, and disappointments are a dime a dozen. But I don't believe you go through this life alone and so my story *must* reflect that.

From the very first time I hesitantly said, "I think I'm writing a book…" (said with great wonder and trepidation) family and friends have encouraged and championed me. To Mom, Marylynn, who read it and said, "Best Seller" (in her best Mom's voice), to Dad, Herb, who gets teary when he talks about his girls (and the good things they get up to), to Wendy who carried the 500 pound binder with her on her two week vacation to Cape Cod *and read it*, to Aunt Evie and Debbie Francis who, between the two of them sent me close to *fifty pages* of corrections and will remain forever as the world's best proofreaders, to my sister, Amy, who after reading all 700 plus pages was furious because the last chapter was "so short", to my wonderful husband, David, who dealt with no dinners, unfolded laundry, and a general lack of care and attention and kept saying, "just tell me when I can retire", to my son, Ian, who said, "If you get famous, do you think I could get to meet J.K. Rowling?", to my daughter, Gracie, who upon opening and reading yet another rejection letter said, "Well…at least she said she liked it before she sent it back to you. She didn't have to do that, you know", to my youngest son, Luke, who when I said I was going to miss him when he went off to kindergarten said, "Don't worry, you'll just have more time to work at your computer", to my friend, Linda who has been so patient – and yet *so certain*, waiting for me to get famous so that she can get on television (Hi, Regis!), to Pam Frueh the world's best editor who seems to be able to get inside my head and make changes and suggestions that still match my style and goal (I really appreciate you even if I groan when I get the hundreds of changes…!) and to my Bible Study ladies who are all powerful women each in their own right and wonderful role models for me to follow: Patti, Beth, Melony, Kate, Jen, Jenn, Maria, Judy, and Kim, and to Laury Vaden, artist extraordinaire who brought the face of Bear to life with her talent and has tirelessly and patiently designed for me The Best Book Covers In The World … For want of better words: THANK YOU.

Sue McG

Cast of Characters: Book II

The People of the Maple Forest
- **Bear** – Elle Grave's Indian name
- **Bright Feather** – Indian brave who joins with Bear
- **Deer** – adopted son of War Woman, also known as William Holland Thomas
- **Raccoon** – Indian brave, mate of Otter
- **Otter** – Indian woman, daughter of War Woman, mate of Raccoon
- **Little Bird** – Raccoon and Otter's son
- **Squirrel** – Raccoon and Otter's daughter
- **Great Elk** – Chief of the Indians of the Maple Forest
- **War Woman** – Mate of Great Elk
- **Cloud** – Indian brave
- **Red Fox** – Indian brave
- **Beaver** – Indian brave
- **One Who Knows** – Indian woman, village healer
- **Double Arrow** – Indian brave rescued from Fort Payne, Tennessee
- **Mary** – Indian woman rescued from Fort Payne, Tennessee
- **Turtle** – Indian woman, daughter of One Who Knows
- **Storm Eli** – Bear and Bright Feather's son

The People of New Echota, Georgia
- **Dark Cloud** – Chief, known in the white world as Major Ridge
- **John Ross** – Elected leader of the entire nation of Real People
- **Weasel** – Indian brave
- **Elias Boudinot** – Indian brave, editor of Cherokee Newspaper *The Cherokee Phoenix*
- **Sequoia** – Also known as Pig's Foot, invented the written language of the Cherokee
- **Reverend James Wilder** – Missionary to the Real People, based in New Echota, Georgia, called The Messenger by the Indians
- **Rebecca Wilder** – James Wilder's wife

❖ **Martin DuBois –** French trader

The People of Ward's Mill, Virginia

❖ **Elle Graves** – daughter of Andrew and Elizabeth Graves
❖ **Andrew Graves –** Elle's Father
❖ **Elizabeth Graves** – Elle's Mother
❖ **Henry Graves** – Elle's brother, four years older
❖ **Eli Graves** – Elle's younger brother, eight years younger
❖ **Cornelius Cooper** – Proprietor of Cooper's General Store
❖ **Naomi Cooper** – Cornelius Cooper's wife
❖ **Johnny Cooper –** Cornelius and Naomi Cooper's son
❖ **Ezekiel West** – resident of Ward's Mill, Virginia
❖ **Jane West** – Ezekiel West's wife
❖ **Daniel Hobson** – resident of Ward's Mill, Virginia

The People of Forest City, North Carolina

❖ **William Holland Thomas** – Proprietor of Trading Post in Forest City, North Carolina, also known as Deer of The Maple Forest
❖ **Possum –** of the Turkey clan of The Real People of The Maple Forest, Deer's mate, also known as Mary Thomas
❖ **James, Red Bird** – Deer and Possum's eldest son
❖ **Eliza, Sleeping Rabbit** – Deer and Possum's daughter
❖ **Richard, Small Turtle** – Deer and Possum's youngest son

The People of Fort Winston, Virginia

❖ **Alexander Everett –** Major, Second United States Cavalry, Division of the Army, Company A. based in Fort Winston, Virginia
❖ **George Maw** – Alexander Everett's interpreter
❖ **Lieutenant George Foster -** Commander of Fort Winston, Virginia, Second United States Cavalry, Company A, and Ninth Virginia Cavalry, Company D
❖ **Joan Foster –** Wife of Lieutenant Foster
❖ **Lydia Foster** – daughter of George and Joan Foster
❖ **Nate Foster** – son of George and Joan Foster

❖ **Paul Foster** – son of George and Joan Foster

Book Timeline: **BOOK II**

Black type = actual facts

BOLD CAPITAL TYPE = NOVEL STORYLINE

▓ *BOOK CHAPTER*

Date	Event
1540	DeSoto explores.
1684	England makes treaty with Cherokees.
1738	Smallpox arrives in South Carolina and ½ of nation dies in one year from small pox.
1754-1761	French and Indian War (Cherokees side with British.)
1763	Proclamation of 1763 a royal decree of George III of Britain, which prohibits colonists from settling west of the Appalachian Mountains and reserves this area for Indians.
1775	Cherokees sell what will become Kentucky to English.
1776-1783	Revolutionary War (Cherokees side with British.)
6/25/1788	Virginia becomes the 10th state of the USA.
4/30/1789	George Washington elected as President.
3/4/1801	Thomas Jefferson elected as President.
1802	**BIRTH OF BRIGHT FEATHER.**
1802	William Holland Thomas born.
1807	**MARRIAGE OF ELLE'S PARENTS: ANDREW AND ELIZABETH GRAVES.**
3/4/1809	James Madison elected as President.
1809	Sequoyah begins work on a Cherokee alphabet.
1809	Cherokees set up a central government that acts for the whole tribe and models the white style of government.
1810	**HENRY GRAVES' BIRTH.**
1810	**WILLIAM HOLLAND THOMAS IS FOUND AND ADOPTED BY GREAT ELK'S VILLAGE.**
6/1812-12/1814	War of 1812
3/27/1814	The Battle of Horseshoe Bend
10/1814	**ELLE GRAVE'S BIRTH**
1817	**WILLIAM THOMAS, KNOWN AS DEER, RETURNS TO THE WHITES IN SEARCH OF HIS WHITE FAMILY.**
1817	**ELLE'S FAMILY MOVES TO HOMESTEAD IN FAR WESTERN VIRGINIA; WARD'S MILL.**

7/8/ 1817	Treaty of 1817, ratified Dec. 26, 1817.
Spring 1818	**WEASEL OF DARK CLOUD'S VILLAGE MARRIES ONE WHO KNOWS' OLDER DAUGHTER; RAVEN, OF GREAT ELK'S VILLAGE.**
6/6/1818	Census taken of all Cherokee.
2/27/1819	Treaty, Proclaimed Mar 10, 1819, tribal lands given up, offer of citizenship made, small number of Indians in North Carolina near the Oconaluftee River take the option for citizenship.
1820	**BRIGHT FEATHER MARRIES ONE WHO KNOWS YOUNGER DAUGHTER, BLACK FOX.**
1821	Cherokee Written` Language, Sequoyah develops a system of 86 symbols that stand for Cherokee syllables.
1821	William Holland Thomas establishes trading post near Indian Territory.
1822	**DISAPPEARANCE OF ONE WHO KNOWS OLDEST DAUGHTER, RAVEN.**
1822	**DEATH OF BRIGHT FEATHER'S MATE, BLACK FOX, AND UNBORN SON.**
1822	**ELLE'S MOTHER'S DEATH, ELI GRAVES' BIRTH.**

BOOK I

3/22/1828	*CAPTIVE*
Late summer 1828	*BEAR*
2/1828	Cherokees print a bilingual newspaper, *The Cherokee Phoenix* with Elias Boudinot as editor.
5/6/1828	**Treaty,** proclaimed May 28, 1828.
Early spring 1829	*POWERFUL WOMAN*
Late summer -Early fall, 1829	*MATE*
	LISTENER

BOOK II

Winter 1829-1830	*ELLE GRAVES*
	GUEST
February 1830	*JOURNEYWOMAN*
	SISTER
5/30/1830	President Andrew Jackson's **Removal Act**
Late Summer 1830	*MOTHER*
1830	**Georgia,** shortly after Jackson's election, passes a series of laws against the Cherokees.
1832-1833	**Georgia Land Lottery**
Today	*ACTUAL FACTS*

Family Tree

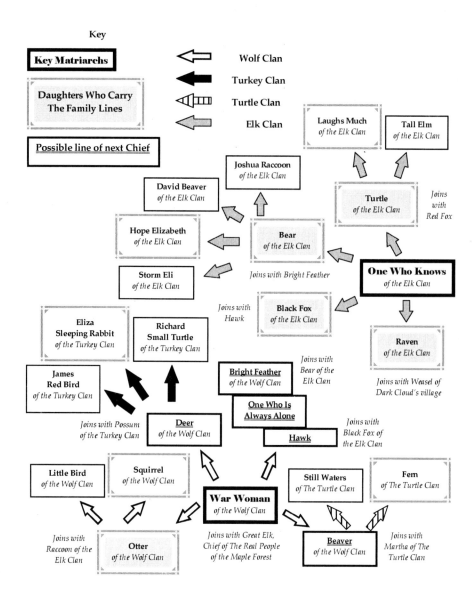

Cherokee Lands in 1791 and in 1838, Before Removal[19]

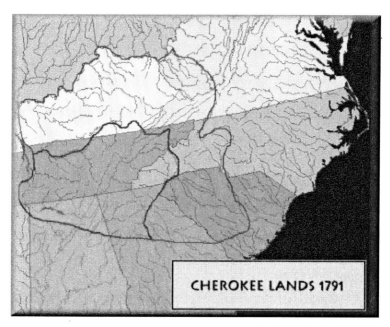

CHEROKEE LANDS 1791

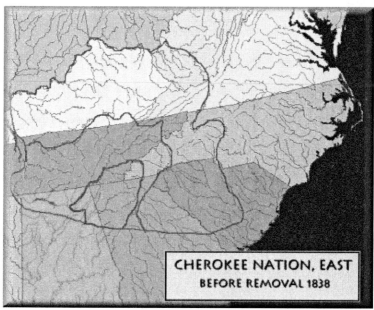

CHEROKEE NATION, EAST
BEFORE REMOVAL 1838

1820 Map of the Five Civilized Tribes[20]

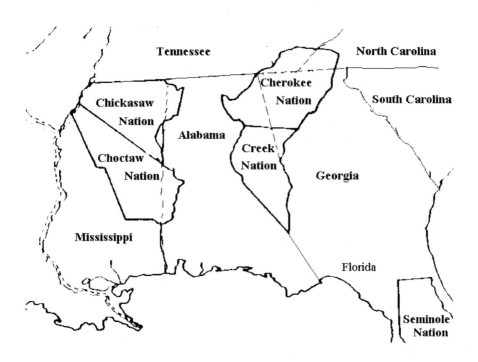

North Carolina Today

The stared counties are all part of the Qualla Boundary, the Eastern Tribe of The Cherokee Nation.

1. Eastern Band of Cherokee

Counties: Swain, Graham, Jackson
Population: 13,400
State Recognition: 1889
Federal Recognition: 1868

"The Eastern Band of Cherokee descended from the Cherokee who in the late 1830s remained in the mountains of North Carolina rather than be forced into Oklahoma along the infamous Trail of Tears. These thousand or so tribal members lived along the Oconaluftee River, some hiding out. The Cherokee eventually gained the Qualla Boundary reservation, the 56,572-acre site where the tribe resides today. The Cherokee are the only indigenous people in America to have their own written language, developed by Sequoyah.

The Eastern Band of Cherokee is the only federally recognized tribe in North Carolina and the only tribe living on land held in trust. The tribe actively promotes tourism on the boundary, with cultural activities, events, and an outdoor drama. In addition, the Cherokee sell traditional arts and crafts such as baskets, pottery, beadwork, stone carvings, and wood carvings. The tribe's involvement in many business ventures helps ensure its livelihood."[21]

About The Author

Susan McGeown is a wife, mother, daughter, sister, friend, aunt, uncle (don't ask), teacher, author … but, most importantly, a "woman after God's own heart." Living in Bridgewater, New Jersey, with her husband of over fifteen years and their three children, writing stories is just about the best way she can imagine spending her free time. Each of Sue's stories champions those emotions nearest and dearest to her: faith, joy, hope and love.

Philippians 1:20-21

For I fully expect and hope that I will never be ashamed, but that I will continue to be bold for Christ, as I have been in the past. And I trust that my life will bring honor to Christ, whether I live or die. For to me, living means living for Christ, and dying is even better.

Footnotes

Portions in the book that tell of stories from the Cherokee: Beaver's story of the Ceremony of Life, One Who Knows story of The Beginning of Time, Bright Feather's story of the Four Sacred Directions, and War Woman's story of Grandmother Corn and her song that she sings are based on the descriptions of these stories given in the book <u>Meditations with The Cherokee, Prayers, Songs, and Stories of Healing and Harmony</u>, by J.T. Garret, Ed.D., Bear and Company Publishers, Rochester, Vermont, 2001.

[1] from a Cherokee Sacred Formula quoted in <u>A Bare Unpainted Table,</u> By Gladys Cardiff, New Issues Press, Western Michigan University, 1999, p. 33

[2] From a poem entitled "Remember Me", Copyright 1989 Renee Womble

[3] 'Twas The Watches of the Night, Isaac Watts, 1674-1748

[4] God My Supporter and My Hope, Isaac Watts, 1674-148

[5] Psalm 23:5, King James Version

[6] From a speech given May 26, 1826, by Elias Boudinot, at the First Presbyterian Church in Philadelphia

[7] "Remember" By Joy Harjo (Creek) <u>*Women in American Indian Society*</u>, By Rayna Green, Chelsea House Publishers, New York, 1992p. 100

[8] <u>Eastern/Central Medicinal Plants and Herbs,</u> Peterson Field Guide, By Steven Foster and James A. Duke, National Audubon Society, Houghton Mifflin Company, New York, 2000

[9] Spoken by General Andrew Jackson to Cherokee chief Junaluska on March 27, 1814 at the end of the Battle of Horseshoe Bend in Alabama.

[10] Psalm 23:5, King James Version

[11] "Teach Me The Measure of My Days", Isaac Watts, 1674-1748

[12] "We Are A Garden Walled Around", Isaac Watts, 1674-1748

[13] "We Are A Garden Walled Around", Isaac Watts, 1674-1748

[14] "Remember" By Joy Harjo (Creek) <u>*Women in American Indian Society*</u>, By Rayna Green, Chelsea House Publishers, New York, 1992p. 100

[15] <u>Meditations with The Cherokee, Prayers, Songs, and Stories of Healing and Harmony</u>, by J.T. Garret, Ed.D., Bear and Company Publishers, Rochester, Vermont, 2001, p. 124

[16] Henry David Thoreau

[17] An author named Lanman, who visited the Eastern Band in 1848·

[18] Cherokee Expression

[19] http://www.cherokeehistory.com

[20] http://www.arkansaspreservation.org/preservation-services/trail-of-tears/images/ahpp_map_area_southeast.gif

[21] http://ncmuseumofhistory.org/workshops/ai/Session1.htm